NOTHING BUT TROUBLE AFTER MIDNIGHT

NOTHING BUT TROUBLE AFTER MIDNIGHT

KIMBERLY BLACKADAR

TWO HARBORS PRESS

Two Harbors Press
212 3rd Avenue North, Suite 290
Minneapolis, MN 55401
612.455.2293
www.TwoHarborsPress.com

ISBN - 978-1-935097-97-6
ISBN - 1-935097-97-0
LCCN - 2009936881

Book sales for North America and international:
Itasca Books, 3501 Highway 100 South, Suite 220
Minneapolis, MN 55416
Phone: 952.345.4488 (toll free 1.800.901.3480)
Fax: 952.920.0541; email to orders@itascabooks.com

Cover Design by Wes Moore
Typeset by Peggy LeTrent

Printed in the United States of America

Acknowledgements

I would like to thank Brett, Jackie, Kelsey, Lindsey, Lori, Melissa, Mindy, and Monika for offering insightful feedback; Jonathon for creating the cover art; and my husband Eric for reading every draft and encouraging me along the way.

-1-

Key Players

I stood there in the middle of the parking lot with my hand stuck to the car door and my face smushed against the window, wondering how someone in their right mind could have possibly locked their keys in the car with the engine still running.

Maybe that was my problem. I wasn't in my right mind; I was in my left, busy analyzing the complexities of my relationship with my boyfriend, who, after the unfortunate incident, did exactly what I expected him to do. He made matters worse, much worse, by rallying the masses around my car like a ringleader at a freak show. "Hey!" he yelled, cupping his hands around his mouth and shouting in every direction. "You gotta' see this!"

Then he turned toward me, flashing a grin. "You know, for someone so freaking smart, you can be really dumb sometimes." Sure, he could be a jerk, but not completely erroneous with his taunts. According to the standardized testing instruments used by the Florida public school system, I was relatively smart, which led me to believe that my intelligence came with a serious drawback: a lack of common sense.

Meanwhile, a sizeable crowd had formed in the back corner of the student parking lot, insuring a campus cop would arrive quickly on the scene. Well, ours took a while since he walked with a noticeable limp. He was shot in the line of duty and decided to finish off his law enforcement career at the high school

1

campus, but he underestimated the students at Riverside High. Here, cops dealt with fights, more drugs than on the streets, and periodic pranks, which were mostly ingenuous stunts like pants up the flag pole, desks assembled on the football field, or frilly unmentionables draped on the larger-than-life statue of Richard Waterhouse, the school's first principal.

As the campus cop neared us, he smiled at me. He probably expected to find two guys pummeling each other's faces into the hot asphalt, and very slowly, he headed over to my idling car. He peered into the window and pulled on the door handle. "Hmm," he started. "I've seen this happen before." I hung onto those words, feeling relief in knowing that some other student had done the same stupid thing as me. "Yeah, it was on one of those TV sitcoms. Real funny show. I just can't remember the name of it."

I sought television for the answer. "So, how did it end?"

"Hmm, can't remember that either." He put a hand on my shoulder. "Listen, young lady, you can either call a locksmith or open it with a spare key. Now, does anyone have a key to your car?"

"No...but..." I turned toward school because someone had a spare key to my house, and as I rushed toward the English wing, I concocted a please-may-I-borrow-your-keys speech. But I didn't have to give it because when I entered Advanced Placement English, Rob was swirling his car keys on his fore-finger. I approached his desk slowly, and he smiled up at me, his dimples sinking deep into his cheeks. "Are you looking for these, Chlo?"

"Yeah." I bit down on my lip.

"You'll owe me."

"I know...anything, Rob."

"*Any*thing?"

"No," I chided back.

"Yeah, I didn't think so."

*   *   *

Back at the parking lot, I climbed into Rob's bright yellow Jeep and clicked off the sports radio. Within a few minutes, I reached the gatehouse of my neighborhood. The guard looked at me quizzically. He recognized the Jeep; he recognized me; but he wasn't used to seeing me in the driver's seat. Rather than letting me pass through the gate, he held up his hand.

"Listen, it's a long story, Clyde," I said.

He tucked the newspaper under his arm and moved closer to me. "Well, I got nothing but time, Miss Preston."

I smiled politely, but before I could formulate a response, he began, "I remember when you were about this tall." He bent over, making me the size of a miniature poodle, and then he shook his head like he was inside a memory. At that moment, I realized I was his captive audience. I had no other choice but to sit there and listen to him, since Clyde controlled the arm of the gatehouse and Rob would be pretty amiss if I plowed through it with his Jeep.

Clyde continued on despite my repertoire of facial expressions. "Each morning you'd arrive at the bus stop, and that Callahan boy would have something for you—a flower, a note, a bag of candy." His eyes drifted toward the street corner where the newest batch of elementary school kids congregated at the bus stop, and we watched the little boys chase the squealing girls as their mothers sipped their coffees and shouted their last disciplinary decrees for the morning.

Then Clyde's eyes fell on me again. "Oh, you couldn't have been much more than six or seven at the time, and I thought that boy would give you just about anything." He stepped forward and rested a hand on the side of the Jeep. "And I guess, even after all these years, he still would."

"Yup, that's what friends are for," I returned and drove on, taking a quick right onto my street. Rob and I lived in a pretty nice subdivision: typical Florida style with pastel-colored stucco homes. Each house had a large front portico, a terracotta-tiled roof, and high-arched windows, but my house was not like the others. It had a shake-shingled roof and floor-to-ceiling windows, making it the lone contemporary atop a heavily treed hill; and

3

even though it was an architectural anomaly in the neighborhood, all of its individuality was lost behind a forest of wide-armed oaks and sky-reaching pines.

I zipped up the long driveway and entered my house with Rob's key. My father gave him a house key when my mother started back to work full-time. I have always had issues with keys, and at first, my parents tried the inconspicuous rock by the front door. But each time I entered the house with the spare key, I forgot to put it back. So the next time I got locked out...

Anyway, Rob was more reliable.

Entering my house was like crossing the time portal into the Victorian era, and even though our contemporary home needed sleek-lined furniture and abstract art, it was decorated with antiques and vibrant oils. Pictures of flowers and fruit bowls covered the creamy walls while dainty benches and fainting sofas rested on tiled floors.

My bedroom was at the top of the stairs and furnished in a similar fashion; with an antique sleigh bed, ornate writer's desk, and a triple dresser, it looked more like the guest accommodations of a New England bed and breakfast than a teenager's retreat. My favorite part of my room was the seat in the bay window, which jutted out into the rear of the home and overlooked the pool and the woods. On either side of the window seat, the built-in shelves housed my books, knick-knacks, and photos.

I grabbed my spare set of keys off the top shelf of my book-case and hurried back to school; and once there, I turned off my car and headed into the main doors of Riverside. It was well into first hour, and the school resembled a ghost town. The only sound was me, jingling like a janitor with three sets of keys in my hand.

For a moment, I paused in the front lobby of my high school. On my right, the administrative offices sprawled endlessly down the hall, but on my left, the glass display cases extended the length of the opposite wall, proudly displaying all the trophies, plaques, and awards from the last forty years.

But it was the massive state championship football trophy that always caught my eye. Shiny and impressive, surrounded by smaller symbols of lesser football seasons, the trophy could have been presented to one player rather than to our entire team. Our star running back single-handedly won it for the school. He knew it. Everyone knew it. And all that knowing promoted my boyfriend to god status at Riverside High.

-2-

First Impressions

I met my boyfriend before he achieved immortality. It was three years ago, the summer before ninth, and Caitlyn Rivers and I were helping her mother in the front office. Her mom's a guidance counselor, and Caitlyn and I filed in exchange for perfect schedules. That morning, we were taking a filing break and sprawled across the speckled blue carpet, sipping on some mocha frappa somethings and flipping through a magazine when a deep Southern voice fell over the counter and landed on the floor. "Hey there."

My eyes lifted from the pages of the magazine to breathing perfection staring down at me. A boy with the brightest blue eyes stood next to his grinning father. I blinked and looked again. He was definitely real, and slowly, he turned up the corners of his mouth. His smile sent a rush of emotions into me. Very pleasant ones. The kind that makes a girl get up and go to school in the morning.

"I need to get my boy here registered for school. We just came from Texas." The father began as he tousled his son's hair. "An' Austin here should be startin' in the ninth grade, ma'am." I snickered at his name, imagining a bunch of older brothers named Houston, Dallas, Antonio, and Galveston. I wondered all sorts of things about him in the minutes before we ever spoke, but mostly, I wondered if the scheduling goddess could put him in some of my classes in the fall.

Mrs. Rivers met them at the counter. "Welcome to Florida. You'll find our weather is just as hot…" Her voice trailed off into more polite adult conversation, and Austin came around the counter toward us. His arms were folded across his chest, and he cocked his head to the right. "You girls into football?"

"Uh, yeah." Caitlyn popped up and gestured across her Riverside Cheer T-shirt. "My boyfriend's Brandon Edwards; he's the starting quarterback on the freshmen team." She had an uncanny knack for dropping the boyfriend bomb into every conversation.

Then his bright blue eyes fell on me. "And what about *your* boyfriend?"

Caitlyn intercepted the question like I was a deaf mute. "Oh, Chloe only dates smart guys." I was barely fourteen, and barely dating, and *if* I had a type, it would definitely include him.

"Well, I'm smart…smart enough to get her to go out with me."

Now, I wanted nothing more than to go on a date with him, so I could stare into those brilliant blue eyes and run my fingers through his golden blonde hair. But one thing fueled my response more than my attraction to him; no matter how hot he was, I couldn't resist a comeback. "You wanna' bet?"

"Aw, c'mon now," he spoke in his slow Southern drawl and smiled again—this one bigger, bolder, and more powerful than before. "If we bet, baby, then someone's gotta' lose, and it ain't gonna' be me."

"Uh." That was my pathetic reply.

"I'll take that as a yes then," he said, smiling.

Caitlyn exchanged numbers with him, and apparently, she gave him mine—my home phone, that is. I wasn't permitted to have a cell back then, and by Friday night, my father was pacing by the front door, eager to put a face to my new frequent caller.

"Son," my father started as Austin entered the house. "Did you put our number on speed dial?" My father meant this sarcastically, which was how he approached any guy who braved the front door.

But Austin replied evenly, "Yup, number seven." Then he

turned to me with his smile-and-wink combo. "It's my favorite number, you know."

I nodded, barely, but yes, I had noticed the golden number seven around his neck on the day I met him. And over the course of our phone calls, he explained how it had always been his jersey number.

Austin gave me a long, lingering stare before he spoke again. "You look real nice tonight."

"Thanks," I said and bit down on my lower lip. I had on a pair of jeans and a white top, and I couldn't ever remember wearing more clothes than my date. He wore a pair of shorts and what was left of a Dallas Cowboys T-shirt. The arm holes were cut so low that I received a full fall preview. I started thinking about football practices on hot August afternoons and how our cross country team always ran by the practice fields...

My father brought me back to the present tense. "Be home by ten, Chloe."

"It's eleven in the summer, Dad."

"Summer's almost over."

"Yeah, but it's a Friday night."

My dad appealed to Austin. "What about you? What time do you have to be home tonight?"

He shrugged. "When I feel like it."

"You know," my father said, moving in closer to my date, and at six and a half feet tall, he used his height for intimidation. "There's nothing but trouble after midnight."

"Well, I kinda'—"

I grabbed Austin's hand and cut in, "Appreciate the reminder, Dad." And we almost made it out the door, but my father had one final question for my date. "Are you driving tonight?"

"No, I'm only going into ninth."

"For the first or second time?"

"Dad!" I was horrified, but Austin just smiled again. "No, Sir, I'm just real mature for my age." And I could attest to that. Most ninth grade boys looked nothing like him, but apparently, the puberty fairy had made all her visits.

8

"Good, good." My father moved in toward Austin, resting a hand on his shoulder. "Then you'll be responsible enough to have my daughter home by ten o'clock."

"Eleven," I repeated as I pulled Austin out the front door and down the steps, but my father's voice followed us. "How about ten thirty?"

"It's not negotiable, Dad."

No worries there. I made it home well before ten o'clock. As soon as my friends and their dates got comfortable in the movie theater, Austin's two arms turned into eight. The octopus offered me an arsenal of cheesy come-ons, which I fought off with sarcastic disdain, and before the movie ended, I excused myself, found a pay phone, and arranged for a ride home.

I didn't want to call my parents, and most of my friends were only legal to drive bumper cars. So I was left with one option: I called on a friend who surrounded himself with upperclassmen. As a freshman, he pitched for the varsity baseball team, but by the time he arrived in his teammate's blue Mustang, the movie had ended. Everyone was waiting outside with me as my friend slipped from the car. With his male bravado in high gear, he singled out my date with narrowing eyes. "Stay away from her."

Austin shrugged. "Why? What's it to you?"

My friend chewed his gum slowly for a minute and stared back at Austin unflinchingly before he took my hand and turned around slowly; offering no reply, he led me toward the blue Mustang, still purring at the curb. We climbed into the back seat, and the driver turned. "Where to, man?"

"My house," my friend replied, and if the guys didn't already know, he added, "She lives right behind me."

That was the moment when Rob Callahan met Austin Walker, and you know what they say about first impressions: they're pretty hard to change. His and mine.

-3-

Better Than Hallmark

When I returned to AP English, I discovered Jessica Jackson in *my* seat. She looked up at me as I paused at my desk. "So," she elongated her "O" into next week. "I hope you don't mind that I'm in your seat." She was leaning on Rob's desk and giving me her big Sunday morning grin. The smile was as fake as our friendship, and even though we grew up in the same church, we hadn't discovered a Christian way to overcome our mutual dislike for each other. So I ignored her completely. It probably wasn't what Jesus would do, but it was better than what I wanted to do.

"Here you go, Rob." I placed his keys as well as my spare set on his desk and dropped the third into my bag. I tossed my bag toward an empty chair against the wall, and as I headed toward Miss Randall's desk, Jessica mumbled some worthless comment about the key incident. *Yeah,* I thought, *At least I dated him once.* Sure, it was a million years ago when going out meant a boy and a girl didn't run in opposite directions on the playground, and back in those days, Rob and I spent our entire recess at the swing set. I loved to swing, and he would push me up, up, up into the sky. When I reached a certain height, he would dare me to jump off, and I usually succumbed to his taunts since that was how I impressed him back then.

"Did I miss anything, Miss Randall?" I asked as I reached my teacher's desk. Her painted lips lifted from her coffee cup. "Nah,

10

not too much, Chloe." She wore a deep aqua suit and kept her hair neatly pulled away from her face. "You know," she started with her pretty smile. "I wouldn't have let you take this class as a junior if you had pulled that stunt last year."

"Aw, c'mon, Miss Randall," I said, sitting down in the conference chair next to her desk. "If school were based solely on common sense, they'd have to keep me in remedial English."

I made my teacher smile and returned to my "seat." I pulled out a spiral and doodled a picture of a ship sailing toward a tiny deserted island, and when the bell sounded, I glanced up at my annoying seat usurper. She was brushing Rob's arm lightly and smiling. It was a different smile than the one she had given me, but I hated it even more. She left my seat and said, "Let me know what you decide, Robbie."

I slid to the scene before Jessica was out of ear-shot. "Decide what, Robbie?" I inquired even though I hadn't used his boyhood moniker since our ages reached the double digits.

He stood up next to me and mumbled softly, "Prom."

"Well," I started slowly. "You wouldn't be in this predicament if you hadn't broken up with your girlfriend over Spring Break." His ex-girlfriend was also a member of our first-hour class, making the scene even more interesting.

"Predicament?" he echoed. "Most guys would be flattered."

"So, are you," I paused before I repeated his word, "flattered?"

He frowned. "No, not really."

Rob and I started toward the math wing, and I handed him a folded piece of notebook paper. "This is for you," I said with a smirk.

He unfolded my note and read the message at the bottom of the page. "Thanks for saving me." A corner of his mouth retreated into his cheek for a moment.

"Do you get it?" I peered over at him and pointed to the picture. "I'm the stick figure with curly hair, and I'm stranded on the deserted island."

"Well." A big smile took over his face. "Those sure are some nice coconuts."

11

"Robert. Wesley. Callahan." I intonated his mother's voice.

"On the tree," he defended. "Why? What were you thinking?"

"I was thinking you were a—" I stopped myself because I was trying to express my gratitude, and jerk wasn't exactly the best way. "So, anyway, you're in the boat wearing your ratty, old Red Sox cap. Of course, that's supposed to be the pirate ship from *Treasure Island*, but my artistic ability is limited, you know."

He folded the picture and put it in the back pocket. "Well, it's better than Hallmark, or at least that's what my mom would say to make *me* feel better."

I placed a playful punch on his arm, and he nudged me with his shoulder. Some things about our relationship never matured beyond the days of playgrounds and pirate stories, and if we overlooked the things that had, our friendship would always remain the same: innocent.

-4-

The Seven C's

Rob slipped into genius math while I hung out in the hallway with Callie Williams, and even though she was talking to me, her brown eyes scanned the halls for Mike Erickson. Mike was her brother's friend and her current crush, and the three of them lived in the upper atmosphere along with the other members of Riverside's basketball teams.

"He wasn't in first." I hated to deliver bad news without a possible upside. "So maybe he had an ortho or something."

"Yeah, maybe." Callie smiled a knowing mouth full of braces and paused in the doorway of my pre-calculus class. She waved over at Caitlyn and Courtney before she headed down the hall to her classroom. We were the four remaining members of "The Seven C's," a circle of friends formed in middle school, which was based entirely on the superficiality of alliteration.

The other three members? Cynthia Westwood transferred to a high school across town when her father accepted the principalship there, and Christina Anderson moved to Alexandria, Virginia in tenth grade. And that left one: Carly Evans. She remained at Riverside, but chose to alienate herself from us. For years, she was Caitlyn's closest friend, but now, she lurked the halls with painted black lips, standing in the sharpest contrast to the pastel predilections of Caitlyn Rivers.

I took my seat across the aisle from Caitlyn. Her short brown hair was pulled back in a headband, and her eyes matched her dark green top. Her hands were massaging her boyfriend's neck and shoulders, and after three long years, she hadn't tired of dating Riverside's mediocre quarterback. Of course, what Brandon Edwards lacked on the field, he made up for in other ways (or so Caitlyn led us to believe). Anyway, he was an honor roll student and good looking enough. He had soft eyes like the ocean and brown hair perfectly gelled into blonde-tipped spikes, and as I pulled out my math book, Brandon lowered his head to his desk for his morning nap.

Caitlyn, relieved of her girlfriend duties, slid her desk next to mine. "You look *so* tired, Chlo." That was her subtle way of telling me I looked like crap. "So, are you losing sleep over this thing with Austin?" The thing was a fight, and apparently, it had gone public.

"Nope," I said and opened my math book, taking a keen interest in parabolic equations.

Her emerald eyes searched my pale blue ones. "I'm sure he's worried too, Chlo." She was ascertaining Austin's emotional state, and that amused me considerably. Brandon too. He snickered a little before he drifted off to sleep. Brandon was Austin's best friend, and I was the girl who morphed into his girlfriend seven months ago. If Austin had much depth, then Brandon and I would have discovered it by now.

After answering a few more math problems, I noticed Courtney Valentine hadn't opened her book yet and remained sideways in her seat. She was twisting her long blonde hair into a haphazard knot and peering over at Ricky Sampson. He brushed the bleached blonde wisps from his dark brown eyes and mouthed an "I love you" from across the room. Ricky was ranked in some surfing circuits, and Courtney was the quintessential surfer girl—the hair, the eyes, the tan, and yes, the killer body to complete every guy's fantasy, especially his.

Courtney turned to face me. "So, I heard."

"Uh-huh," I acknowledged flatly. That was my new plan. I was going to appear uninterested in what people had to say to me, since I was going to be the butt of all jokes until someone did something stupider than lock their keys in a running car.

14

"That was nice of Rob," Courtney said. Geographically speaking, Rob Callahan was her boy-next-door. "What are we going to do without him next year?"

"Rely on each other," Caitlyn joked. Courtney made a dreadful face, and we all laughed. Courtney and I lacked common sense, and together, we made even less sense than we did apart.

Caitlyn's eyes drifted back to her boyfriend; then she heaved a heavy sigh as she fumbled through her purse for a tissue. She swiped the drool from his chin and off the desk before she folded the tissue into a square and tossed it into the trash. Returning to her seat, she rested her chin on folded hands and smiled. "Isn't he peaceful when he's sleeping?"

"Uh, that's what people say about their children," I said.

Courtney tilted her head in drool boy's direction. "Well, he *is* like a child."

"Yeah, but he's *my* child." Caitlyn smiled and noticed the clock. "Okay, sweetie. Time to wake up."

Courtney and I hung back by ourselves, funneling slowly into the crowded hallway. "And when are you putting *yours* up for adoption?" she asked, and I found the comment amusing until I noticed my big responsibility lounging against my locker.

-5-

Tabula Rasa

"**W**hy don't you make yourself useful, Austin?" I unloaded an armful of books into his empty hands, and the corners of his mouth curled into his notorious smile. And just like that, I forgot my next class.

I stood there, staring into my open locker, since Austin's presence was unbelievably distracting, and I couldn't imagine being on an actual study date with him. But then again, he rarely had any homework, and the only library we ever visited was in the "Land of Lies." After all, a date to the library sounded much better than "I'll be at Austin's place," since his apartment turned into Party Central whenever his dad shacked up with some woman. Currently, Whitney, a waitress from Riverside Diner, was offering Mr. Walker some fine Southern hospitality; nevertheless, I kept Austin's family dynamics as far from mine as possible.

Caitlyn shoved her books into the locker, and then Callie lowered a heavy American Lit text over my head. Our locker was totally communal—like the locker room showers that girls only used in the movies (you know the kind).

I spied a tattered, brown text at the bottom of the pile, and then I remembered I had Latin third hour. I grabbed my book, where one of the previous owners had scribbled the likes of Julius Caesar and Caligula into the "Property of" column, mixing Roman rulers with Latin losers who only took the dead language to increase their verbal SAT score.

16

Then Austin held my hand and my books down the hall, and for someone with incredible speed on the field, he moved like a slug everywhere else. He led me to our usual spot for goodbyes, but when his mouth started toward mine, I stopped his advancing lips with my fingertips. "I'm still mad at you."

He shrugged. "Cause of last night?"

"Uh, last night...this morning...last week...last month...take your pick."

"Yeah, yeah, whatever," he mumbled, and I turned on a heel and into third hour. But the bell beat me to my seat, and after I received a referral for chronic tardiness, I pushed back through the door and caught up to Austin's sauntering gait. "I'm not sitting in detention because of you!"

"Aw, calm down, baby. I'll take care of it." He grabbed my referral and walked me over to the front office. Once there, he leaned on the gray counter and flashed his sweet-boy grin at the secretarial pool. "Good morning, ladies. May I speak with Mr. Jenkins for a moment?"

"Sure, sugar, head on back."

Mr. Jenkins was sorting through a pile of mail when Austin sunk into a wing chair and pushed the referral up the desk. Our principal gave it a quick once-over and looked at Austin. "How can I be of assistance this morning?"

"Sir, this was all my fault," Austin began with an earnest smile, spreading his hands to the side. "Chloe tutors me, so I can stay academically eligible. Sometimes I need her help between classes, and I'd hate to see her to get in trouble for it."

"Sure, I'll explain it to Mrs. Evans."

"Thanks," I said meekly as I watched him rip up the referral and file it in the trash can under his desk. Then Mr. Jenkins leaned forward and rubbed his hands together. "Can't wait for next season."

"Yeah, me neither." Austin grinned.

"We lost a few starters, but Coach thinks..." The conversation went on and on as the minutes elapsed slowly from my third-hour class. The day was almost half over, and I had spent most of it outside the classroom; but when the principal got an important phone call, he ushered us to the door, saving his last words for me. "And keep him out of trouble, you hear?"

I nodded, but *really*, what was I supposed to do? The only boundaries Austin ever encountered were mine, and he whined at every roadblock like a little brat used to getting his way.

At the doorway, Austin extended a hand. "Thanks, Sir. I really appreciate it."

As we headed down the hall, I said, "That was almost hard to watch."

He winked over at me. "I *can* be nice."

"Yeah," I returned. "When you want something."

"You know what I really want?"

"No, I can't imagine." I played dumb as he pulled me into a remote girls' bathroom. He spat his gum into the trash can, smiled, and pressed me up against the wall. The pale yellow tiles felt cool against my backside, and the smell of industrial-strength cleaner hung in the air from last night's janitorial visit. His cinnamon tongue slid into my mouth, making it a good spicy kiss despite the locale, but after a few minutes of his tongue swirling around mine, I found his ear. "I'm going to class. Maybe you should try it for a change."

As I entered Latin again, Mrs. Evans summoned me with a curling finger, and I sat down next to her desk. "So, Mr. Jenkins gave you a tabula rasa, huh? You do know what that is, don't you, Miss Preston?"

I nodded slowly, but I didn't need three years of Latin to understand the English equivalents. I had received a blank slate; a mulligan; a fresh start. And it was all because of who I dated.

Mrs. Evans leaned in, lowering her head and her husky voice. "Therefore, I'm supposed to ignore all of your previous tardies since you were—how did Mr. Jenkins put it?—tutoring Mr. Walker. Well, maybe you should refrain from tutoring him right outside my class then."

"Yes, Mrs. Evans," I replied softly, finding my seat in the center of the classroom. Since we sat in alphabetical order, the desk in front of me belonged to Brad Preston, a sophomore and my only sibling.

When Brad and I escaped from Latin purgatorium, we ran into a waiting Austin who grinned at my brother menacingly— like a fraternity brother at a measly pledge. "Guess who will be running the offensive drills at football camp this summer?"

Brad considered the news. "Hmm, I think I'll go out for the band then."

"Yeah, what are you going to play?" I wondered.

"The tuba?"

I poked at his flat tummy. "Then we'll have to fatten you up over the summer, you little turkey." Austin shook his head at us, and my brother took it as his cue to leave.

Austin draped an arm around my shoulders, and together, without exchanging a word, we strolled toward the lunchroom at the far end of campus. Once inside, he left me for the food line and cut to the front with his ridiculous sense of entitlement, and I headed in the opposite direction, landing at my usual seat. There, I dumped the contents of my lunch onto the table.

Yes, I was the loser who brought my lunch to school every day, but I brown-bagged on financial principles alone. I received a set monthly allowance, which covered all my expenditures, including lunch money, so I saved it for clothes, my most basic need, and that spending pattern earned me the nickname of "best-dressed skeleton" in my father's third book, *Preston's Principles for Teens*. My dad wrote a series of titles on financial freedom, creating other volumes for children, newlyweds, and retirees, and when I got bored, I mused over new titles. My favorite was *Preston's Principles for the Homeless*. It could be a relatively thin book, and then after our teachers droned on and on about the pending teacher strike this past fall, I devised *Preston's Principles for the Overworked and Underpaid Teachers of America*. Amazingly, neither my father nor his publisher considered any of my suggestions.

Callie joined me at the lunch table first. "He was at the dentist."

"Ooh, a good day for a first kiss then."

19

"Every day is *that* day." She glanced down at the other end of the table as Mike slid into his seat. Then he slowly turned up one corner of his mouth, offering his asymmetrical grin.

"Mm-hmm, I saw that," I assured her ego, and she squeezed all of her excitement into my hand, eating her lunch under the spell of Mike Erickson's half smile. Austin found a seat on my other side. He had a plate of pepperoni pizza in one hand and chocolate cake in the other, and before he got too comfortable, I informed, "We need to talk."

He folded a slice and took a bite. "About what?"

"You know what!"

"I thought we were good." His hand climbed my thigh and found its usual resting place. "We kissed, and you usually withhold when you're mad at me."

"Oh, that." I waved my hand dismissively. "That wasn't a make-up kiss. That was a thank-you kiss."

"Well, baby," he managed between mouthfuls. "They all taste good to me."

I turned and offered the evil eye, but somehow he mistook my eyebrow-raising scowl for something else. He lunged forward and planted a greasy kiss on my lips.

"Yuck." I wiped my mouth with a napkin. "You know I hate pepperoni." And that was how all of our serious talks ended. He annoyed me as a means of distraction. It was like stomping on someone's toe to divert the pain of a broken arm. Our relationship was still in pieces, but since he irritated me so much, I didn't feel like fixing it anymore.

Brandon leaned forward, getting our table's attention. "The party will be at *my* house tonight." A loud whoop exploded around the table, and then Austin peered over at me with intensity in his bright blue eyes. "And don't invite him."

"Huh?" I wondered for a moment, but when I saw my best friend perched at the end of the table, I had my answer.

"A no-hitter, huh?" Callie inquired and sunk her teeth into her slice of pizza.

"No, but it was close," Courtney answered quickly. She must

have made the game last night, but I went to the "library" instead. We spent hours reviewing anatomy, and Austin got upset when I wouldn't let him advance to the next chapter.

Rob clarified, "Yeah, well, Kennedy got a hit with one out in the ninth."

"Wow! That *was* close!" I remembered when the Sox played Kansas City and Jon Lester pitched a no-hitter. Rob said it was the ultimate rush for a pitcher, yet now, he just shrugged it off. "Nah, I just got lucky. Plus, their best hitter was out."

"Well, it's still amazing." I toned it down a bit, since I had the peanut gallery behind me. "Anyway, I'm sorry I missed it. I'll make the next game, I promise."

Austin draped his arm around my shoulders and pulled me into his chest. "You know, Chloe never misses my games."

"Dude!" Ricky Sampson was up to bat next. "That's because she *loooves* you, man."

"Yeah, and I don't have to give her the keys to my truck either." Austin received a few laughs at my expense, but Rob just glared back at him. "Why would you brag about that?"

Austin shrugged. "Because you do all the work, and I get all the benefits."

I was *so* annoyed with him that I heaved his heavy arm off my shoulders, and Rob leaned forward, grinning. "And is rejection one of those so-called benefits?"

Austin stood up and did the stare-down with Rob, and silence swept down the entire length of the table. "You got something to say to me, Callahan?"

"Yeah, where do I begin, Walker?"

"How 'bout with your last words before I kick your—"

"Ooh, and look at the time!" Courtney jumped up and faced Rob. "You mind walking us to class?" Her eyes drifted back to Austin. "Because there are a lot of jerks on this campus."

Rob smiled, and as soon as we reached the main aisle of the cafeteria, he hung an arm around each of us. "You two have the worst taste in guys."

"Maybe, but we have the best taste in friends," Courtney

returned with a smile, and Rob did an obligatory "aw." Then we split up in the science wing: Rob went to AP Biology, and Courtney and I ducked into our physics classroom.

Once inside, Courtney's eyes remained at the front of the room, but her words were aimed at me. "You didn't make this easy for him when you started seeing Austin."

I defended myself. "It's not like his girlfriends are ever nice to me."

"Well, I wouldn't be either," she said as she slid her spiral onto the lab table. "You were his first girlfriend, and no matter what you two say, you still have that weird connection."

I looked at the intern and found her ear. "Like you and Mr. Martinez?"

Her response was a single huff, since our young teacher was on his way to our table with a stack of papers. "And Chloe, out of all my classes, you got the highest score on the test."

"Well, that's because I studied with a genius," I admitted quickly, always feeling a little uncomfortable in our teacher's presence. He was tall, dark, and chiseled to perfection.

"Your boyfriend?" he asked tenaciously.

Callie found her seat across from us and laughed uncontrollably. "Seriously, do you know who her boyfriend is?"

"No, but I know about her car troubles this morning," our teacher replied with a suppressed grin.

"Oh, that's a gentle way of putting it," I decided. "But you realize, in the halls of Riverside, I'll be forever known as the stupid girl who locked her keys in a running car."

He leaned on his elbows. "So, really, how'd you do it?"

"I can't answer that." I gave him one of those "I'm an idiot" expressions, and we shared an acceptable student-teacher laugh. This might sound weird, but I never minded mocking my own intelligence since I wasn't insecure about it at all. It's like how rail-thin girls look at themselves sideways in the mirror and mutter, "God, I'm so fat."

Then without a word, he pushed Courtney's test across the table. My eyes followed her paper, a respectable B plus, but she tucked it away like she had failed miserably; and when he walked away, she mumbled, "Maybe if I had your brain, then he'd notice me more." But it wasn't a lack of brains or beauty that kept Mr. Martinez from returning her advances; it was something Courtney couldn't change—except one slow year at a time.

*   *   *

After watching Courtney sulk and sigh for the rest of the class period, I headed to AP American History. It was taught by this retired military guy, and about halfway through the class, he put on a documentary about some war. But I fell asleep before I figured out which one, and when the lights flipped back on, I headed to my last class of the day.

I had sixth-hour journalism, and since it was Friday, I joined Caitlyn at the round table for our weekly staff meeting. I was rubbing my eyes and feeling groggy from the short video nap when Rob assumed his role as editor of *The Riverside Review*. "Okay, everyone, let's get started." I sat directly across from him, trying to conceal my successive yawns. "And Chloe, let's begin with you."

"Really, Rob?" I frowned because I wasn't ready to pitch an article, and Rob always had a sixth sense about it. I was in charge of the "Student Life" section, and prom was the major headline in our last issue. Even though I hadn't planned my articles, Caitlyn and I aptly covered prom all week long: we decided on a place for dinner, the time to meet up at my house for pictures, and the location for the after party. Caitlyn even created a spreadsheet, so everyone had the exact times and locations for each activity. After we finished with prom, we decided Caitlyn should become a wedding planner, and we planned our double wedding to our boyfriends.

"Well, I was thinking of interviewing a couple about their prom experience," I started talking as I tossed ideas around in my head. "Like a his-and-hers perspective on the night."

23

"But it can't be either of us." Caitlyn gestured between her and me. "Because we'll both be on Junior Court, and it doesn't seem fair to showcase us twice in the same issue." There are two things to realize about her statement: first, if I made Court, then it would have been based on my boyfriend's popularity and not my own; and second, the only reason Caitlyn took journalism was to make sure she was well showcased in every issue.

"Yeah, well, I don't want to interview you two anyway," I said to Caitlyn before addressing the whole table again. "Plus, I was thinking about two friends or a couple in the early stages of a relationship." I peered across the table at our fearless leader as my next idea surfaced. "You know, I should interview you and your date." Curiosity fueled my next question. "So, who's the lucky girl, Rob?"

He shrugged. "I haven't decided yet."

"Just flip a coin," our sports editor offered.

"Uh, mucho problemo," I began in a language I had never taken. "A coin has two sides, and I know more than two girls have asked him to prom."

He leaned back in his seat and crossed his arms like he was annoyed with my acute awareness of his social life, but then again, our lives ran as parallel as the roads on which we lived.

"Oh, I know, I know," Caitlyn repeated enthusiastically. "You should draw names, Rob." She pulled out a ruler and a pair of scissors from the office supply caddy at the center of the round table and began making perfect strips of paper, and while Caitlyn exhibited her obsessive compulsive tendencies, another idea popped into my head. "Or better yet, we could make it a contest—like an essay contest. And we could print the winning entry in the paper." I smirked and drew my hand across the air. "Why should Rob Callahan take me to the prom?"

"Hmm, that *is* a good question." Rob rested on his elbows. "Why should I take you?"

"Well, you can't take Chloe because…" Caitlyn interjected unsuccessfully, her voice muffling like Charlie Brown's teacher as our eyes locked for verbal warfare.

I went first. "Because I'm nice, Rob."

"*You're* nice?" he echoed incredulously. "Think of all the things I do for you." He enumerated each one on his fingertips. "Tutoring. Taxi Services. Car Loans." A few snickered at the mention of the car thing. My key incident—still not old yet.

"Yeah, well, I do plenty of things for you," I returned.

He tossed a "like what" expression across the table and handed me my assignment. "Why don't you explain it in your essay then?"

"Well, she can't win the contest," Caitlyn reminded.

I leaned in toward Rob. "Yeah? How many words?"

"Haven't I taught you anything? 'Brevity is the soul of wit.'" He leaned back and turned his attention to the entire table. "Now, that we've covered *my* student life, let's move on to Sports…"

After we wrapped up our Friday meeting, I followed Rob over to the counter at the back of the classroom. "Hey, chief," I said, sliding next to him.

He was busy sorting through articles. "Whatcha' need, Chlo?"

"Nothing, really. I just wanted to let you know that I got the highest score on the physics test." I rose up on my tippy toes and whispered the rest. "And I even answered the bonus question correctly."

He turned, offering his dimpled grin. "Wow, I'm really proud of you." His fatherly tone gave me a warm feeling and caused a catch in my throat. My dad was in the middle of a four-week-long speaking tour.

"I really miss my dad," I said with a prominent pout.

"Yeah, me too." He draped his arm around my shoulders. "Taking care of you is a lot of work."

-6-

Brown Paper Bag

After school, Brad and I lounged on the L-shaped leather sectional in the family room. It was one of the few pieces of furniture from this century, and it was the perfect configuration for after school slothfulness. Brad took the long side since, at fifteen, he had surpassed the six-foot mark, and I always got the short end since I was only five and a half feet tall, never growing an inch after my big middle school growth spurt.

For the rest of the afternoon, Brad and I remained on the couch with an open bag of tortilla chips and a big bowl of salsa between us, and when my mother came home, I was busy picking miniscule bits of chips off my hot pink T-shirt while Brad flipped channels at an impressive rate.

My mother entered the room with a loud sigh and several bags of groceries. She was dressed in a pair of gray slacks and a lavender blouse, and her blonde hair was cut in a short wedge. My mom had no use for makeup beyond lip gloss and a little mascara; she wasn't one of those Monet moms who looked like a blank canvas in the morning. All she required was a single cup of coffee, and she was herself again: a totally conservative librarian.

Brad and I left the couch begrudgingly and helped my mom unload the groceries from the trunk of her silver Civic. It was a hybrid, of course, since our household was as green as the two saplings sitting on the backseat, and at the sight of the tiny trees, our faces twisted into question marks.

26

"Oh, come on kids, it's Earth Day!" A smile spread across her face, and she acted like the holiday rivaled one with presents. "And we're going to do something nice for the environment by planting trees in our yard."

"Like we need any more of those," Brad mumbled under his breath, and my mother offered her parental frown.

As we headed into the kitchen, I asked, "So, Mom, did you consult Dad before you bought these trees? Sure, they're cute little saplings now, but one day they'll grow into big, *big* trees."

"Oh, I see where you're going with this." She placed the bags on the island in the kitchen.

"Yeah, I bet you do." A few years back, my dad returned from one of his book tours and was surprised to find a tiny dog in the backyard. Even though my mom was a librarian, we neglected to research Fluffball's breed ahead of time, and when our pup matured into a full-grown, menacing Chow Chow, my dad sent our beloved pet to live out the rest of his days on a nice, roomy farm. There, he could dig holes and bite people without my father worrying about the inevitable lawsuit.

My mom started putting groceries away while my brother foraged for snacks, and quite casually, Brad mentioned, "Mom, ask Chlo about her day."

She turned toward me. "Why? What happened?"

"Well," I started plainly. "I locked my keys in the car."

"Oh, you've done that before." She waved her hand dismissingly. She was holding a carton of eggs in her other hand, so Brad waited until the eggs were securely on the shelf before he added, "Yeah, but her car was still running."

Her mouth dropped open.

"I know, Mom." He put his hand on her shoulder like it was a delicate situation. "It's Earth Day, and Chloe is polluting the environment with unnecessary car fumes."

My mom started laughing like she wasn't all that concerned about the environment *or* my feelings. Brad had my mom going, so he followed it up with a preposterous tale about the book mobile, which is like a library on wheels. The big buses visit

27

parking lots of grocery stores and day cares, bringing books to children who may not have access to them otherwise. Brad began the story with a smile, "Well, it's still not as funny as that kid who tried to use the book mobile bathroom, and by the time he was all done, he found himself in the Winn Dixie parking lot way across town."

"C'mon Brad, do bookmobiles even have bathrooms?" I asked.

"Sure, they're fully equipped like an RV, and if they run short on TP, the kids probably use the—"

"Okay, okay, that's enough." My mother held up her hand. "After a long day of work, I could use a little peace and quiet right now."

"Seriously, Mom, you're a librarian. Isn't that what you get all day long?" I couldn't hold back the laughs even though there was a serious déjà vu feeling to this comment.

"Oh, go do your homework, kids."

"It's Friday night, Mom," Brad reminded her. "I'm going to the movies."

"Yeah, and I'm spending the night at Courtney's."

Brad and I left the kitchen together and crossed into the family room. "Courtney's house, huh?" He eyed me carefully. "What will you do to buy my silence?"

"You can use my car tonight." I paused. "Oh, that's right. You can't drive."

My brother stepped in closer, whispering, "And what about your little referral today?"

"You want rides to school, don't you?"

"Yep, but I want to keep the spare set of keys."

"You'll have to get them from Rob then."

"Sure, that makes sense, since Callahan acts more like your boyfriend than that Neanderthal you date."

I glared back at my brother as I reached for the ringing phone in my back pocket. "Hey, I was just thinking about you." I poured on the syrup in front of my brother and then left the room.

"You coming?" Austin asked.

"Yeah."

"Then hurry your sweet, little—"

I cut him off. "Okay, okay, I'll be right there."

* * *

Two hours later, Courtney and I arrived at the party, grabbed a pair of chaise lounges by the pool, and slid into our sunbathing poses. We were soaking in the rays of the setting sun when Austin lowered himself to the end of my chair. "Glad you made it, baby." He placed a beer between his thighs and started admiring his own pecs. "Guess what?" I shrugged a shoulder. "I benched 18 reps of 225 today."

"Is that good?"

"Hell yeah! Running backs are doing 20 to 25 at the NFL combine."

"The NFL?" Courtney wondered. "Are you going out for the draft or something?"

"No, I gotta' go to college first." He looked at her like she was mentally challenged, but Courtney was clueless about the sports world. Then again, she was *that* hot, and guys didn't really care if she conversed in their language or not.

Austin continued on, "I'll put in my three years and then head out for the draft." He ran his fingers up my leg and found a resting place on my inner thigh. "But I have to bulk up for next year. The scouts will be at the games, and I want my pick of anywhere in the state." He glanced at Courtney. "That way Chloe and I can stay close to home." His eyes found mine again as he leaned forward slowly, his lips landing on the top of my knee.

"Heads up!" Brandon shouted from across the pool, and Austin lunged forward and caught a whirling football headed for my face.

"Thanks." I smiled at Austin as he flipped the ball in the palm of his hand.

"I never miss. You know that, baby."

"Yeah, three years of games, home and away, and when you

guys made State, I went to all your playoff games too. Do you realize how many nights I have spent watching you run up and down that field?"

"A lot." He sipped his beer and smiled.

"Yeah, and in those three years, what have you done for me?"

"I went to all your track meets."

Courtney lifted her sunglasses, which were more an accessory than a necessity. "That's because you run track, Walker."

He cackled, chugged the rest of his beer, and wandered off to form a pick-up game in Brandon's backyard. Moments later, Caitlyn Rivers and Aimee Peterson, the captain of the cheer squad, showed up with too much pep for a non-football Friday night. "C'mon, let's watch the boys." Caitlyn turned toward the game, and a huge grin filled her face as Brandon, Austin, and Ricky pulled off their shirts. "Ooh, and it looks like our guys will be on the Skins' team."

"Oh, big deal! We live in Florida," Courtney returned quickly. "Half-naked guys are more common than orange trees."

Aimee rolled her eyes to the sky, and Caitlyn frowned at us. Apparently, we lacked the proper rah-rah attitude. They left, and Callie arrived next. She shoved my feet aside and plopped down at the end of my chair. Her face was red from something other than the setting sun, and she was pushing out exhales like she was trying to avoid a massive panic attack. "Okay, you guys need to stay totally calm."

"Like you?" I questioned with an unavoidable snicker.

"Oh, shut up! You will *not* ruin this for me." She glanced back at a circle of guys, none of whom were under six feet, and then back to us as she squealed, "Mike just asked me to the prom!" Her bare feet were tap dancing the Chattahoochee rock, and there was no way she could hold back her excitement, so I grabbed her hand and suggested, "We should go inside and scream like crazy."

Not even close to calm or cool, we slipped away for a synchronized potty session, and once inside the pool bath, we looked at one another and committed a long succession of ear-splitting shrieks. Our mouths hung open; our screams flowed freely; and we jumped up and down with more excitement than when Caitlyn won concert tickets over the radio. This was probably the best news of our entire junior year, and Courtney was the first one to stop freaking out. "Okay, give us all the details, Cal."

Callie drew a deep breath. "Well, Mike told me that after he and Amber broke up, he wanted to ask me out, but he was all concerned about my brother and everything, and I'm like who cares, but I mean he does because he and Landon are tight, you know. So, he actually talked to my brother before he asked me to prom." Her hand touched her chest, and I imagined her heart was beating like a bass drum. She drew another deep breath and fell onto the toilet. "I've never been so happy in my whole life." And that's when the happy tears started flowing freely, and we consoled her during her time of great joy. "This stuff only happens in the movies. I mean, Mike is my ideal. He's so cute and smart, and most importantly, he's tall and can take me in a game of one-on-one."

Courtney chewed on the end of her fingernail. "So, are you gonna' let him dunk it in your basket then?" Courtney was a master of the innuendo and harassed us mercilessly about our sexual status, acting like we were the last two members of the Virgin Sisterhood.

"Hmm, maybe on prom night." Callie turned toward me with a mischievous smirk. "Then you'll be the last one."

"Oh, I don't know," Courtney started with a smile. "Haven't you heard all the rumors?"

"C'mon Courtney." I was tired of the Riverside rumor mill turning out stories about Austin and me.

"Come to think of it, Landon said Austin was running his mouth in the weight room this afternoon." Callie looked at me with those dark brown eyes of judgment. "I mean, you're spending the night here, aren't you?"

"That doesn't mean we'll actually do *it*," I defended. "Austin talks the big talk, but he knows I want to wait until..." I let my

31

voice linger, since they would only mock me for wanting to wait until marriage anyway.

Courtney rubbed her chin. "Austin doesn't seem like the patient type to me."

"I know what you should do, Chlo." Callie shot up from the toilet seat. "You should go through his stuff and see what he has planned for tonight."

"No way! I am not doing that!"

"Fine!" Courtney grabbed Callie's hand and headed into Austin's room. "Then we'll do it for you."

Brandon was an only child, and the Edwards let Austin crash in the bedroom by the pool. The whole arrangement bonded them like brothers, and while Brandon's parents were out of town for the weekend, Austin moved in, redecorating the place with his crap everywhere. His unzipped duffle bag sat on the dresser like an open invitation, and Courtney rummaged through the contents quickly. She pulled out a brown paper bag and peeked inside. "Okay girls, I'll give you three guesses." She shook the bag. "What's inside?"

I wasn't interested in playing, so I folded my arms across my chest like a grump at a comedy club; but Callie, on the other hand, licked her lips in anticipation. "Antifungal foot cream."

"Nope."

"Fast-Acting Tinactin for his jock itch." She gulped for air dramatically like a contestant making bid on the *Price Is Right*. "Oh, I know Ex-Lax!"

"Not even close, but I'll give you one more try."

She scratched her head for the desired effect. "Hmm, could it be Rogaine?"

Courtney dumped the contents onto the unmade bed. "Nope, you lose." A big lavender box of condoms sat on top of the pale blue comforter, and Callie examined the jumbo pack of prophylactics. "'Her pleasure.' Well, *that* was thoughtful of him."

Courtney walked over to me and draped her arm around my shoulder. "So, he's either planning on having sex with you *or* with someone else. Either way…" Her voice drifted off while I stared at the box of condoms, and I thought about last night and

32

the fight we had. I thought about how much he begged me to still come to the party, and all of it made sense. He was obviously ready to have sex. Now, the question was, was I?

Austin stepped into the room. "What's going on in here?"

"I was looking for some, uh, toothpaste," I tried.

Callie tossed the condoms onto the bed and gestured toward Courtney. "And we were looking for the bathroom." They shut the door behind them.

He looked over at the bed and then back at me. "You still need toothpaste?"

"Nah, I'm not too concerned about oral hygiene right now." I grabbed the box of condoms and held them up like I was on a commercial. "Why do you have these?"

He spread his hands out to the sides. "Because you're not on the pill."

"And why would I be on the pill? I'm not having sex with anyone."

"Yeah, don't you think I know that better than anyone? I'm the one who's been denied for seven friggin' months!"

"You are such a jerk," I muttered through clenched teeth like I was an accomplished ventriloquist, and then I searched his hardened expression for a reason not to continue. But his face offered no alternative. "It's over, Austin! I really mean it this time!"

I was pissed about the tears welling in my eyes, and I would be lying if I said I hadn't imagined our break-up scene a few times in the last few months. Every time, I wore a smug expression and was armed with wit. But here, as the scene unfolded, I had too much emotion and too little wit. I grabbed my overnight bag off the bedroom floor and flung it over my shoulder. "I'm leaving."

"Good. Go home. I won't stop you," he said, gesturing at the box in my hand. "Because those would expire before I used them with you."

"Oh, shut up!" I chucked the box of condoms at him. I aimed at his crotch, and needless to say, after years of tossing the ball with Rob Callahan, I didn't throw like a girl. But Austin's hand flew up ever-so-quickly, snatching the projectile prophylactics

33

in midair. "Thanks, I'll need these tonight."

I stared back at him, wishing I could shoot daggers from my eyes or blow fire from my nose, but I wasn't given any superpowers at conception, just the X-chromosome that caused crying at the most inconvenient times.

Courtney drove me to her house, which was where I was supposed to be anyway, and we sat in her driveway for a while as I wiped away tears with the back of my hand.

"I have some napkins in the glove box," Courtney said as she reached for my hand. "Chlo, we've been friends for a long time and through lots of guys together, but I've never seen you cry this much over any of them."

"But this started that summer before ninth," I admitted slowly. "I know we only had that one date…well, mostly because I thought he was a jerk."

"And?"

"He can be. Trust me. But there is another side to him, the side that no one sees. And that's why I'm crying, Court. All those memories—" I broke off, thinking of my room. It was a shrine to Riverside's football god. I had framed photos on my bookcase and an entire bulletin board of his newspaper clippings.

Courtney knew. "Just put everything into an old shoe box. Cry hard over it tonight, and then seal it with duct tape. Someday you'll be able to open it again, and you'll smile about it. The heart has a way of forgetting about the bad times, Chlo, and all you'll have left are the good memories of Austin Walker."

I heaved out an "O-k-k-ay."

"Or better yet, we could hit the clubs tonight," she started with a mischievous grin, "since I believe in the replacement theory myself."

"No thanks," I said quickly. "I don't need another Austin Walker."

"Oh, don't worry, Chlo. He's one-of-a-kind."

A slight grin transformed my face, and I grabbed my bag from the tiny backseat of her red convertible. "I think I should just go home."

34

She led me toward the side of her house where her lawn met Rob's yard. It was the grassy expanse where we played soccer and ran through sprinklers on hot summer days, and it was like walking on childhood.

I lifted my eyes slowly and glimpsed over at the darkened house next door, and Courtney answered my thoughts. "The Callahans went out for dinner." We continued across Rob's yard until we reached the woods, and at the edge of his property stood a huge oak with a tree house in its boughs. As children, it was our place. It was where we laughed uncontrollably at each other's jokes and whispered our secrets, and a little part of me wanted to flick off my flip flops and climb inside, but the majority of me felt sixteen and thought better of it.

I stepped gingerly into the woods and followed the pine needle path to my backyard. I hugged Courtney goodbye at the gate and entered my dimly lit house. The only light came from the master bedroom where I found my mother propped up on several pillows and engrossed in the latest Grisham novel.

"Mom, I just wanted to let you know that I was home." I forced out a fictitious yawn that manifested into a real one. "I was too tired to stay up with the girls."

"Okay, Chlobear." She smiled and lifted her eyes from the page. "Go get some rest, hon, and I'll see you in the morning."

"Okay, goodnight, Mom."

I made a pit stop in the kitchen, pulled the tub of Rocky Road out of the freezer, and grabbed a big girl spoon. Armed with the quintessential break-up food, I headed up to my room. Once there, I removed pictures from frames and newspaper clippings from the bulletin board, and then cried over the last three years while I shoved heaping spoonfuls of chocolate heaven into my mouth. It was the pleasure-over-pain principle, and when I finished with my tears and had consumed over four servings of ice cream, I tucked the shoe box on a shelf in my closet, hiding it behind a pair of barely worn winter boots.

Now, what? I wondered, but I knew enough about break-ups to avoid music at all costs. There's no actual study on this, but the majority of songs were probably written after a bad break-up, which is why I dismissed my other favorite alone time activity: writing. With music and writing out, I decided to try reading. I walked over to my bookcase to find *John Steinbeck: A Biography*, but it was buried under my copy of *Wuthering Heights* and my spare set of keys. There was a note sticking out of Emily Bronte's famed novel, and it was from the other member of my book club. Since our *Dr. Seuss* days, Rob and I have exchanged favorite titles; but lately, he concentrated on the novels of the American literary canon, and I fired back with classical romances.

> *Dear Hopeless Romantic-*
> *I just finished those three hun-*
> *dred pages of exquisite torture*
> *and can't wait for the next book.*
> *-Rob*

I slid his note back into the book, and I wondered if he was right. Was I just a hopeless romantic doomed for one disappointing relationship after another? Maybe if I had spent more time watching the TV's version of love, I wouldn't be so jaded each time I came close to finding it. I was sixteen, almost seventeen, and even though I had a few relationships behind me, I had never been in love. I had never come close to finding anything that I had experienced in the pages of my books, and I had to wonder if my expectations of love actually kept me from falling in it.

-7-

Making the Grade

The next afternoon, I was sprawled across Courtney's pink satin comforter, perusing through a stack of magazines. I was looking for the answers to the "love" question, but after flipping through several *Cosmo's* and the big prom issue of *Seventeen*, I didn't have any answers—just more questions. So I decided to take the "Rate Your Date" quiz at the end of the prom issue, and since I hadn't secured another date for the dance, I used Austin as my point-of-reference.

"And what do you know...Austin Walker failed another test," I said to myself, but loud enough for Courtney to overhear. She was on the phone, orbiting the house like Halley's Comet, so I expected her to return at some point. What I didn't expect was the particular sound of her laugh upon reentering the room. It was deep and breathy, and clearly belonged to her next-door neighbor and not her.

"What are you doing here?" I snapped.

"Well, hello to you too, Frankenstein."

That's when I remembered the pale green glop caked on my face. I flung off the bed and rushed into the bathroom as the blood rose in my cheeks.

"What does that stuff do anyway?" Rob inquired from a closer proximity than I would have liked.

"It helps with my complexion," I answered as I washed my face and patted it dry with a pink hand towel.

"Well, it worked, Chlo." He smiled widely, offering the grand entrance of his dimples. "Your cheeks are much redder than normal."

I stepped toward him. He was consuming the doorway and blocking my way into Courtney's room. "Oh, you're so funny." I pushed my pointer finger into his chest. Extremely hard. His chest—not my jab, and for some reason, curiosity urged me to test it again. So, like a little researcher, I advanced my finger to the same exact spot. This time he drew his shoulders inward and flexed his pecs like he wanted me to draw a particular conclusion about his muscular density.

A little "impressive" slipped from my lips even though I had not given my mouth permission to report my findings, and a smile spread across his lips. His hand rested lightly on my bare shoulder, and that's when I noticed I was missing a shirt. I was only dressed in a pink spandex camisole, and the weather dials on my chest were forecasting the temperature in the room. Mine hinted at chilly.

I pushed him aside and grabbed my shirt off the bed. Quickly, I slipped into my blouse and started at the buttons. "Aren't you going to ask me about last night?"

"Nah, Courtney told me what happened." He paused for a moment. "And she didn't leave out any of the gory details."

"Great," I muttered sarcastically as my nimble fingers finished the last buttons. But as I looked up at him again, his brown eyes fell to my chest. "Hey, you missed one, Chlo." And before I could check my own handiwork, he reached across and slowly slid the button through the small slit. As I watched his fingers flutter near my heart, that feeling surfaced again. It was indescribable in words. It was just the way I felt around him sometimes. He was the first boy to hold my hand and profess his affections for me, and all I knew was the feeling started in childhood. But since I had no name for the feeling and couldn't describe it with words, I simply recognized its existence and waited for it to pass again.

Courtney entered the room, and we both stepped back and looked away from each other. She covered the mouthpiece of the phone and shout-whispered, "Did I interrupt something?" It was completely rhetorical, but she liked to pose those questions on occasion. Courtney was around when Rob and I were "dating," and she acted like she owned the teasing rights to our playground romance.

"Mom said dinner would be ready in an hour or so." Rob turned toward Courtney. "But Josh has been ready for *you* all day." Josh was his cousin on his father's side, yet a few months younger than Rob, and like most normal, healthy teenage boys, he was infatuated with Rob's neighbor.

At the mention of Josh, Courtney bit down on her lip and left the room with her phone, and I proceeded to the bathroom for a few minor touch-ups as Rob resumed his post in the doorway again. I slid a tube of gloss across my lips, pressed them together, and let out a smack. I looked up at him in the mirror and spoke to his reflection. "I have something for you," I said and pulled a white envelope out of my bag.

Rob eyed it with curiosity, and I replied, "It's my entry for the contest, silly."

"Oh," he said with a smile, sliding a finger across the seal and pulling out the folded paper. I watched his expression as he read the following:

"Why Should Rob Callahan Take Me to the Prom?"
by Chloe Preston

1. *He won't get lost on the way to my house.*
2. *I actually get his sense of humor. I just don't find it all that funny.*
3. *I'm a fast runner. So, if we need to dine and dash, then I could make it out the door in time.*
4. *He already knows my curfew, and he uses it to make fun of me. (Refer to #2)*
5. *I don't have any known food allergies or previous medical conditions that would interfere with the whole prom experience.*

39

6. *My dancing is totally normal, meaning it's not good enough or bad enough to put us in the spotlight.*
7. *He knows my parents, which saves considerable time at the front door.*
8. *I'm not hideous looking, so he won't be embarrassed to show his prom picture to his grandkids.*
9. *Taking the girl next door is fiscally responsible; after all, it saves money on gas.*
10. *And most importantly, I'm his best friend. (So, does he really need any other reason to take me to the prom?)*

"What do you think?" I wondered.

"Somewhat amusing."

"Yeah, but the real question is…" I drum-rolled the counter-top. "Did I win the contest?"

"C'mon, there is no contest."

"Yeah, I know. I made it up to annoy you, but that still doesn't answer my question."

"Actually, I think it does." He smiled again, and I bit down on my lip as the other meaning popped into my head. Agreeably, I was the best candidate in the prom race, since I was way more fun than Jessica Jacobs or any of the other smarties from the senior class.

"Okay, I get it," I replied as I flung my bag over my shoulder and headed out the opposite door of the Jack and Jill bath.

"Oh, no, you're not getting away that easy," he said as his hand rested on my shoulder. "You still have to ask me."

Slowly, I turned to face him. My pale blue eyes connected with his chocolate brown pair, and I swallowed down the little knot growing in my throat. "Rob, will you go to prom with me?"

"Sure," he said with a wry smile and a wink. "I thought you'd never ask."

-8-

Table Talk

"Chloe, let me take a look at you, dear." Aunt Nancy intercepted me as soon as I walked into the Callahan's kitchen. "You get more and more beautiful every time I see you."

"Thank you," I replied demurely as Courtney brushed past our conversation; she was on her way to find Josh. His family, which included Aunt Nancy, Uncle Mike, younger brother Jake and little sister Julia, lived north of Orlando. But they visited Rob's house quite often, making Josh a nice addition to Courtney's ever-expansive collection of guys.

Then I crossed the kitchen toward Mrs. Callahan. She gave me a one-armed hug; her other hand was stirring a simmering pot of homemade pasta sauce. Rob's mother had prepared an Italian feast for her dinner guests. In addition to her family of four, she had invited Josh's family, Grandpa Callahan, Courtney, and me. She extended an invitation to the two of us, since my mom was at one of Brad's tennis tournaments and Courtney's parents were out of town, which was more the norm than the exception these days.

"Need any help with dinner?" I asked, but she just shook her head gently. "No thanks, hon. Why don't you go upstairs and say hello to Grandpa?"

I took the hidden staircase behind the kitchen, since it led up to the master suite. Off their bedroom, Rob's parents had a study where Grandpa Callahan spent the majority of his visits.

41

"Hi, Grandpa," I said softly as I opened the French door. He sat comfortably in a leather wing chair in the middle of the windowless room. The built-in bookcases wrapped around the walls, and a Tiffany lamp offered the only light.

"Well, hello, Chloe." He adjusted his reading glasses and glanced up at me. "And what have you been reading lately?" Grandpa had been an English professor at a few colleges in Boston and finished his tenure at Stetson University, so he took a keen interest in my literary progress.

I crossed the room and ran my fingers across a row of books. "Oh, I just finished Steinbeck's biography last night. Not my choice, but your grandson's." I pulled the book out of my bag and slid it back onto the shelf.

"Good. Then you should read his novels next." Rob's voice entered the study, and he started pulling a couple of books off the shelf. He turned toward his grandfather. "*East of Eden* or *The Grapes of Wrath*?"

Grandpa addressed me. "Surely, you read *Grapes of Wrath* in American Literature this year."

Rob spoke first. "She skipped Am Lit and took AP this year, but don't worry, Grandpa." Rob handed me both novels. "I'll educate her properly."

Grandpa chuckled as I tucked both books into my bag, and Rob fell into the other chair and opened his newspaper. If a hint of favoritism could be detected, then I would have guessed that Grandpa preferred the company of his eldest grandson. The reasons would have been numerous: a love of literature, a passion for baseball, or perhaps, the man overcompensated for a boy who bore no relation to him at all. When Dr. Callahan married Rob's mother, he adopted her young son and added his good family name to the end of Robert William Wesley.

"And what do you recommend for Robert?" Grandpa asked me.

My fingertips lightly touched the spines of the books as I moved toward the beginning of the alphabet. I rose up on my tippy toes and reached for Jane Austen's *Pride and Prejudice*.

"Here." I dropped the book in my best friend's lap. "I think you have a lot in common with Mr. Darcy." I teased Rob endlessly about his air of superiority, and Jane Austen's male protagonist was the embodiment of pride.

"Hmm," Grandpa interjected as I crossed the room toward the French doors. "That's interesting, since I've always regarded you as a bit of a Lizzie Bennet myself." She was the main character of Austen's novel and could banter better than any Shakespearean heroine, so any comparison to Miss Bennet was a huge compliment in my book.

"Well, thank you very much," I said with a slight curtsy and headed out of the room. I bolted down the stairs and almost ran into Rob's mom near the bottom. Mrs. Callahan had stopped to straighten the pictures along the walls of the stairwell, which were like a family photo gallery.

"Chloe, do you remember this one?" she asked as she adjusted a dark mahogany frame.

I looked at the photograph on the wall. It was taken about ten years ago, and Rob and I were sitting on the edge of my pool with our feet dangling in the water. He was shirtless with a Red Sox cap on his head, and I had on a bright floral sundress with my hair up in pigtails. Our arms were wrapped around each other like we were the best of friends—even then. It was pretty cute actually, and it reminded me of one of those old-timey photographs on a romantic greeting card. "Yeah, I have it in one of my scrapbooks," I said.

"You know, someday you'll be glad your mother did those for you."

"Yeah, I know." It was hard to argue that point with my mother's scrapbooker-in-crime, and I followed her into the kitchen as the oven beeped. "Would you like me to call everyone for dinner?"

"Sure, that would be nice, Chloe."

I headed to Riley's room first. She was in ninth grade and had to follow in the footsteps of her brilliant brother, but she chose a different path at Riverside—not a bad one, just a more creative

43

route. She dabbled in the performing arts like her mother, and as a freshman, she received one of the lead roles in the spring musical.

As I neared her bedroom, the sounds of music wafted into the hallway, and I caught a pungent whiff of nail polish. Luckily, I caught Riley and her cousin Julia between their first and second coat, and they were able to depart for the dinner table without compromising their manicures.

I knocked on Rob's door next. "Hey, it's Chlo."

"Come in," they returned, and as I opened the door to a dimly lit bedroom, I found Courtney and Josh nestled on Rob's bed while the television droned on in the background.

Together, we headed into the dining room where Rob pulled out a chair for me. He sat on my left, and Jake, Josh's younger brother, took the seat on my other side. Josh and Jake were Irish twins, separated by eleven months and a school year. They had shaggy light brown hair and a dusting of freckles across their noses, and their light green eyes smiled at each other across the table. Actually, Josh couldn't stop smiling, and it probably had everything to do with his alone time with Courtney.

"David, will you lead us in grace, please?" Mrs. Callahan requested as she peered across the table at her husband, who returned her gaze with an adoring smile. They had a really good marriage, like my parents, but completely different. My parents functioned separately whereas Rob's parents worked well together, and if I had to choose one over the other, I'd follow the Callahan model of marriage.

After the blessing, the serving dishes moved in a clockwise fashion like at Thanksgiving, and in their family tradition, constant conversation followed the food around the table. Aunt Nancy leaned forward to get her nephew's attention. "So, are you going to prom, Rob?"

"Um," Rob stalled, but she didn't wait for his reply. "Well, Josh has already been invited to two proms this year."

"C'mon, Mom." Josh looked embarrassed. Even his neck and the rims of his ears colored.

"Aunt Nancy, Rob doesn't have a date for prom…probably because no one is good enough for him." And no one raised an eyebrow at his sister's conjecture.

"What about you girls?" Rob's mother asked from the other end, and Riley answered for us as well. "Courtney is still undecided, but Chloe is going with Austin Walker." Her palm hit her chest. "Of course, *she's* the luckiest girl in the whole school."

"Tell me, who's this Austin Walker fellow?" Grandpa asked.

Rob held his napkin up to his lips. "A gigantic A-hole."

"I agree," I whispered in return, but Riley didn't. "He's like the hottest guy in school," she said, subscribing to the popular opinion at Riverside.

Grandpa was eager to dissect her statement. "Therefore, he's not *the* hottest guy in school; he just looks like him." The lesson in grammar divided the table, and depending upon age, Grandpa received either laughter or groans.

While Grandpa Callahan divulged more thoughts on teenage vernacular, Rob leaned into me. "I totally disagree. Austin looks nothing like me."

"That's true," I said plainly.

"Because we all know I'm much better looking than him."

I offered no response.

"What? You don't want to offer your opinion?" He gave me that dreamy look, which caused girls to swoon, so I stared back at his nose. It was the most ordinary feature on his widely appreciated face and was the single spot that did not cause me to get too distracted. I was not blind to his good looks or his charms. He had thick auburn hair, which curled up at the ends, and those warm, chocolate brown eyes, and whenever he smiled, his deep-set dimples made an appearance.

"As for my opinion of you, I gave it ten years ago." I eyed him up and down. "And nothing's changed, right?"

"Gee, thanks."

I swirled the spaghetti around my fork, but before I took another bite, Rob's mother asked, "So, I heard that you and Austin

45

broke up, huh?" Apparently, the rest of the table had moved on with their conversations while Rob and I had ours.

I nodded, and Courtney, in her love for perpetuating topics others would rather not discuss, added, "Now, Chloe has joined me. We are both dateless for the prom." Such a status provided excitement for my friend, since she enjoyed her time of deliberation. I, on the other hand, was glad to be off the prom market.

Aunt Nancy piped up. "Ooh, I have the perfect idea. Why don't the boys take you girls to your prom?" Jake patted my hand in agreement with his mother. "And Josh, at this point, we should just buy you a tux." Aunt Nancy was one of those annoying statistic moms. *Oh, my son walked right out of the womb, started reading at age two, and attended x number of proms in one year.* She was *that* kind of mom, the one to avoid on the bleachers, but most of all, she was the polar opposite of Rob's mom.

"Um," I started slowly, wishing I had Emily Post's take on the matter. I mean, how exactly should I turn down a mother who asked me to prom on her son's behalf? Well, I went with the direct approach: "Thanks for the offer, but I already have a date."

Courtney's huge blue eyes popped open. "Who?"

I responded with a silent *later*, but she continued her investigation, starting with the guy on my left. Slowly, and with a smile spreading across her face, she extended a painted finger in his direction.

"Hey, it's not polite to point," Rob returned with a grin and answered the questioning stares from an unusually quiet dinner table. "But yes, Chloe and I are going to prom together."

A chorus of aw's erupted around the dining room table, but I held up my hand. "C'mon, it's not like that. We're just friends."

-9-

First Kiss

After dinner, Rob and I headed down the same path that Courtney and I had taken the night before; we walked across the green grass, past the old tree house, and into the quiet woods. There was a low hum of crickets and the sound of our feet crunching on fallen leaves, and for most of the way, neither of us spoke. Still, I knew something was on his mind by the way he raked his fingers through his hair, and each time he did so, his hair returned to the same exact spot.

"It sure is hot," he offered eventually. (Surely, he had not been contemplating the weather for the last five minutes.) "But next year will be nice. With the change of seasons and all."

"Uh-huh," I muttered flatly.

"Like the leaves in the fall and the cherry blossoms in the spring," he added, but I said nothing more. The trivial talk of weather turned into the subject of next year, and even though Rob and I were the same age, he was a year ahead of me in school. He had skipped the third grade and was in the waning weeks of his senior year. In the fall, he was off to Georgetown University, and considering the school was up in Washington D.C., it didn't take a psychic to figure out how it would affect our friendship. And I knew it was wrong of me, but I never wanted to discuss his college plans. Sure, I was happy for him, just not outwardly excited, since the thought of next year caused a sudden hollowing in my stomach every time he broached it.

I changed the subject. "I'm glad Josh is taking Courtney to prom, aren't you?"

"Anyone is an improvement over Ricky, but I wouldn't say I'm happy about it."

"Why not?"

"She's not right for him."

"You mean not good enough."

"I didn't say that."

"Then what are you saying?"

"Nothing." He looked down the path. "I just know how Josh feels about her, and I don't want him to get hurt."

"Oh." His sincerity silenced me quickly.

"She was the first girl he ever kissed," he added after a long pause.

"I know."

"And some people are weird about that stuff."

"Are you?"

"*No*," he returned emphatically.

"Yeah, me neither."

Then I considered our stories for a moment as we walked along the path. His first kiss was with Kelly Winters, a girl who lived in a neighborhood next to ours. I can still remember her face, round and lightly freckled and eyes the color of wheat, and when she moved away, she sent him mushy love letters on Hello Kitty stationery.

My first kiss, however, was with a boy I see all the time. I dated Callie's brother Landon after my growth spurt in seventh grade. He liked my long legs, but not my crappy jump shot. And I still think we broke up over my lack of skill on the court, but he said it was reverse height discrimination. Apparently, I told him that he was too tall to kiss and that I didn't feel like searching for tree stumps or step ladders every time we parted ways.

"You know everybody thinks you were the first boy I kissed," I broached casually but with an intended goal in mind.

"*Everybody*, huh?"

"You know what I'm saying, Rob." I was thinking about the picture in the stairwell and the countless pages in my scrapbook when I continued, "There are some really cute stories about us."

And to that, he added nothing to the conversation.

"You ever think about those days?" I paused and flicked my head in the direction we had just traveled. "Like the time up in the tree house when we almost..." I purposefully let my voice linger and glanced over at him.

He shrugged, and my mind drifted to a summer long ago—it's long when you're only sixteen...

Back then, Rob and I roamed the neighborhood, wasting days with soccer games in the yard and Marco Polo in the pool. But one afternoon, we snuck away from the neighborhood gang, and with muddy feet and wet swimsuits, we climbed into the tree house all by ourselves...

I interrupted my own thoughts. "You honestly don't remember?"

He shrugged again.

"You can recite sports statistics like a walking ESPN almanac, but you have no recollection of anything *romantic*." I wondered about the last word, but my internal Thesaurus wasn't offering any other suggestions.

"Romantic?" he repeated, finally joining the one-sided conversation already in progress. "You need to stop reading Bronte and Austen. They're clouding your judgment."

I was on the defensive. "It *is* romantic, because you were my first boyfriend."

He countered quickly, "Chlo, we were little kids, and we played doctor until our parents caught us, and you went around topless just because I could. That's not a relationship. It's what kids do because they don't know any better."

"So, you were that way with other girls?"

"No, *you* were too possessive, and you got jealous if I hung out with anyone else." A smile spread into his eyes. "And sometimes, you still do."

"Oh, you're so full of yourself." I stopped and stared at him until his smirk faded. "And to think I was gonna' tell you the truth after all these years."

His voice softened. "The truth about what?"

"About why we never kissed."

"Listen, it doesn't take a genius to figure that out." His smile appeared again, contagious actually, and that was the way it had been so many summers ago...

We were smiling and laughing uncontrollably, our expressions feeding each other. Very slowly, he reached across and held my tiny hand in his. He held it very lightly and sweetly, then whispered, "May I kiss you?" I said nothing as his lips neared mine. I watched his soft brown eyes close and his face move toward me, distorting his familiar features into obscurity, and as inches separated our lips, I yanked my hand from his and turned my head swiftly to the side...

"Do you want me to tell you or not?"

"Why not," he deadpanned.

"Okay." I looked at the grass and mumbled the reason like I had ingested truth serum. "I thought I could get pregnant."

"You what?"

"You heard me." Then I defended my childhood self. "And I was upset at you for trying to kiss me. I wasn't trying to be mean or anything, but I wasn't prepared to have a baby at six."

"That's pretty funny. Of course, it would have been even funnier if it had happened to someone besides me."

"I wasn't trying to hurt you, Rob. I was just trying to be responsible."

He smiled. "So I'm assuming you've heard about the birds and bees by now." He teased with a mocking glance, and my eyes narrowed back at him. "You've kissed lots of guys since then, and you don't have a house full of mutant children."

"Funny," I said as I turned toward my house.

"Hey." His hand rested on my shoulder. "You ever wonder what it would have been like?"

"What?"

"That first kiss."

Yes was the truth, but I turned and gave him a different

answer. "It would have felt like kissing your sister."

"Maybe," he started. "But there's only one way to find out." He stepped toward me, cupping his hands on my shoulders. I looked up at him, and he smiled down at me. Then he leaned forward and placed a kiss on my forehead. It was soft and warm and completely fraternal. "Goodnight, Chlo."

-10-

Much Ado about Nothing

On Monday morning, I trudged up the hill behind my English classroom since the blackboard read: CLASS OUTSIDE TODAY, and had we lived a few lines of latitude to the north, this may have been a swell idea. But at seven, nearly eight, in the morning, it was unbearably hot, and I was glistening from something other than the final step of my skin regimen.

I reached the top of the hill, glanced around at all the full picnic tables, and felt like the last kid to be picked for kickball, but after a few moments, Mike Erickson motioned for me to sit at his table. It was all guys and all fairly cute, and now, that I was single again, I had to be more observant of my surroundings.

"Thanks," I said to the table and slowly pulled my lower lip across my teeth. It was something I had seen Courtney do, and I decided I should try it now—you know, the whole flirting thing. Single girls give off a certain vibe to show availability, and since I was single again, I would have to learn the tricks of the trade. But I had always been couple material: I was more of a Caitlyn than a Courtney, and it was only a matter of time before I entered into another relationship. I glanced around the picnic table of senior boys; each one was plagued with Senioritis and probably looking forward to what college girls had to offer him. So, I considered the junior class for maybe a millisecond before I decided to look outside Riverside for once. Why not try a nice boy from church who attended Central or Kennedy? And in the time it took Miss Randall to cross the picnic area and land at my table, I actually decided on my next boyfriend. He didn't have a name yet—just a profile.

Miss Randall placed a small cardboard box at the end of our table. It had *Much Ado about Nothing* sprawled across the side of it, and she started discussing the next two weeks of class as well as the non-required, but highly recommended, performance at the Orlando Shakespeare Festival. She wrapped up her overview and dropped a worn-out copy of the play in front of me. "Chloe, you will be reading the part of Beatrice."

Did I volunteer? No, of course not. High school English teachers didn't need volunteers. They assigned parts like evil fairies giving out anti-wishes. I just wanted to sit there and listen to other people fumble through their *thee's* and *thou's* on that horribly humid morning, but soon, I accepted my fate and flipped through the pages. I found out that Beatrice had a lot to say, and there were these entire sections where she said it to this guy named Benedict.

"And for the part of Benedict," Miss Randall began as she crossed the lawn and landed at a table with only two guys at it. On one side sat Tom Richardson, our slated valedictorian. But she didn't select the well-spoken orator about to give a lengthy speech in four weeks. No, she chose the other boy at the table, and when she did, I heard that familiar laugh from across the lawn. After a few scenes into the play, I realized why Rob found our roles so amusing. Our characters bickered back and forth endlessly, making us look like complete amateurs at the sport of verbal volleyball, and when first hour ended, I headed over to Rob's table. "Nice reading, Benedict." I purposefully omitted the final consonant of his character's name.

"Yeah, you too, Beatrice." His enunciation was much more precise, allowing for a noticeable hiss at the end of mine.

"Anyway, I need to talk to you about my article. You know, the one about prom."

"Yeah, what about it?"

"Callie and Mike agreed to do it."

"Why, Chlo? You don't want to interview yourself?"

"Uh, no," I said with a scrunched-up face, not ready to embrace the irony of the whole prom situation.

"So, what are you going to do about prom?" Jessica asked as she leaned across the table, showing considerable cleavage in her low-cut chartreuse top.

"Dunno," I said with a quick shrug. I figured it was Rob's responsibility to tell her about our prom plans. I would *love* to do it, but he would definitely frown upon my delivery. Trust me, I had thought about it though. I do that often. I think about conversations ahead of time. The only problem is they rarely live up to my expectations. Take my break-up with Austin, for instance. I had so many great comebacks that I will never be able to use. That is, unless I enter into a relationship with another jerk like him. But jerk didn't fit my new profile. Now, did it?

"I mean, what can you do? You're Austin Walker's ex, and he'd probably beat up any guy who even looked in your direction." She glanced up at me with that twisted smirk. "It's not fair and all, but what guy would take that risk?"

"Well," I said, spreading out the word like a substitute teacher trying to fill space during a class period. "I can think of one." Then my eyes rested on the boy sitting across from her. "So Rob, will you take me to prom?"

Rob nodded, and Jessica rose from the table with an audible huff.

I left English with a big smile plastered across my face and remained in a relatively good mood until lunch. Like usual, I sat down in my regular seat and unpacked my lunch: a turkey sandwich, an apple, and some homemade oatmeal raisin cookies. I was utterly famished, and since I was in a huge rush to get to school, I didn't have time for breakfast. My stomach grumbled all during the Latin quiz, and it's hard to concentrate on the conjugations of verbs when your stomach converses with you in Gurglish. I guess it was pretty noticeable since the Latin loser next to me shushed me during the quiz. (Like I have any control over my digestive system.)

Anyway, I was sitting at the lunch table about to sink my teeth into my turkey sandwich, which was made on fresh sourdough bread, when Austin roared, "Get up, Chloe." Apparently, his manners weren't going to improve after our break-up, and when I lifted my eyes to meet his, I noticed Ricky Sampson and Brandon Edwards on either side of him, rounding out their usual trio of jerkitude.

"Hi," I said casually and bit into my sandwich. It was quite tasty.

Austin lowered his head. "You know I'm with someone else now."

"Yeah, and I'm *so* happy for you."

He ignored my sarcasm as usual and cut to the chase. "Aimee doesn't want you to sit here." He placed his palms on the table and leaned forward. "And neither do I."

"But this was our table—first!" The conversation belonged in an elementary school cafeteria, but in ninth grade, the original Seven C's claimed the table on our first day of high school, and we vowed to sit together until our last day as seniors. As our group of seven dwindled down to only four, the guys invaded our territory, pushing us to the end.

Brandon eyed me. "Should we take a vote, Chlo?"

"Yeah, like on *Survivor*," Ricky added with his retarded laugh.

Brandon offered a list. "You'd get Courtney and Callie. And maybe Mike and Landon, but that's it."

He was right. All the rest of my friends, even Caitlyn, would side with Austin and Aimee. So I packed up my lunch and decided to leave the table with some dignity, but as I started down the aisle, Ricky teased, "You gonna' start crying again?"

I whipped around and glared at him. No tears, just anger in my narrowing eyes. I thought back to Friday night, remembering how Ricky acted all sweet to me in front of Courtney. But that was how those three were: complete chameleons, changing from jerks to gems in a blink of an eye. And Austin was the worst of them all. He could be pure honey, full of all the right lines and moves, and I prided myself with not falling for it for the longest time. But this year he tried a different approach with me: honesty. And I fell for it. Hard.

"You want something to cry about?" I tossed at Ricky. "Courtney's going to prom with Rob Callahan's cousin."

"Uh, I don't care." His tone wasn't all that convincing, and Brandon didn't buy it either. "Yeah, you do, man." They started tossing insults about each other's virility and sexual orientation as Austin started toward me. "You going to prom?"

"Yeah," I said and left it there.

His fist smacked his palm. "Who?"

"Rob."

Then his expression changed. "Oh, like on a pity date?"

I stared back at him. Not sure what to say.

"C'mon, Chlo. He doesn't want to take you. No guy wants to go with a friend."

"That's not true."

"Now, there are only two reasons why a guy takes a friend to prom: either he can't get a real date or he's gay. So which is it?"

Right then I wanted to have a prom date for another reason, the reason why prom existed in the first place, the reason why girls dreamt about the night since they learned of its existence; but instead, I was going to prom for the lamest reason of all. "He's taking me because he's nice."

"Yeah, whatever, it's still a total sympathy date. And his mom probably made him do it."

"Oh, just shut up." After months of fighting, it was all I had left in me. I turned around and felt like a huge loser. I had been exiled from my lunch table and was holding my lunch instead of eating it. I needed to be alone, but even in a huge high school like Riverside, there was only one place to find real solitude: the girls' bathroom. I opened the door to the stall, and fully clothed, plopped down on the lidless seat.

From my vantage point, I could hear all the conversations— mostly hey's, hi's, and how was your weekend? And the longer I sat there, the more the scents filled the air. It was the usual blend of fruity body spray, perfume, and hair spray.

"Girl, you are still glowing," a familiar voiced entered the bathroom, and I pulled my feet off the floor, hugging my legs to my chest. As they talked, they sprayed, leaving a few clean air molecules left for consumption. My nose itched. My throat tickled. And I was doing my best to keep silent, but I was suffering from scent overload.

"Brit, you make it sound like she's pregnant," said another.

"Well, I could be." And that was the voice of Aimee Peterson, my replacement and the reason I had been ousted from my lunch table.

"Surely, you used."

"Yep, every single time."

"Ooh," they chorused, and then Brit Blackwell spoke again. "Tell us everything."

"All I can say is that what girls say about him is *not* true." She paused, and I could just see Aimee working her crowd. "No one could possibly describe what he is like. Austin Walker is beyond words."

But I had the words: he's experienced and completely in control; he treats a girl's body like a blank canvas, and he paints it with his fingers and his lips.

"Well, you got him at the best time. He was ripe for the picking after seven frosty months with the Ice Queen."

I gasped for breath, but quickly covered my mouth.

Aimee's voice fell to a whisper, and I strained to hear the rest. "I can trust you girls, right?"

"Oh, yeah." They chorused in the most unconvincing tone.

"Actually, Chloe gave it up to him a while back, and that's why they stayed together for so long. He didn't want to hurt her because he was her first and all. But she went psycho in the end. You know how much they were fighting, and he just had to end it with her. He's really torn up inside."

My face was on fire, and I wanted to hit something. Correction: I wanted to hit someone.

"You'll just have to find a way to make him feel better, won't you?"

"Don't worry. I already have." Aimee was on cloud nine, but then her tone changed. "Listen, he doesn't want anyone to know about him and Chloe, so don't say a word."

"Oh, we won't. We promise." Those were the famous last words from the biggest gossip leaks at Riverside. The truth was Aimee wanted everyone to know, and so did Austin. And at that moment, I wanted to jump out of the stall and set her straight, but really, who's she going to believe? The guy who gave her the best sex of her life or his raging mad ex-girlfriend?

When the coast (and the air) was clear, I slid off the toilet seat and opened the stall of the bathroom slowly. I considered my lunch options around campus. The library didn't permit food, and since my stomach was set on continuous growl, that option was out. The band, chorus, and drama rooms attracted students, but it was pretty uncool to eat there when you didn't take those classes. Therefore, I had one option left: Loser Lawn. It was the place for outcasts, and apparently, since my break-up with Austin, I had hit the bottom rung of the social ladder.

I walked over to the English wing and through the back doors to the picnic area where first hour had been held. It had been dubbed the Loser Lawn years ago, and as I climbed up the grassy hill, the regulars looked at me with raised eyebrows. Then I wished I had worn something less vibrant than a bright aqua top and white shorts. But it was late April, and it seemed fashionably irresponsible to go drab in the spring.

I noticed Carly Evans sitting at a picnic table with her new friends, and even though we hadn't spoken in a couple of years, I offered her a slight smile. It went unreturned, and at a moment when I didn't think I could feel any worse, I actually did. I held back those silly tears and found a spot under an oak tree. I started eating my lunch and opened up *East of Eden*, trying to concentrate on Steinbeck's imagery of the Salinas Valley rather than the last few minutes of my crappy life. But it was impossible to consider anything other than what Austin had said about me. He was out to ruin my reputation, which was something I had fought to keep over the last few months, and even though my eyes were on the pages of the book, I still noticed when the familiar pair of brown Crocs advanced on me. "You okay?"

"Spectacular," I said and turned the page.

"You want to talk about it?" Rob asked as he found a seat next to me.

"No." I just stared down at the book, but when my eyes watered with the inevitable tears and the words went blurry, I closed the book. Rob put an arm around me and brought me to his shoulder. "I heard what Austin said." I buried my face in the crook of his neck, and I cried a lot harder than I should have, but he didn't say a word. And we remained there for a while: me crying, and him saying nothing. And when I stopped sobbing, he asked, "Do you remember Kirsten? That girl I dated in ninth."

"Not really," I lied.

"Well, anyway, when I broke up with her, she told everyone I was gay."

I cracked a slight smile, knowing why he was telling me this awful story. "So, is that the real reason why we're going to prom?" I lifted my head off his shoulder and wiped away tears with the back of my hand. "Is it because you're—"

"No, we're going to prom because you asked me." He picked up the napkin from my lunch and handed it to me, and I blotted the corners of my eyes. "And if you want to get technical about it..."

"Let's not."

He did anyway. "*You* asked me twice."

59

-11-

Big Brother

The week marched on. I left the Loser Lawn and joined Rob's lunch table, which consisted of the Smart Jocks and their Hollister-outfitted girlfriends. By midweek, the rumors about me had been replaced with the one about the physics intern and a certain friend of mine, proving that some rumors were not altogether false. And by Friday morning, Rob and I were reading our parts with increasing fervor, and at the end of first hour, Miss Randall announced, "Rob. Chloe. I need to see you after class."

At that, Mike Erickson did a quick one-eighty in his seat. "Ooh, you're in trouble, girl!" I stuck out my tongue at him as Rob walked past our seats, and Mike retorted, "Save that for Callahan!" Fortunately, Rob showed no sign of awareness, and then I lowered my head and offered a response. "We are *not* dating!"

"I don't know. First you ask him to prom. Then you start eating at his lunch table." Mike slid off his seat and offered me his lopsided grin. "I mean, really, what's next?"

"Nothing," I said with utter finality, but Miss Randall had the answer up at her desk; and when I reached the front of the classroom, I arrived in the middle of a hyper compliment. Our teacher was laying it on so thick that I knew a request was about to escape her lips. It was something that deserved an immediate no, but after receiving such lofty accolades, we couldn't refuse her.

60

The tactic was pretty common, and guys used it all the time. Like when some guy tells a girl she should be a model or looks like a famous actress, it's just a prelude to "Will you go out with me?"

"…And you two read so beautifully. Do either of you have any acting experience?"

I thumbed at Rob. "His mom was a theater major."

"And Chloe's always been a drama queen."

"Have not," I said as my hands hit my hips, proving *his* point, not mine.

Miss Randall continued, "Anyway, I was hoping you two could recite a scene from Act IV on Wednesday. I know that's only five days from now, but you're my best readers." I scrunched up my nose like someone had just passed some rancid gas, and Rob ran his fingers through his hair. Taking our expressions into account, she added, "C'mon guys, I'll give you some extra credit." She looked at Rob. "Well, it's not like *you* need it."

"Uh, thanks," I muttered. "Some of us have a life outside school."

"You mean *had* a life."

"Ooh, you can be such a—" I stopped myself since Miss Randall was sitting in front of us, so I folded my arms across my chest and rattled off a list of names inside my head. It wasn't as rewarding, but it saved me from a teacher condemnation.

"Hmm, I see why these parts come naturally for the two of you." She smirked at us. "But remember, if you keep it up, you might end up like our two characters in the play."

"What? In a double suicide?" I laughed at my own joke, but apparently no one else saw the humor in it, and sight unseen, I agreed to perform a duet scene from Act IV for our entire class.

Getting what she wanted from us, we got what we wanted from her—two excuse slips. But in her haste, Miss Randall forgot to jot down the time. With free time on our hands, we headed to the vending machines at the opposite end of campus. I got a Lipton Iced Tea, and he bought some M & M's. He poured a bunch in his hand and plucked out the red ones for me.

"You finish the play yet?" he asked.

"No, Rob. The rest of us are reading it *in* class."

"You ever see the movie?"

"No."

"But you know it's a comedy, right?"

"Yeah, so?"

"And all Shakespearean comedies end the same way."

"Yeah, it's very original."

"No, it's formulaic, Chlo, and since comedies close with a wedding, our characters will get married in the end; therefore, Miss Randall is saying that if we don't stop fighting, then we'll end up the same way."

"I know."

"Which part?"

"The part about getting married in the end."

He smiled at my obvious ambiguity and emptied the bag of M & M's into his hand, offering me the last few red ones. "But maybe we should stop arguing so much...just to be on the safe side."

"Okay, but what will we talk about then?" I wondered.

"Something that won't cause an argument."

"People can argue over anything."

"I'm sure we can find an agreeable topic."

"Doubt it."

I looked over at him. He was biting down on his lower lip, and his eyes shifted to the right. "Hey, save your brain cells for Calculus, Callahan. The fact is we always argue. It's what we do together. Some friends go to the movies. Some go shopping. We argue, and the truth is, we do it well."

"Yeah, you're right."

"See, *that's* something we can agree on," I said with a crooked smile. He returned one, complete with dimples, and escaped into his AP Calculus classroom. I had to make a quick stop at my locker before I went to the math class for the less-than-brilliant people, but as I turned the corner, I spotted Austin Walker waiting for me.

"Hey, baby," he said as if the whole week hadn't happened. Or like we were two characters on a daytime soap, and the writers changed their minds about our break-up after the ratings dropped. The only problem was I hadn't received the new script. "What do you want?"

"*You*," he crooned in his bedroom voice.

"Wow, there's a line I haven't heard before!" I fidgeted with my combination, but I could feel the weight of his stare on me.

"You missed a number," he gibed.

"Go to hell, Austin." I started the combination process over again and concentrated on the task like it was a life-and-death situation.

"Why are you so pissed off? You broke up with me, remember?"

"But that's not what you told everyone."

"I have a reputation, baby."

I flung open my locker and tossed him the coldest look I owned. "Yeah, and thanks to you, so do I."

The jerk chuckled for a moment and leaned against my open locker door. He watched me fumbling with my stack of books and reached over to tuck an errant strand of hair behind my ear. "I love it when you get all mad."

I glared at him.

"So—" He licked his lips quickly. "What's this crap I hear about you and Callahan?"

I didn't bother to dispel the rumor. "Oh, like you're one to talk. Look at you and Aimee. I mean, did you even wait until I was out the door?"

"I was pissed, Chlo."

"Yeah, well, that's a great reason to start seeing someone." I looked at him. "You know, I feel sorry for her."

"Don't. I'm giving her what she wants." He moved in closer to me. "Of course, it's what you wanted, but you were too afraid. You and I both know that's why you got so upset last week." The night flashed in my head, and I could almost feel his hands across my skin. "You weren't really mad at me. You were upset with yourself, because you wanted me too." His hot breath entered my ear. "All of me."

I pushed at him. "Get away from me."

He sucked a breath between his teeth. "You know that only turns me on more."

"Stop it. I *really* mean it, Austin." There was a noticeable shakiness in my voice, and I started breathing unevenly as he reached for me, his confidence trumping mine. He pulled me toward him, wedging my arms against his chest, and then he smiled his triumphal grin. Oh, how I hated that smile! It sent shivers down my spine and caused my stomach to flip. But Austin was enjoying it. Way too much. And I had to wonder what he had hoped to accomplish, but before another word escaped his lips, Rob grabbed me and whooshed me across the hall. Austin muttered a harsh obscenity, and the two of them squared off for another round of a three-year-old fight. Rob stepped closer, and with a finger a millimeter from Austin's nose, he seethed, "I don't ever want to see you near her again. You understand me, Walker?"

Austin smacked Rob's hand out of his face and stepped forward. "Then I'll wait until you're not looking."

Rob glanced over at me and then back at Austin. "Then I won't let her out of my sight."

There was a long stare-down, where time stood still, and then Austin shook his head, cackling. "Well, big brother can't always be watching." That was Austin's pet name for Rob, but don't believe for a minute that it was some astute allusion to George Orwell's *1984*. It was just an accurate depiction of Rob's self-appointed role in my life. Austin continued, "Because someday you'll be off at college, and Chloe will be all alone with no one to watch over her. Well, except for me, of course." Austin glanced over at me with that accomplished smile-and-wink combo. "Right, baby?"

I offered him such a cold glare that I gave myself the chills, but Austin simply turned and headed down the hall, completely unfazed.

"Not out of your sight, huh?" I said as I closed in on Rob. "Am I allowed to go to the bathroom by myself? How about showers? And sleeping arrangements may be a problem." I looked up at him, hoping he would crack a smile. "I don't know about your parents, but mine are against cohabitation."

"Uh-huh," he said flatly like he wasn't listening to me at all. His gaze was fixed on Austin, who took his sweet time walking down the hall. Finally, Rob turned to me and handed me an excuse slip, and at that moment, I realized why he had been there in the first place. "Just wait here for me after class," he started. "And I'll walk you to Latin."

"Oh, that won't be necessary"

"Yes, it will." He shot me his eye-narrowing look. "And you can thank me later."

So, after every class, I thanked him profusely. I even tried different accents to show my appreciation: southern, British, and Irish (in honor of his ancestry). I made big, pouty lips and batted my eyelashes. I did my best to portray the damsel-in-distress role, figuring at some point in the day, he would tire of my theatrics. But unfortunately for me, Rob never did. He took great pleasure in annoying me, and at the end of sixth hour, he walked me to the front of the school like a bodyguard for a Hollywood starlet. His arms were folded across his chest, and he leaned against the brick pillar, waiting with me in the parent pick-up line. "Why's your dad picking you up today?"

"He's taking me dress shopping." I glanced at my date. "I'm going to the prom with this overprotective ogre."

"Has to be better than my date. She's this ungrateful, little snot."

I pursed my lips together. "Ouch, that hurts."

"Uh-huh, the truth usually does," he said flatly and flicked his head toward the line of oncoming cars. "Here comes your dad now."

"Well," I said, starting toward the curb. "Good luck with your game tonight."

He followed closely behind me. "Your dad's the one who needs all the luck. Shopping with you is an acceptable form of torture for the eternally damned."

"Oh, you're so hilarious."

Rob opened the car door for me, and his tone changed dramatically. "Well, hello, Mr. Preston. Welcome back."

"Thank you, Rob, and how have you been?"

"Great, Sir," he said with a grin plastered across his face. I gave him the evil eye for acting so dreadfully polite, but he just smiled back at me. "Have a great time shopping this afternoon."

"Oh, we will," my father chirped cheerfully, but several hours later, my father was singing a different tune. I was standing in the dressing room of the third—no, maybe the fourth—dress shop along Park Avenue. I was running out of stores, and my father was running out of patience. I could almost hear his foot tapping outside my spacious dressing room, which was about the size of my bedroom and had an upholstered chair in the corner in case I needed to rest between trying on dresses.

But I didn't have time to rest, or to even think. I had to make a choice—and fast. So I hung the black strapless number on one hook and a powder blue gown on the other and was about to recite "Eeny Meeny Miny Mo" when my father lowered a third option over the dressing room curtain.

"Where'd you find this?" I asked, clutching the silky gown to my chest.

"In the next section." The dress shop had various levels. Symbolic actually, since every time you went up a step or two, so did the price.

"It's so perfect." My voice rose to an unnatural octave.

"Well, it ought to be for the price," my father grumble-mumbled as he returned to his waiting chair. I stepped into the ivory gown, pulling the weightless fabric the length of my bare skin. I slid my arms through the intricately braided straps of ivory and gold, and once on, the simple sheath fell gently to the floor. The waistline was higher, empire style with a wide brocade band of golden gossamer threads and shiny beads. I twirled out of the dressing room, holding the back of the dress together with one hand. When I reached the three-way mirror,

66

the saleslady buttoned the row of fabric covered buttons. "This dress is absolutely gorgeous, but look at all of these buttons. It'll take forever to get on you."

My father arched an eyebrow. "Good, then the inverse will hold true."

"Dad, that's not even remotely funny. I'm going to prom with Rob."

"Yeah, yeah. I could have used that line when you went to Homecoming with that juvenile delinquent." I just shook my head. Why did fathers joke about the one thing that frightened them the most? Was it some sort of bizarre coping mechanism or something?

I twisted and turned in front of the three-way mirror for a while, long enough to receive my share of compliments from passing customers. The saleslady sat down in a vacant chair next to my father. "It's so nice to see a father taking his daughter out prom dress shopping."

"Trust me, nice is *not* the right word for it." I tossed over my shoulder, since "nice" is not synonymous with overprotective in my dictionary. My father liked to put his stamp of approval on what I wore out of the house—especially to dances.

"Oh," she replied and then dawdled off to assist other customers, mostly brides who were behind schedule on selecting a dress for their summer weddings. But then again, who was I to judge? Prom was only two weeks away.

I looked again at my reflection. Hands down, it was the most beautiful dress I had ever worn. With a few school dances behind me and a junior bridesmaid dress hanging in the back of the closet, I had never owned anything that looked as timeless as this. But for some reason, I started to doubt the selection. "I don't know, Dad."

"It's perfect, Chloe," my father stated emphatically and rose from the chair.

"But it's so pricey."

"Do you understand opportunity costs?"

"A little," I said, knowing it should have seeped into my

brain during dinner-table osmosis.

"Well, put it this way. The cost of the dress is somewhat insignificant if it affords me the opportunity to leave this store." After a quick lesson in economics, my father paid the saleslady, and we were zipping down the interstate in my father's Explorer.

I stared out the window, watching the blue sky turn into a soft grey as the sun dipped behind the pines, and as night followed day, I sighed out loud. It was officially Friday night, and I had no plans. All my friends had dates for the evening, and even though I didn't miss Austin, I did miss the routine of the relationship and the comfort that comes with having a boyfriend.

My dad glanced at me. "You got a hot date tonight?"

"No."

"Then you want to catch a bite to eat before we head home."

"Sure," I said as my father exited the interstate.

"Great, because I already have a place in mind. It's very economical, *and* all the proceeds go to a good cause."

-12-

Dinner

"What a bargain, huh? They even include ketchup and mustard in the price." That was my father's comment to me as the red-shirted booster parent exchanged my father's twenty for a couple of hot dogs and some ice cold drinks, and then with dinner in hand, we edged behind the back stop. My father took a bite of his hot dog, expressed his appreciation for the ball park frank, and flicked his head toward the pitcher's mound. "He's having one helluva' season, isn't he?"

"Yeah," I said back.

"You make that game last week? The one where he nearly pitched a no-hitter?"

"No, I was at the library…you know, studying."

"Yeah, I guess you won't be doing that anymore." He gave me his knowing smile, and I tossed him a "whatever" look. My father lived a much fuller life than my mother did; she actually spent her formative years at the library, and therefore, believed I was there several nights a week for the last seven months. I blamed my frequent visits on my tough class load and stayed there until ten o'clock, which was my weeknight curfew. On weekends my curfew was still eleven, but my parents agreed on twelve for special occasions. But it was nearing the end of my junior year, and I still hadn't received a curfew extension.

Still eating dinner, my father and I climbed to the top of the bleachers and sat with the Callahan family. "I can't believe this is the first game I've made all season, Dave," my dad started the conversation with Dr. Callahan.

"You've been working too hard, my friend," Rob's father returned, but I decided neither one of them had any business discussing the matter. Rob's dad was an obstetrician in a two-man practice and on call every other weekend, and my father was a financial planner turned writer. "You been riding at all?"

My father stretched out his long legs. "Does the stationary bike count?'

"*No*," Dave Callahan chided as he patted my father on the back. "You're going to slow us down, old man." They went on to discuss their training regimen for their bike trip in July, a two-day ride along the scenic back roads of North Florida. My whole family, minus me, attended the annual biking ritual, but I was always visiting my grandmother in Kentucky that weekend.

I left them to their training talks and slid down the row. Grandpa Callahan sat up with Rob's mom, Riley and her clique of baseball sisters occupied a few rows below them, and I sat next to Courtney and a still-smiling Josh. "You wanna' hear about my dress?"

"Sure," she said and drew a sip from her soda.

"The dress is ivory and—"

"Ivory?" Riley whipped around so fast it was a wonder she didn't suffer whiplash. "Are you going to the prom or getting married to my brother?"

I said nothing while the conversation ensued, gaining interest from her fellow ninth grade cohorts who thought prom and weddings were fascinating topics for discussion. Courtney spoke to the crowd. "Well, if Chloe marries Rob, then I'll be the maid of honor."

Riley dropped her jaw. "But he's *my* brother."

"But they're my best friends."

Josh leaned forward. "Aren't you two forgetting something?"

"What?" they snapped back.

"They're not even dating."

70

"Thank you, Josh." I said and moved up a row, but when I arrived next to Mrs. Callahan, I noticed her hand stifling a laugh. I glanced around the bleachers and back at Rob's mom. "Maybe I'll sit with another family.

"Now, now, Chloe." She patted my thigh in a succession of light taps. "You know why it's funny. Your mother and I have been joking about you and Rob getting married since the day you two met."

"Yeah, I know," I mumbled and thought about that day. It's not like I have any recollection of the second year of my life, but I've heard the story countless times over the years. Apparently, I was sitting on a swing at the park, waiting impatiently for my mother to push me. I was crying and whining and carrying-on while my mother tended to the squeakier wheel—also known as my baby brother—when this little, brown-eyed boy waddled over and pushed the swing for me. So, on that day, Rob and I became playmates, and our mothers became friends; and after all these years, nothing much had changed—except for the term governing our relationship, of course.

His mom smiled at me. "Why don't you tell me about your dress?" I gave her all the details, and when I finished, she decided, "Maybe Rob should wear a cream tux shirt to match your dress. And—" She paused, her enthusiasm growing a little. "Have you seen those tuxes in dark brown? It would match his hair."

"Yeah, and his eyes," I added, and then felt regretfully self-conscious after mentioning her son's eyes, but really, she had to have known. They were like liquid chocolate.

I looked out onto the field; Rob was on deck and warming up. Chip North got out in three quick strikes, and with two outs on the board for Riverside, Rob advanced to the plate. He watched the first pitch carefully and decided not to swing. The ump called a strike, but Rob connected with the second pitch, nailing a line drive down the third base line. He made it to second, spat into the grass, and adjusted his ball cap.

Mrs. Callahan turned toward me. "And do boys and girls still exchange corsages and boutonnières at dances?"

71

"If they want."

"Oh, tell Rob that Chloe *loves* red roses." The comment came from the obnoxious blonde in front of me, and I nudged her with my flip-flopped foot. Courtney turned around, complete with a grin. "Yeah, Austin bought her a rose every time he messed up, which was all the time, so he should've planted a rose bush in her backyard and been done with it."

Mrs. Callahan summed up my feelings. "Okay, no roses then."

I nodded.

"And your mom said pictures will be at your house?"

"Mm-hmm." I paused and watched Rich Masterson launch a ball deep into the outfield, sending Rob on a path to home plate. As he rounded third, I cupped my hands around my mouth. "Bring it home, Callahan!" I sent out a loud whoop as he crossed home plate. "Wow, he's having another great game," I said to his mother. "It's no wonder he's so conceited."

She laughed, and I continued on with more prom details. "Oh, and before the pictures, we'll serve refreshments, and I don't know if my mom told you this part, but you're welcome to come and take pictures too."

"Sounds like you have it all planned out."

"Well, yeah," I said and looked over at her quizzically. "Didn't he show you the prom schedule?"

"No, hon. Boys never share anything with their mothers," she said with a slight frown. "Half the time, he forgets to show me his report card."

"Well, it's not like there are any surprises," I muttered. Rob pulled straight A's all four years of high school and missed out on making words on report card day. My marks have spelled ABBA several times and CAB only once since "C's are not permitted in *this* house, young lady."

Mrs. Callahan and I continued our prom discussion as Rob resumed his position on the pitcher's mound. "And after prom, you two will go to the church lock-in. That'll be fun, don't you think?"

"Yes, it would be fun…" I started slowly, remembering Rob's comment: "We're not going to tell our parents that we're at the church when we're actually at the beach." That was my original idea, but dates change and so do plans. "But the girls and I were planning to stay at Courtney's beach house after prom, and her parents said it would be okay if the guys wanted to tag along too." I wondered if I succeeded in making it sound as innocent as a co-ed softball game.

"And Courtney?" Mrs. Callahan addressed. "Will your parents be there?"

"Yeah, my mom will," she answered. Her step-dad was a commercial pilot and scheduled to be across the Atlantic at the end of the month, but her mom would definitely be at the beach. When her mother wasn't traveling with her third husband, she liked to spend time at her other house, the one she ascertained during her second marriage. But whenever we stayed the night, Courtney's mom preferred the solace of her neighbor's place over a house full of giggly insomniacs.

Mrs. Callahan studied me for a moment. "Are your parents okay with this?"

"Well, I haven't *exactly* asked them yet."

She appealed to Courtney again. "Where will everyone sleep?"

I was over at Callie's house when her mother asked the same question. "The bedrooms are for the girls, and the guys can crash on the couches or on the floor of the family room."

His mother nodded and turned her attention toward the game, watching Rob as he struck out the third batter in a row. "Well, if your parents let you go, then I don't have a problem with it."

* * *

"Daddy?" I asked softly.

"Yes?" He hung an arm around my shoulders and drew me closer to him.

"I was wondering if I could go to Courtney's beach house

after prom." I took a breath and waited for the negative reply.

"Did you ask your mother?"

"No, she always says to ask you, so I figured I'd just eliminate the middle man."

"Hmm, that makes sense." His eyes remained on the field. "Will Rob be there?"

I was trying to figure out if this information would fall into the pro or con column. "Uh, yeah…I think so."

"Well, tell him to have you back in time for church then."

"Oh-okay," I managed and slid next to Courtney again, and when I told her about my dad's second act of kindness, the first being the pricey prom dress, she said now would be a good time to ask for something else I wanted. After all, wishes come in three's, but I, of course, reminded her that so did bad omens.

"Whatever," she said and found my ear. "So, when you get married, I'll be your maid of honor, right?"

"Yeah," I said back.

She put her arm around my shoulders. "Good. You'll be mine too." With that decided, she placed an open palm in front of me, and I tapped it with two fingers. I flipped my hand over, palm facing up, and she thumped two fingers in the center of mine. We formed a "C" with our fingers and tapped our hands on top of another. That was the secret handshake of the Seven C's, and we used it to close any friendship deal.

I watched the remainder of the ball game next to Courtney, and Riverside took it easily: 7-1. After the game, Rob climbed the bleachers with his bat bag slung over his shoulder. He set one foot on the bench next to me and rested a forearm on bended knee. "You catch any of the game?"

"Yeah." I yanked the brim of his hat down over his eyes. "You played all right."

"Aw, that means so much coming from my number one fan." He lifted up the red Riverside cap, ran his fingers through his hair, and replaced the hat in the same exact place.

"Do you want to work on English tonight?"

"Yeah, I guess so."

"Hey, don't sound so excited."

"Oh, I'm sorry, but doing homework on a Friday night makes me feel like a loser."

"But it's not homework, Chlo." He leaned in closer to me. "It's for extra credit."

I brought a finger to my lips. "Shh, that's even worse."

-13-

And a Movie

After the game, I slid down the wall outside the training room and got comfortable since Rob's last words were: "It could be a while." I scanned the halls for conversation, and soon one started toward me. It was Tom Richardson with his newest girlfriend Katie. Her arm was threaded through his, and her head was propped on his shoulder.

"Waiting for Rob?" Tom asked.

"Yeah."

"What are you guys doing tonight?"

I shrugged. "Just hanging out, I guess." I wasn't willing to admit our plans to anyone, not even the studious valedictorian of the senior class.

"We're all headed to Chip's house," Tom invited and then turned to strike up a conversation with one of his passing teammates.

Katie slipped from his side. "And just so you know, it'll be a small crowd. You know, ours." Her crowd included the likes of Jessica and Kendra, and their little clique reminded me of those kids on *Dawson's Creek* since they conversed in SAT words and exchanged partners faster than in square dancing.

My friends were the complete opposite. We avoided polysyllabic words outside the classroom and *never* dated the same guys; we viewed guy swapping as the cardinal sin of friendship.

I looked up at Katie and uttered, "Uh, that's nice," wondering if I had ever used the phrase and really meant it. I probably would have considered other phrases of vernacular irony, but Tom found his way back to the conversation and added earnestly, "Hope you guys can make it."

"Yeah, we'll see." And speaking of SAT words, one little gem popped into my head: abacinate. It meant having your eyes gorged out with hot, metal pokers. Yes, a gruesome form of torture, but it was comparable to attending Chip's little gathering.

I opened *Much Ado about Nothing* and decided to look at my lines, and by the time I had read over the passage twice, Rob emerged with his right side wrapped in a bulky pack of ice from shoulder to elbow. "You up for going to Chip's tonight?"

My eyes were on our scene for class, which was the first reason why I was fuming mad at him, and he was trying to give me another one. I lifted my head slowly as my eyes narrowed into a slits.

"Is that a yes or a no?"

I closed my book and chucked it at him. He picked up the play, which had ricocheted off his shin and into the middle of the hall. "Oh, that's right. We're supposed to be doing this tonight."

"Yeah, *that*," I said, gesturing at the book in his hands, "is the real reason I'm mad at you."

"Why?" He tossed it into my open bag and chugged some Gatorade.

"*Why?*" I repeated. "You've read it, so you knew what was in that scene."

He shrugged.

"Rob, our characters tell each other that they..."

"So?" He smiled. "I've said it to you before."

"Like ten years ago."

"And nothing's changed, right?" He teased with a twisted smirk. His line sounded familiar—only because it was mine from Saturday night. But love at six is completely different from love at sixteen, and maybe my feelings for him had never changed, and maybe I still loved him *that* way, but it didn't mean I felt

77

comfortable saying it to him—especially not in a room full of immature seniors who were looking for any excuse to laugh at the lowly junior in the class!

Still chuckling to himself, he handed me his keys, and I drove to his house, parking his Jeep in the third stall of his garage. I followed him inside, and we chatted with his parents for a moment before heading to his room. I plopped down on the edge of his bed and checked my texts while he sat at his computer.

I glanced up at him. "Whoya' writing?"

"Just someone I met at campus," he answered evenly. Rob went for a campus tour of Georgetown last month and came back with a few cyberspace pen pals.

"Is it a girl?" I chided in that annoying voice I had reserved for my brother.

"Yeah...so?"

"A little weekend hook up?"

"No, I don't do that."

"Is she your girlfriend then?"

"No, because at the time, I had a girlfriend."

I offered him the skeptical tone. "Oh, so she's just a friend."

"I am capable of being friends with a girl." He tossed me a glance over his shoulder. "*You* should know that."

"Yeah, but I don't count."

"Why not?" He spun around in his chair, smiling. "Is there something anatomically wrong with you?" I rolled my eyes as he got up from his chair. "I'm going to take this off," he said, gesturing toward his saran-wrapped arm. "You want anything from the kitchen?"

"Nah." I slid off the end of his bed and walked around his room. It had changed over the years, but I could still remember when his walls were painted sky blue with cumulus clouds and wooden planes dangled from his ceiling. Then his mother redecorated with a baseball motif, but now, his collection of autographed baseballs and team trophies had been relegated to the bottom shelf of his bookcase, and his walls were a soft grey. A picture of Mount McKinley hung over his bed, and his comforter was

78

a muted plaid of soft blues and grays. His room was extremely neat, and the only trace of clutter was on his bulletin board over his desk, where he had pinned up some sports tickets and photos. There were photos of friends, team photographs, some shots of him on bike trails and hikes, youth group pictures, and a Homecoming picture of him and Kendra. I lifted up on my tippy toes and noticed all the pictures of me. There was a real skuzzy shot of me after a cross country meet, and I considered removing the evidence from the board as his voice reentered the room. "You know, I have more pictures of you than of anyone else."

"Really?" I started counting.

"Uh-huh, Kendra pointed that out to me."

I didn't conceal the grin, since my back was turned to him. "I bet that caused a fight, right?"

"Yeah, but we fought all the time."

I thought about the last few months with Austin. "Yeah, I know how that is."

"At least, *we* don't fight like that. You know…over stuff that matters."

"Yeah, that's because we're not dating."

"And if we were, then you'd probably get mad if I did this." I felt the slightest tap on the back of my head, and when I turned around, I saw a gargantuan grin on his face. He was on his bed with his hand buried in a bowl of popcorn.

"Here, catch," he teased; then a piece hit my forehead.

"You have rotten aim, Callahan." I jumped onto the bed and scooped up a handful of hot ammunition.

"That's because I have to rest my right, Chlo." He launched a fistful into my hair, and I dumped some on top of his head.

He reached for more, and I did the same.

Then our eyes met. "All right. This *is* war," I declared. And it was—the sort of war that resulted in laughing, play wrestling, and a lot of popcorn casualties all over his room.

"Stop," I tried, but he ignored my comment and chucked more at me. I laughed and picked up pieces off the bed and pelted him in the nose. He started laughing uncontrollably and pointed a finger in my direction. "You have so much in your hair (a big belly laugh)…that you look like a Christmas tree (another obnoxious laugh)…wrapped in popcorn garland." I shook my head like a wet dog and gave him a pelting popcorn shower.

A loud knock hit the door, and we froze like statues.

"I hope it's not your mom," I whispered.

He faced the door. "Uh, come in."

Riley entered the room, and her eyes grew into saucers, and for the first time, I noticed his bedroom. It was popcorn, popcorn everywhere. I glanced at the bowl. And not a bite to eat.

"Watcha' need, Ry?" he asked evenly.

"Um, I smelled popcorn and I…" she muttered.

He showed her the empty bowl. "Sorry, it's all gone."

She examined us for a long moment, and then she left the room without another word. We waited a whole nanosecond before we collapsed on the bed and started laughing. Rob and I lay in opposite directions—with my head at his feet and his at mine—and after considerable laughter, we were holding our stomachs because our bellies actually hurt. So I lay there, wondering if my stomach felt like I had done a hundred crunches, would my abs show similar results? Because if so, I should laugh more and exercise less. And still thinking, I rolled up on my side and spoke to his feet, which were a bit hairy—not exceedingly ape-like or anything, just very manly like his legs, arms, and chest. "Listen, I'll help you clean up this whole mess even though *you* were the one who started it."

"Wow, you're such a good friend, Chlo," he returned sarcastically because if anyone were keeping track, he would beat me in the kindness race.

I collected some pieces off the bed. "It's the least I could do…after what you did today."

"And what was that?"

"What you always do." I dumped a handful of popcorn into the bowl, and he slid off the bed with a knowing smile.

"Listen," he started as he collected popcorn off the floor. "I have a question for you."

"Yeah?"

"Why'd you date him?"

"Why does every girl date him?"

"Yeah, but you're not every girl," he returned evenly.

I heaved out a heavy sigh. "Actually, I ask myself that all the time." I should have left it there, but for some reason, I continued. Rob had that effect on me. Talking to him was like being under oath, and I had to tell him the truth. "At first, it was just physical attraction, but after a while, we became friends, close friends, and I guess, it just went from there."

"Sometimes it happens," he said, and I thought to myself, *Yeah, and sometimes it doesn't.*

When most of the popcorn was off the floor, I realized I had a piece caught in my bra wallet—you know, the place between the cups where girls can stash cash when they don't have a purse or any pockets. I dislodged the piece and dropped it into a bowl, feeling the need to explain. "Things always get stuck in there."

"Oh," he said. "Guys don't have that problem."

"Yeah, well, I'd rather have ours than yours." That was a real conversation stopper, and we picked up the remaining pieces in silence.

Then he placed the bowl on top of his dresser and said, "Well, I think that does it, so I guess we should work on that scene now."

I reached into my bag and pulled out my copy of *Much Ado about Nothing*. I sat down on the end of his bed, and he sat next to me. I opened my book to Act IV, and he glanced over at me. "Okay, you need to start crying, so I can say my first line."

His line was: "Lady Beatrice, have you wept all this while," but instead of crying, I informed, "Rob, I can't cry on a command."

"Why not? You're a girl, aren't you?"

I pushed out a loud and long exhale like I was experimenting with my lung capacity, which was quite good since I'm a long distance runner and all.

"Listen, why don't you try Method Acting? It's a technique

81

where you think about something sad, and by drawing on your own personal experience, you'll portray the correct emotion in the scene."

"Should I think about my break-up with Austin then?"

"Yeah, I guess so."

"Or how I felt when my dad got rid of my dog? He was a really bad dog, but still." I wiped away a little tear and looked over at him. "But if I'm really in the mood to cry, I think about my Grandpa Preston. I miss his little one-liners, and I wish I would have written them all down because I can't remember half of them anymore." He brought me to his shoulder and patted my back. "Oh, and I miss your Grandma too. She sang all those beautiful folk songs with her Irish lilt." I started blubbering through the first few lines of the "Irish Lullaby." I heard audible swallows coming from him. His hands were folded in his lap, and I wondered if I should hold his hand, like I did on the day of his grandmother's funeral...

Grandma Callahan's funeral was held in a big Catholic church across town. Rob wore a dark suit, and I wore a black dress for the first time in my life. I was only nine, and I spent the entire service staring at my shiny black patent leather shoes. But when his mother began to sing "On Eagle's Wings," Rob started sobbing. I held his hand in mine and whispered, "I'm sorry. I'm so very, very sorry." And that was the first and only time I had ever seen my best friend cry...

"Hey," Rob said, slapping his thighs. "Maybe we should forget reading this scene tonight and work on memorizing our lines first."

"Yeah...okay."

"We could watch a movie." He gestured toward the top of his dresser. "And look, we already have popcorn." At the mention of popcorn, I smiled, thinking of all the places those pieces had been.

He grabbed the remote off the top of the TV and propped up some pillows against the wall. He took the right side, and I got comfortable on the left. He started flipping through a million channels at a voracious rate. I saw many options that we didn't have at my house, since my mother didn't believe in TV and my father didn't believe in paying for it. If the satellite company offered a PBS / Sports pack, that would be adequate for the Preston family.

Minutes passed, and after watching a millisecond of a million programs, I began to stare at him, hoping he'd feel the weight of my evil glare.

Rob faced me and arched an eyebrow. "You see something you like?"

I stared back at him, zeroing in on the little freckle at the tip of his nose. "Nope."

Then he turned away again, laughing.

Finally, we settled on a teen romance that neither of us had seen before, but about half way through it, I decided I could have gone my whole life without ever watching it. It was like an extended cliché on dating, and after experiencing some of my own relationships and seeing my friends with their boyfriends, I decided it held no resemblance to real life.

"Oh, c'mon," I scoffed at the television screen. "No guy would ever say that." Rob didn't offer a response, so I turned and found out why. He had fallen asleep. I slid off my side of the bed and pulled a navy blanket off the top shelf of his closet. I draped it over him, and when I did, a little corner of his mouth retreated in his cheek. I whispered, "You're welcome, Rob."

I returned to my spot and pulled the blanket over my legs. The movie droned on, but my eyes fell on him. I watched his face as he slept soundly next to me, noticing how his eyelashes fluttered and his expressions changed, and I leaned over and lightly touched his face with the back of my hand. It felt like soft sandpaper, and I wondered what it would feel like to kiss his face. Slowly, I lowered my head to his shoulder, his good one, and let my imagination travel to places where my lips dared not.

-14-

The Bet

My phone rang several times before I flipped off the side of the bed and scooped it out of my bag. "Uh, hello."

"Do you know what time it is, young lady?"

"Uh, no."

"Why not? The Callahans don't have any clocks over there?"

Clocks? I spotted one on Rob's night stand, and it was almost midnight. "Uh...sorry, Dad," I muttered.

"It's okay. I'll see you in a few minutes."

"Yeah, um, a few minutes," I repeated, and the conversation ended there. I felt confused. I stood there, replaying the words in my head. I was quite sure my father left out the part where he explains how rules are there to protect me, and how he's disappointed in me, and even though he wishes he didn't have to punish me, I had left him no other choice this time.

"That was my dad," I told Rob.

"Yeah, I figured," he said inside a yawn and walked over to me. "You okay?"

"I don't know."

"Why? Was your dad upset?"

"Uh, no."

"Then what's wrong?"

"Uh, I don't know," I stammered and searched the floor for my shoes.

Rob walked over with a pair of pink flip flops. "Maybe I should let you wake up before I ask you any more questions."

I nodded, and we left his bedroom and tiptoed across his dark house. He opened the sliding glass door, and we walked back to my house in silence until I realized, "Listen, Rob, my dad was just being nice over the phone, but he's still going to ground me for the rest of my life—which means you need to find another prom date!"

"That sounds a little harsh."

"You don't know my dad."

"Trust me, I do." He stepped in front of me and placed his hands on my shoulders. "And he's not going to be that upset."

"What makes you so sure?"

"Because you were with me."

"So?"

"*So,* your dad loves me."

"Only because I'm not dating you."

"Let me get this straight. If we were dating," he started, gesturing between us, "then your dad wouldn't like me anymore."

"Yup."

"You wanna' bet?"

"Sure," I accepted quickly. It was a rhetorical bet anyway, and unlike other wagers in the past, I had absolutely nothing to lose this time.

As we came to the end of the path, I noticed my father sitting on our back porch. My dad was dressed in weekend wear, a white T-shirt and a pair of plaid lounge pants, and as we entered my fenced-in backyard, he stood up, greeting us with a smile.

"I'm sorry, Mr. Preston," Rob apologized as he closed the gate behind us. "But we fell asleep during a movie."

"Must have been a lousy one."

"Yeah, but it would make a great cure for insomnia." Rob offered, and my father replied with a low chuckle. Rob was a master at polite adult humor, but I, on the other hand, had only one comedic weapon in my arsenal of humor: sarcasm.

"Then we should get it for Mom. It'd be much cheaper than

85

Ambien." As soon as I said it, I knew it was the kind of joke that wasn't really funny because it was too close to the truth. Lately, my mom suffered with my father's long absences and filled the void with medicinal friends like Ambien and Prozac.

"If only it were that easy," my father said quietly and maneuvered the conversation in another direction. "You pitched a great game tonight. How's your arm holding up?"

"It just has to last through the playoffs."

"Are you expecting to take regionals this year?"

I shot a finger in the air. "And on that note, I'm going to bed."

"Okay, goodnight, sweetheart."

"Night, Dad." I planted a quick kiss on my father's cheek and offered Rob a smile. "See you tomorrow."

He returned the smile and stepped toward me. "Goodnight, Chloe." Now, there was something different about the way he said my name, and then it hit me—about the same time as his kiss landed on my cheek. It was soft and warm and completely boyfriend material. His lips drifted to my ear. "And sweet dreams."

I entered my house in a complete fog as an odd feeling crept over me, something similar to having the flu. My whole body felt weak, but somehow, I managed to make it up the stairs and into my bedroom. I didn't bother to turn on the lights as I sprawled across the window seat. There, I waited for Rob to turn toward home, and since it was completely dark in my room, I knew he wouldn't see me. But as he walked out into the open, he lifted his head toward my bedroom window. My heart raced faster and faster as his eyes remained on my room, and when he offered a little wave, I gasped out loud and fell to the floor.

*   *   *

Early the next morning, I downed a tall glass of frosty water and headed out the garage door. Both of the road bikes were off their hooks, and my mother was kneeling next to a bed of bright pink impatiens in the front yard, proving that the familial definition of early and mine were off by a full hour or two.

I strolled down the driveway, waved at my mother through the trees, and set my GPS watch for the Riverside Trail. No ipod. No distractions. I needed time to think. Last night, my best friend posed as my boyfriend, and I had to figure out if it were to win a bet or if it were something more, and as much as I needed help sorting through this little dilemma, I couldn't imagine talking to anyone about my feelings for Rob. Trust me, I knew I had them; I just didn't know what to do with them, and the last thing I wanted was to put them out there in the open.

I took the sidewalk to the front of my neighborhood and glanced over at the gate house. Clyde was busy with a line of incoming cars, so I crossed the main road without the usual wave and entered the Riverside Trail at the head. I joined bikers, roller-bladers, walkers, and fellow runners for my Saturday morning ritual.

The seven-mile trail was a converted railroad track and ran parallel with the main road for about a mile, swerved in and out of canopied trees, and then crossed over the river before it ended in a loop around a small botanical garden. The Riverside Garden Club, of which my mother is a member, cultivated an impressive array of native wildflowers and seasonal blooms in beds scattered around benches. The park-like setting attracted insects, butterflies, tired rail-trailers, and couples in love, and each time I rounded the curve, I noticed an ample representation of each.

It was one of the nicest trails in the area, but the internal debate kept me from enjoying the scenery, and after forty-nine minutes and thirteen seconds of deliberation, I returned home without an answer.

I headed into the garage and grabbed a bottle of water from the drink fridge, and taking successive swigs of water, I meandered into the yard where I found my mother pruning bushes by the front entryway. "You need help, Mom?"

"Sure, that would be nice."

I pulled a few weeds from the bed and made a small pile on

a stepping stone. I glanced at the street. "Shouldn't the boys be back by now?"

"Which ones?"

"Hmm, I wonder." I pretended to consider the question. My father and brother biked with a group of guys from my dad's Rotary club every Saturday morning, and over the years, the guys formed two packs, based on speed, which was usually, but not entirely, dependent upon age. Mr. Dixon was a few years older than my father and led the fast pack. I knew his daughter from the cross country team. She was two years older than me, but during my freshmen year, we roomed together at the state meet. That was when she told me this horrible story about how her father actually lifted her boyfriend's prints off a glass and ran a full criminal check on him. Mr. Dixon's a detective by profession, and after hearing several stories about her dad, I realized that I didn't have it too bad.

I looked toward the street again, seeing slivers of yellow, red, and blue flow by the trees, and then the steady stream of bright colors climbed the driveway. I turned to my mom. "I'm gonna' head in now."

Her eyes dropped to a tiny pile of weeds next to me. "Hmm, thanks for all your help, dear." I think sarcasm runs on both sides of my family; thus, according to the Punnett square, it was genetically impossible for me to avoid.

"Yeah, don't mention it," I said and started toward the driveway.

The reason I left my weeding post was around six feet tall and dripping with sweat, and as I approached him, he was in the middle of a water bottle shower, squirting cool liquid on his face, the top of his head, and down his neck.

"Hi," I said.

"Hey," he said back while the last few droplets of water dripped from his bottle.

"You need another one?"

He nodded, and I went to the fridge. I grabbed an arm load of water bottles and passed them out like candy to trick-or-treaters.

"Thanks," Rob said, twisting off the cap and consuming half the bottle. He glanced at the other guys; they were huddled together and talking about the conditions of the ride. "In case you were wondering, your dad's still talking to me."

"So?"

"So," he repeated. "It proves that I won the bet." That wasn't the answer I wanted to hear, and I felt rejection take hold of my heart.

I looked down, sweeping a leaf with my running shoe. "What's the payback this time?" I figured he was going to make me wash his car again. That was my payment for the whole borrowing-the-keys incident, but Rob waited until he and Tom went trail riding on a drizzly afternoon. So, while he cleaned the mud off his mountain bike, I washed and waxed his whole Jeep. Then when he finished with his chore, he pulled up a lawn chair and sat under the coach lights of his garage. He read *Pride and Prejudice*, making intermittent jibes at my literary tastes as well as my car-washing capabilities.

"Well, the Jeep's still clean." He flicked his head in the direction of his house and laughed. "But the lawn—"

"You know what?" A hodgepodge of feelings, but namely rejection, fueled my next response. "I'm not doing anything for you. It was a dumb bet, and it proved absolutely nothing."

"No, it proved *you* were wrong."

I stepped closer to him, whispering my next statement. "I'm not wrong because we're not actually dating, and if we were, then my father wouldn't like you anymore."

"Yes, he would."

"No, he wouldn't."

"Would too."

"Would not."

We were headed toward conversational infinity, so Rob held up a hand. "Listen, Chlo, I think I know a way we can settle this."

"Yeah, how?"

"I'll show you tonight. Say around five o' clock."

My eyes narrowed in skepticism "For what?"

"A date."

"Like a real date?"

He nodded.

"To where?"

"I haven't decided yet."

"Then how will I know what to wear?"

"Just wear a dress."

"What kind of dress?" For a girl, this was a very logical question since certain events necessitated a certain style of apparel.

"I don't know. How about one of the bazillion dresses you have hanging in your closet?" He put on his bike helmet. "I'll see you later, okay?" He started coasting down the driveway on his bright yellow Trek, and my mother sidled up next to me. "I wasn't trying to eavesdrop..."

"But?"

"Are you and Rob going out tonight...like on a date?"

"Yeah," I said, and my mother smiled, like she did when I brought home all A's on my report card.

She peeled off her gardening gloves. "I guess we better get going then."

I offered a perplexed look.

"Because we don't have much time to find you a dress for tonight."

-15-

Real Date

By a quarter till five, I was sitting in the family room, since it was the perfect vantage point to wait for Rob. The back of the room had double French doors, which opened onto the patio, and the front was a wall of windows, looking out onto the front walkway. From the couch, I could spot him—whether he arrived by foot or by car like a normal date. Either way, I didn't want to be surprised, and I kept watch like an owl, swiveling my head from side to side. But when I spotted him coming up the front steps, I took an immediate interest in the television and concentrated on each breath.

When the doorbell chimed, I jumped a little, and my father emitted a low chuckle.

"Uh, could you get that, Dad?"

"Why don't you get it? It's for you anyway."

"But *I* can't answer the door."

"Why not?"

I heaved out an exasperated sigh. "Because."

My mother rose from the couch, thus ending the pointless discussion, and a few moments later, Rob entered the family room, freshly showered and dressed in grey slacks and a crisp, white button-down shirt. His sleeves were rolled up to his elbows, and his hands were buried in his pockets.

"Hi," I said first.

"Hey," he said back. "And uh…hello, Mr. Preston."

91

My father smiled graciously. "Make yourself at home, Rob."

Rob sat down next to me, leaving enough space for the dog. That is, if our pup hadn't been sent to a farm several years ago. Rob leaned forward and rested his elbows on his knees. "When did the Yanks score?"

"Bottom of the second. Must have been while you were driving here." My father gave him an inquisitive look. "Didn't you have it on in the car?"

"Nah, someone doesn't appreciate sports radio."

"Trust me. I know where she gets that from." Then my father mimicked my mother, who was in the kitchen and out of ear-shot at the time. "'It would be nice if we could talk for a change.' But whenever I turn it off, you know what she does?"

Rob knew. "Reads a book."

"Exactly," my father replied.

Rob and my father watched the game again until the next commercial, and then he slapped his thighs. "Well, I guess, we better get going."

The three of us rose on cue, and my mother emerged into the room again, wiping her hands on a dish towel. I smoothed down my dress, and Rob examined me for a moment. "Is that a new dress?"

"Yeah…why?" I fished for a compliment.

He shrugged. "Just wondering."

Then my father placed his hands on my shoulders. "Yeah, her mom took her out shopping this afternoon. I wouldn't have agreed to this one." It was deep red, a halter top style, and much shorter than the other dresses in my closet.

Rob's eyes drifted toward my mother. "Well, in that case, thanks, Mrs. Preston." She smiled, and my cheeks colored, probably turning the same shade as the aforementioned dress. Then we headed for the front door, and miraculously, we left without a review of my curfew. It was smooth. It was easy. And it was really nice for a change. But halfway down the steps, my father stopped us. "And Rob?"

"Yes, Mr. Preston."

"Have her home by midnight."

"Yes, Sir."

I was in shock, but Rob wasn't. And that's when I had the big a-ha moment. Yes, sadly it took me until the curfew thing to figure it all out. The pricey prom dress, the after-prom party, the new dress for the date, and yippee, the curfew extension had everything to do with my parents' feelings for Rob (and not me). My parents adored him, trusted him. After all, the boy had a key to my house, and I was about to embark on a new chapter in my dating life.

With a grin only plastic surgery could enhance, I climbed into the Jeep. My favorite band was playing, and we headed down the interstate toward Downtown Orlando. He veered off the highway and found a parking spot by Lake Eola, and as he cut the engine, I smiled over at him. "You know the play starts in a couple of hours," I said smartly, already figuring out his plans for the evening.

"Yeah, well, I like to be early." He came around to open my car door, and I followed him to the back where he unloaded a picnic basket and a blanket. "But I also like to eat."

"Aw, how sweet."

"Yeah, while you were out shopping, I was slaving in the kitchen all afternoon. I was just going to make a couple of sandwiches, so you can thank my mom for revising the menu."

We found a quiet spot near the edge of the lake where he laid out the blanket, and then gestured for me to open the picnic basket. Inside, it was like food Christmas. I pulled out a thermos of homemade raspberry lemonade, chicken salad on lightly toasted Panini, fresh fruit salad, and decadent brownies. We heaped food onto our plates and ate ravenously. Then remembering my manners, I said, "And my compliments to the chef."

"I'll thank my mom for you, but seriously, wouldn't you have been just as happy with a couple of baloney sandwiches?"

"No," I dismissed decisively and stabbed at a fresh strawberry with my fork.

He sighed. "Listen, I'm not going to do this every time."

I smiled at the thought of there being a next time, but decided against expressing any of those feelings. "Well, of course not, Rob," I teased. "Because that wouldn't be very original. Now, would it?" He shook his head and sunk his teeth into his sandwich, and before I took another bite, I tried to shift the conversational gears. "No, seriously, I appreciate everything you did for tonight."

"Yeah, I appreciate what you did too."

"What? Spend the afternoon shopping?"

"Yeah, because you look great in that dress." He swiped his lips with a napkin and smiled.

"Thanks." I gestured toward him with my fork. "And you don't look half bad yourself."

I got a low chuckle out of him. "Only you would say a thing like that."

"Really? What do you expect me to say? Some line to feed your massive ego?"

"Do you really think I'm *that* conceited?"

I inhaled through my nose, held it for a moment, and let it out with the truth. "No, not really, but I think you're confident though." I shrugged. "Probably because you happen to excel at everything. Like sports, school…" I rolled my eyes as I added the last example, "…and girls."

"It's not any different for you."

"Well." I bit down on my lip. "I tend to coast on my natural abilities. I don't really push myself that hard."

He set his plate aside and lowered himself to the blanket, propping himself up on an elbow. "Maybe it's better that way, Chlo."

"Huh?" I responded, lowering myself to the blanket and mirroring his position. "What do you mean?"

He licked his lips. "When you strive to be the best all the time, then you set yourself up for an inevitable fall. Because someone will always be smarter, funnier, faster…" He grimaced. "And maybe, even better looking."

I gave him a look of mock-horror. "Oh, no! That's just not possible!"

He winked at me. "Nah, not while I'm in my prime."

"So it's all downhill from here, huh?"

His dimples sunk deep into his cheeks, and he laughed. "Oh, you're funny."

I raised an eyebrow. "But am I *the* funniest person you know?"

"Well, Chloe." His smile softened. "I bet you have made me laugh more times than anyone else."

"Yeah, that's probably true."

He continued on, "And when you were little, you used to make up all the songs about everything. And while you were singing, you would strum along on that pink guitar of yours."

"Which I never really learned to play, by the way"

"Yeah, but it didn't matter to me," he assured me.

"Because I was the best singer in the whole world, huh?"

"No," he paused. "Just the most creative."

I tried to hide my overwhelming smile by looking down at the blanket, but soon, I noticed his hand, inching toward mine. He didn't hold my hand; instead, his fingers traveled across it slowly. His touch was gentle, somewhat explorative, and after a while, I joined in the playfulness of the moment. I enjoyed the warmth of his skin and noticed the subtle calluses on his palm, and eventually, his fingers slid slowly through mine, joining our two hands as one.

As we held hands, we never spoke, and I wondered if we didn't know what to say to each other as we crossed into new territory. Things were changing between us, and it was as if our words were intimidated by our actions.

"Should we get going?" he asked.

"Uh, yeah," I said, but I really wanted to stay with him on the blanket. After all, I was more concerned about missing what might evolve between us than what Shakespeare penned four hundred years ago.

He sat up. "You want anything else to eat?"

I reached into the open container of brownies. "Maybe I'll have one more of these." He closed the lid, and then the two of us started repacking the basket. After he folded the blanket neatly, he thumbed toward the parking lot. "I'll take this back to the Jeep if you want to wait here."

"Okay," I said as he started walking away from me, and I examined him like he was a hot guy strolling by me at the mall. I liked his walk, his steady gait and fluid movements, since it exuded both confidence and a sense of maturity beyond his years. I always believed that a guy's walk revealed a lot about who he truly was, and Rob conveyed himself accurately with every step he took.

I watched him load up the Jeep, and as he returned toward me, I offered him an overzealous wave, which he returned with a subtle nod of the head, and for some reason, I kept my eyes on him. I didn't divert my attention toward the lake; instead, I watched him, noticing the broadness of his shoulders tapering toward his waist and his developing muscular frame.

He reached my side. "You ready?" He nodded toward the outdoor amphitheater, and as we started down the wide sidewalk, moving closer to each other, our shoulders brushed a few times until our hands joined together. We resembled an official couple on a date, and then I felt exceedingly giddy like a girl holding her first boyfriend's hand down the hall in school.

Once we arrived at the box office, I spotted Miss Randall, our English teacher. Rob joined her in line while I waited by a group of Riverside's faculty, which were mostly old relics from the English department. I noticed Mr. Martinez, our widely appreciated physics intern, off to the side. He offered me a slight smile, and I knew Courtney would tear off a limb if I didn't take advantage of this chance meeting.

"Hey, Mr. Martinez." I flicked my head toward my single, and very pretty, English teacher. I intended to ask the obvious, since they were the only members of the faculty in their twenties. Riverside was like teacher utopia, and teachers never left—well except for death or retirement, whichever came first. "Are you dating my teacher?"

96

"I am your teacher." That wasn't the point. Plus, I never saw him as a typical teacher. I think it had something to do with first meeting him on the beach when he wasn't wearing a shirt.

"Well, isn't there some rule against faculty fraternization'?" I wondered.

He frowned. "Nope, just with students."

I went for a new topic. "You like Shakespeare?"

"Not really. It's just a faculty night out."

"Yeah, I get it. It's not your scene. You'd rather be—"

He tapped the side of my head. "Listen, just tell Courtney if she wants to talk to me, she still can. As long as she remembers that I'm her teacher now. Comprendé?"

I nodded.

Rob sidled up next to me as Mr. Martinez joined his colleagues. "Who was that?"

"Just the physics intern."

"Now, I know why you two rush to class every day."

"Oh, it's not me," I said, shaking my head. "He's not *my* type."

"Why? What's wrong with him?"

I squeezed Rob's dimpled cheeks. "He doesn't have any of these."

"Well, I guess, I'm in luck then." He grinned and took my hand again, leading me to our seats. I saw our teachers a few rows ahead of us and noticed that Mr. Martinez sat a few seats away from Miss Randall, dismissing my earlier suspicions. I gazed across the audience and spotted a group of girls from our English class. In a loud stage-whisper, I turned to Rob, "Jessica's here."

"Yeah," he said. "She already had plans, so I had to take you."

I punched him in the arm, but soon apologized, "Oh, I'm so sorry."

"Why?"

"Because we're on a date."

"So we should act differently now?"

97

"Yeah, I think so."

"Nah, that wouldn't be any fun!" His hand slid down my left side, and he found one of my terribly ticklish spots. I sputtered a cacophonous laugh and caused a "blue hair" to shush me with narrowing eyes.

The play hadn't even started yet, and for the duration of it, we remained relatively quiet. But when our scene from Act IV appeared on stage, I looked at him and he looked at me, and we mouthed our first few lines to each other, since that was the extent of my memorization.

During the final act, I nudged him. "You better not fall asleep."

"I won't." He winked at me. "I want to see how it ends."

"Ha, ha, ha," I returned flatly.

After the play, Miss Randall and her Riverside cohorts intercepted us while his warm hand was still in mine. "Rob Callahan and Chloe Preston, are you two...? Well, I'll be. I just paired you up because I thought you'd make a cute couple." I thought back to ninth grade when I played the part of Juliet in the final act of *Romeo and Juliet*. My teacher paired me up with this kid named George, who actually wore a T-shirt with the Periodic Table of Elements on it. He was like the anti-Romeo, and I was just glad that I got to play dead for most of the scene.

"Miss Randall," Rob started with his dimpled grin. "Are you trying to collect a matchmaking fee?"

Her eyes narrowed at him, but Mr. Martinez seemed to appreciate his sense of humor. "Are you the one who helps her with physics homework?"

Rob extended a hand. "Rob Callahan."

"Alex Martinez."

Rob draped an arm around my shoulders. "So, tell me, how is she in class?"

"Well, since you asked, she's a pain in the neck. She sits next to Courtney Valentine, and the two of them whisper and giggle all hour."

"Tell me about it. I live by both of them." And Rob shared a few gems from our formative years. Mr. Martinez wished us a good night, and Rob and I strolled around the perimeter of the lake, stopping by the playground at the far end of the park. I pulled him through the open gate and over to the long row of resting swings. I sat down and looked at up him with pouty lips. "Oh, please, Rob?"

"Sure, why not?" His hands found my waist, and he pushed me up into the air several times. I pumped my legs enthusiastically. Then his phone rang, and even though I was curious about his conversation, the swinging back and forth turned his sentences into fragments. All I heard was, "No way…I can't believe it…" He spoke dramatically and eventually rounded the swing set, standing in front of me with the explanation. "The game went into extra innings."

"Oh," I said, relieved it wasn't something important.

"You mind if I…" He thumbed at the bench.

"No, not at all." I closed my eyes, leaning all the way back in the swing with my legs stretching out in front of me and my body parallel to the ground as I glided back and forth through the humid night air. There was something about the swings that transported me back in time, and I could almost hear the laughter of children and feel the sunshine on my face.

"Hey, I dare you to jump," he said abruptly.

I opened my eyes. "But I'm in a dress, Rob."

"Yeah, like that's ever stopped you before."

I came up with another reason. "Well, I'm trying to act like a lady on our date."

He found that somewhat amusing. "Did you decide that before or after you punched me?"

Before the swing completely stopped, I jumped off, showing little evidence of any ballet training, and landed most ungracefully on my feet, then bottom, and lastly hands into the warm sand. I sprang to my feet, continuously brushing the sand off as I moved closer to him. He masked his chuckle with his hand. "I'm sorry."

I gave him a little shove. "No, you're not."

"Yeah, you're right. I'm not."

"So did the Sox win?"

He nodded.

"Good, I'd hate for some game to ruin our date."

"Don't worry, Chloe. Nothing could ruin tonight," he said sweetly and took my hand again, leading me over to a park bench on the edge of the wide sidewalk. Sitting close to each other, he gently draped his arm around my shoulder, and I leaned against his chest. He filed his fingers through mine, and I glanced all around us, noticing the stars dotting the heavens and the colorful blooms in the gardens, and in the center of the lake, the wondrous fountain shot a continuous stream of water into the night sky. No one crossed our path now, and the moment was cinematic perfection.

"Did you have a good time tonight?" he asked softly.

"Yeah." I swallowed down a little knot in my throat. "And you?"

He placed a soft kiss on my temple, his lips traveling closer to my ear and his warm breath reaching my neck. "Of course, I did. And do you know why?"

"No…why?" I asked softly.

"Because I was out with my best friend." And for some reason, those last two words gave birth to doubt. It began in the pit of my stomach and swirled around until I felt the full effects of it. He whispered something in my ear, something like "It's a nice night," but I didn't hear him as I rose from the bench. "Can we go home now?"

"W-w-why? What's wrong?"

"Nothing." I started toward a bright yellow spot across the lake. "I'm just ready to go. That's all."

On my run this morning, I never considered the third and most obvious possibility. Rob wanted the best of both worlds; he wanted to be friends who dated. No commitments, just all the benefits. And it all made sense to me now. He was going away to school in a few months and probably didn't want some girlfriend back home. I cursed my own stupidity, and I wanted to cry because, in the course of a perfect evening, the best date

100

of my life, I opened up some sealed off part of my heart. I had let out those feelings, the ones I had been trying to ignore for the last ten years, and in doing so, I realized I was completely in love with him. At six. And *still* at sixteen.

He caught up to me. "Do you want to go somewhere else?"

"No."

He placed a hand on my shoulder. "What's wrong?"

"Nothing."

"C'mon, just tell me."

"It's complicated."

"Yeah, well, the truth usually is."

Neither of us said anything for a long moment, and then I turned around to face him. He spoke again, very softly this time, "Let's go some place where we can talk, Chlo."

I nodded slowly, and even though we never said another word on the way back to the Jeep, I knew exactly where he was taking me.

-16-

Rewriting History

He rolled up my driveway, and the two of us walked through the woods, only stopping when we reached the base of the old oak tree. His eyes lifted slowly to the opening in the tree house. "After you," he said, and I climbed the side of the tree, stepping on the wooden two by fours that served as the ladder. When I was about half way up, I glanced down at him, and he was looking away, just as he had done when I wore a dress as a little girl.

My head emerged into the small opening, and the inside felt even smaller than I had remembered, and I took a deep breath of the past. The air was warm and muggy, and the smell inside reminded me of the lumber aisle at Home Depot.

On all fours, I crept across the wooden planks and found my spot against the wall, and when I stretched out my legs, they reached halfway across the floor of our childhood hideout. He joined me, taking his seat on my right, his long legs reaching way past mine now. Our shoulders touched lightly, and he offered his hand, laying an open-faced palm gently on my thigh. I rested my hand on top of his, and his warm fingers encircled mine.

The sounds of the night surrounded us. There was a rustling of the leaves, and the crickets strummed their only tune, but neither of us spoke a word. My head raced with thoughts, which never formed into complete sentences, as he peered out of the window on the right. The small opening had served as our lookout for years and was there in case we were ever attacked by neighboring invaders.

I drew a deep breath and squeezed his hand. "You're my best friend, Rob. You were the only person who cared enough about me to find me on Monday. I was really hurt, more than you'll ever know, but you made it better."

"You're my best friend too, and I'm closer to you than to anyone else."

"But I don't want to date my best friend."

His voice registered his disappointment. "Okay."

"Unless..." I felt the need to explain further. "We're not just friends anymore, because I don't believe in the whole friends-with-benefits movement."

He turned, his eyes finding mine. "I don't either."

"But isn't that what you meant earlier?"

"No." He shook his head and smiled. "I know you're not like that, and you should know that I'm not either."

"But you're leaving for school—"

"In four months."

"But—" I tried.

"None of that matters, Chlo, because I want to be your boyfriend." He smiled sweetly before he added, "Again."

I smiled back. "But you have to promise me something."

"What?"

"Promise me that we'll still be friends no matter what happens."

"I promise." My heart fluttered as he spoke earnestly into my eyes, and very gently, he rested a palm on the side of my face. His thumb swept across my lips, and he looked like he intended to kiss me. "And..."

"Yes?"

"I do remember that day." His smile warmed my insides. "You were wearing a pink swimsuit with a little ruffle across the top, and your hair was up in pigtails, and we were telling each other stupid knock-knock jokes. We were both cracking up, and I remember thinking that you were the coolest girl in the world and that I…anyway, I remember, Chloe."

"Guess what?"

"What?"

"I know a good knock-knock joke."

"There are no good knock-knock jokes."

I started one anyway. "Knock, knock."

"Who's there?" he mumbled.

"Yeah."

"Yeah who?"

"Aw, I'm happy too, Rob."

"Oh, you're so funny." He went for my ribs, and I started laughing. I targeted his belly, but unfortunately, he didn't have any good ticklish spots on his entire body. (Well, as far as I could tell.)

"Do you know what was *really* funny?" I asked, giggling.

"What?"

"The look on Riley's face when she came into your room last night."

"Yeah, I know." We both started laughing, and my head tilted back as his lips found my ear. "May I kiss you?"

I felt six all over again, and even though it's impossible to go back in time and relive the past, it is entirely possible to recreate the same exact moment and make it better. Much better. With his lips still near my ear, he added. "I've thought about this moment for a long time."

I didn't hesitate with my reply. "Me too, Rob." I closed my eyes, completely under the spell of his intentions, and waited for his lips to meet mine…finally.

"But," he began, and I opened my eyes slowly. My gaze fell downward, and then he lifted my chin with his hand. "We'll only have one first kiss, Chlo, so this moment will only happen once for us." I smiled at his beautiful, calculating mind. "Think about it. Is this," he hesitated, "exactly the way you imagined it?"

"Well, my imagination is usually better than reality…" He looked dejected, and I rested my hand against his smooth cheek, and very softly, I added, "…until now." Then I wrapped my

104

hands around his neck, feeling the warmth of his skin under my fingertips, and while his hands cradled my face, I closed my eyes. Then his warm lips pressed against mine.

"See, I didn't turn away this time," I whispered against his mouth.

He patted my cheeks. "Don't worry. I wouldn't have let you."

Our mouths smiled against each other as his lips parted slightly. He kissed my upper lip a few times, gently moving to my lower, softly sucking it. Slowly, he explored the contours of my mouth, and I let him, without thinking, without forcing my thoughts on him. I let him control the moment, knowing his sweet intentions and not wanting to spoil the moment with my growing desire for him. Gradually, his fingers crept from my face and into my hair. He found the tendrils on the nape of my neck and twirled them playfully with his fingers. As his mouth closed, he planted a final kiss on my eager lips. Even though his kiss bore the sweetness of a boy with his first girlfriend, we were no longer children experimenting with puppy love because desire tugged at our innocence. And while his lips lingered by mine, he pushed out a breath and spoke, "We need to take this slow."

"I know."

He guided me onto his shoulder, and gently, he caressed my hair. Words were unnecessary now, and I soaked in the after-thoughts of our first kiss. And now, with my lips dangerously close to his neck, my eyes wandered freely across his still body. Surely, my fingers and lips grew jealous of the places where eyes could travel without reproach: down his chest, I thought of the swirls of brown hair that I wanted to explore; and across his lap, the mystery of a man's body still lay hidden to me; and out the length of his long legs, I envisioned our bodies intertwined while our fingertips discovered each other for the very first time. All my fears succumbed to fantasies, and I felt the warmest rush of affections for him. His hand caressed my back now, and his soft lips touched my forehead. I wanted him to kiss me again and cross the line of innocence, but into our quiet moment, a notorious neighborhood invader chanted in a singsong voice:

105

Rob and Chloe
Up in their tree
K-I-S-S-I-N-G
First comes love
Then comes marriage
Then comes baby
In the baby carriage.

Quickly, we separated like two kids getting caught in the act, and following the song, Courtney leaned all the way into the opening of the tree house. "Aw, I've always wanted to sing that to you two." Then she giggled back down the tree.

Rob turned toward me with an enormous smile. "Too bad she didn't sing it ten years ago. Then you would've known that the baby comes after marriage and *not* the K-I-S-S-I-N-G."

I shoved him into the corner and scampered across the floor, meeting Courtney at the base of the tree.

She bit down on her lip. "So, tell me, how was your date?"

"It was nice," I said evenly.

Then Rob joined us. "Yeah, we had a good time."

Courtney looked at us with narrowing eyes. "That's all I get."

"Yup," we chorused.

"My two best friends go out on a real date, and *that* is all I get!"

We nodded in unison.

"Wanna' know what Josh and I did tonight?"

"Sure." Rob took the bait.

"Each other." She spun on a heel and marched home.

"She's kidding, right?"

I nodded, and he followed me into the woods with another question. "How do you know?"

"Because we tell each other everything."

"Everything?" he repeated uneasily.

"Yeah," I said. "Is that a problem?"

"Not yet," he returned with a smile, and then he led me toward the garage door. Under the coach lights, he offered one last kiss on my lips and repeated his line from the previous night: "Goodnight, Chloe, and sweet dreams."

He got into his Jeep, and I entered my house, dark and quiet, and climbed the stairs to my bedroom. I sprawled across my window seat, pulling up the blinds a few inches and gazing into the woods behind my house. I watched as the faint glow of his headlights illuminated the darkness, and while touching the humid glass, I whispered a soft "I love you."

-17-

The Four F's

Days later, I professed my love for him, several times actually, and in front of the brightest kids in the whole senior class. Even Jessica and Kendra stood up during our standing ovation, and everyone remarked on our acting ability, which was quite ironic, since neither one of us was acting anymore. Consequently, Rob and I had reached a level of honesty that we hadn't known in years—ten years to be exact. And sometimes, I had to remind myself that I was sixteen now, and I couldn't blurt out my real feelings for him.

At six, there were no rules. We could fall in love and talk about marriage and how many kids we wanted to have, and whenever it was my turn to pick the game, I always wanted to play house. He was the daddy, and I was the mommy, and if Brad or Riley joined in, then they played our children. Each day, Rob would climb down the ladder of our tree house and go off to work while I tended to our house. Even then he was a thoughtful husband, bringing me wildflowers from the woods and fresh blooms from his backyard, and I, in return, prepared his favorite meal from fallen debris off the forest floor.

But at sixteen, there are lots of rules, and you don't discuss marriage or the number of children you want to have. You're supposed to talk about movies and music, and right now everyone was talking about one thing: PROM!

At present, I was sitting on a padded, pink bench and reading *East of Eden*—which is a considerably long book—while Courtney, Caitlyn, and Callie were in their dressing rooms.

Courtney popped out her head. "I need your advice." I placed my book face-down on the bench and stuck my head in her dressing room where she posed like an actual Victoria Secret's model. "Is this the last thing I should be wearing when *he* loses his virginity?"

My mouth dropped open. "No."

"How about this?" She held up something black and equally seductive, and I slid into her tiny dressing room and scolded her. "Don't even think about it."

"Why?" she asked in mock innocence.

"Because he's completely in love with you, and I know you don't love him."

"I might."

"What about Mr. Martinez? And Operation Intern?"

"That plan goes into effect in a few weeks…after the school year ends. But I need something to do until then."

"You mean some*one*."

She chewed on a nail. "Maybe."

"Have you ever considered a real hobby?"

"Well, I…"

I quipped back, "Something other than collecting broken hearts."

She smiled knowingly and pulled off her slinky negligee. She stood there like a marbled Aphrodite, wearing just a bright pink thong. She spun around and narrowed her eyes at me. "Well, what about you? Why are you out there reading a book when you should be in here trying on something for the big night?"

"But we're not going to do anything."

She rested her hand on my shoulder. "Listen, just because you're not going to have sex *with* him, doesn't mean you can't be sexy *for* him."

"I know."

But I didn't, and I was glad when her tutorial continued, "I know you've jumped on that whole waiting-until-marriage

109

bandwagon, but being sexy starts with these." She snapped the elastic of her own unmentionable. "I bet you still wear those horrid granny panties, don't you?"

"Bikini cut," I corrected as Courtney slipped back into her sundress. She dragged me to a table of neatly folded underwear and handed me a red pair. I examined it. "It's like a triangle with string." I glanced at the price in comparison to my typical selection. "And they even charge more for these."

Courtney winked. "Yeah, sometimes, less is more."

Yeah, what did I know? I bought three: deep red, soft ivory, and basic black. I used up most of the cash in my wallet to buy three pairs of underwear that I might never wear. Because if I did, I would have to hand wash them in my sink and dry them with a hairdryer in the privacy of my bathroom. Then I'd have to store them in a secret place, since it's not like G-string underwear can quietly enter the laundry world without getting noticed by my mother.

After we left Victoria Secrets, we walked around the mall for a while, and then headed to the food court for dinner. As Caitlyn sipped her soda, she zeroed in on Callie. "So, how far have you and Mike gone?"

Callie grinned and held up two fingers. Caitlyn's green eyes slid around the table and found mine, and I shot one finger into the air. The middle one.

"Technically, you haven't even made it that far." Courtney patted my other hand in successive taps. "It's French, feel, finger, and—" She mouthed the final f-word, not because she was opposed to saying it, but there were little ears sitting behind us.

"Omigod, he kisses you without tongue." Caitlyn was appalled at the information, but then she smiled like only Caitlyn can—condescendingly. "What kind of guy does that?"

I swirled the ice in my lemonade and thought about our promise to take things slow. "A very, *very* good one."

-18-

The Schedule

About Rob being a good guy, that was never an issue until I came down with a bad case of Promitis. Now, the day started out fine. The girls and I followed the schedule: manicures at eleven; followed by lunch, which was pointless since we were full of butterflies; and then we headed to the hair salon for our two o' clock appointments.

I, of course, opted out of the whole salon experience since I have naturally curly hair and hairdressers only envision two things when they see me in their chair; they either want to straighten my curls or tease them to Medusa proportions—neither of which was acceptable to me.

Anyway, guess what I did during their hour-long appointment? Yup, I read my book. Well, I *tried* to read my book, but the lady next to me wanted to chat. "Are you reading that for school?" she asked sweetly.

"Nope. For my boyfriend."

"Well, isn't that nice," she said, introducing herself as Betty. Her hand felt limp in mine, and her dull, yellowy eyes revealed her age. "Are those your friends in there?"

"Yes, we have our prom tonight." I told her about my friends and their dates. I even flashed a picture of Rob, and she smiled, telling me he was very handsome and reminded her of a young Lawrence Olivier. I was only familiar with the older one who portrayed the aging King Lear in the Shakespearean film, but

111

I thanked her anyway. She was sweet and reminded me of my Grandma Preston, since she had a knack for getting me to talk about myself. But when Betty got called for her appointment, I returned to my book. I was reading intently when Caitlyn taunted, "Hey there, geek."

I kept my eyes on the page. "Geek is most often associated with those who are knowledgeable about computers, of which I am not; therefore, I am not a geek, but a nerd. So, if you plan on insulting me, please use the correct terminology."

She let out a single huff, and I smiled victoriously as I slid the bookmark into the four-hundred-page novel and glanced up at my friends. Courtney looked like a real beauty queen with her traditional updo, and Caitlyn was cuter than usual with her jagged part and bobby-pinned style, but Callie had been totally transformed. She had exchanged her ponytail for a half-up, half-down style, and the hairdresser added random spirals throughout her locks, drawing most of her dark brown hair into a clip and leaving a few wispy tendrils to frame her heart-shaped face.

I stood up in front of Callie. "Wow."

"Is that all you can say?"

"Hey, it's more than what Mike'll say." She looked concerned. "C'mon, Cal, he's going to be speechless."

"You really think so?"

"Yeah, I know so."

For my three friends, prom meant something completely different. For Callie, it was about the fulfillment of a fantasy. For Courtney, it was about the glamour. And for Caitlyn, it was about the schedule. And speaking of schedules, we arrived back at my house at a quarter after three, getting an early start on our makeup. Courtney and I took over my bath upstairs, and Caitlyn and Callie claimed my brother's for the afternoon.

Since Courtney and Caitlyn showed up at school in full makeup every morning, we regarded them as the experts on the matter. Callie, on the other hand, had always been a bit of a tomboy, and I viewed face paint as somewhat optional, ranking it below ironing, coffee consumption, and the morning paper.

112

Later on, I sat there in my bathroom, watching Courtney apply her makeup from the vantage point of my vanity stool. Picking up a tube of gloss, I slid it over my lips while Courtney leaned into the mirror, examining her face closely. She smiled, apparently pleased with what she saw, and then she turned her eyes on me and frowned. "I know you're into that whole natural girl look, but it's prom, Chlo. You should let me do your eyes for you."

I pushed out an exhale and dropped my shoulders, feeling like the next contestant on the makeover game, and Courtney popped open her makeup tackle box with an enormous grin. She pulled out a myriad of brushes and palettes of eye shadow, and I closed my eyes as she swept a base coat over them. Then I felt the cool, wet brush draw lines in the creases of my lids, and like an artist creating a masterpiece, she chose her colors carefully and painted my eyes with artful strokes.

"Okay, open up," she requested. "I need to line your eyes and brush on a little mascara." She finished my eyes, and slowly, I turned on the stool like at a beauty salon. Seeing my reflection in the mirror for the first time, I had to give Courtney her kudos: my light eyes popped from my face.

Then she rested a chin on my shoulder and said, "We really should have taken a before photo." And with that said, my mind drifted back to one of Courtney's middle school slumber parties when we did just that. "Do you remember when we raided your step sister's closet and pretended it was our prom night?"

"Yeah," she returned, and then she gasped dramatically. "Do you have those pictures in your scrapbook?"

I nodded enthusiastically, and Courtney and I bolted down the stairs and rushed into the family room. After grabbing the scrapbook from the bookcase, we headed into the other bathroom. "Look at this," I said, holding the page open to the two-page spread.

Caitlyn ran her fingers across the photos and sighed. "Look, it's all seven of us."

"We thought we were so cool," I said.

113

Courtney added, "Yeah, what did we know?"

"Nothing, but we were lucky to have one another. Middle school can be so awkward," Callie said. She had always been the tallest girl in the class, and the complete opposite of Caitlyn, who had always been promoted to the top of every pyramid.

"You know what? We're still lucky," I added as we fell into a group hug.

"Okay, okay, break it up, girls." Caitlyn said, sounding like a lame administrator trying to limit PDA in the halls. "Because I didn't make time for this in my schedule."

Courtney and I saluted the little general and headed up the stairs to put on our dresses.

Once inside my bedroom, I lifted the corner of my mattress, and Courtney raised an eyebrow. "Is that where you keep your secret stash?"

"No, it's where I keep these." I pulled out a flattened pink bag and removed a silky pair of ivory panties.

"So, will tonight be your first time?"

I narrowed my eyes at her.

"Listen, Chlo, it'll probably hurt a little at first, but after a while, you'll get used to it, and eventually, you won't even notice it's there."

"Are we still talking about the underwear?"

"Yeah, but when you're ready to do the other thing, it'll be the same speech—except for the part about not noticing. Well, unless the guy is really—"

"Great," I cut in. "Now, Caitlyn can omit the sex pep talk from my wedding day schedule."

"C'mon, you're not going to wait that long."

"Yes, I am."

"You know, it's not a sin to do it before then."

"Actually," I said, spreading my hands to the sides, "it is."

A knock hit the door, and I slid the bag under my mattress and shoved the balled-up underwear into my pocket. "Who is it?"

"It's me…Caitlyn." She sounded emotional, a sad kind of angry.

"What did Brandon do now?" Courtney accused as she opened the door. Caitlyn sat down on the edge of my bed. She dropped her face into her hands for a moment, and then quickly regained her composure. "He waited until now to pick up his tux. Apparently, there were some major waves down at the jetty, and then they hit traffic on I-95..." After three years, we had heard lots of stories about long lines, lost items, and bad traffic, so Courtney and I nodded during the whole story. "...Anyway, his pants were like a half a foot too short, and the seamstress is home with a sick kid, so they're trying to locate someone from another store to come in and do the alterations for him."

Just then my mom stepped into my room, glancing at Courtney and me with a huge smile. "Girls, you should get dressed now. The Callahans are here."

Caitlyn heaved out a heavy sigh. "Oh, just go to the prom without us then."

"Nonsense." Courtney put a hand on her shoulder. "I'm sure you made time for unforeseen problems in that schedule of yours."

"Problems. Yes. Major wardrobe malfunctions. No."

"Well, he could start a new trend," Courtney said with a smirk. She and I felt the same way about Brandon Edwards and would like nothing more than to see him show up at prom in a pair of floods. "Since capris tux pants are all the rage over in Europe."

I gave a decisive nod, and Caitlyn bought it. "Maybe in a few years when the runways of Paris reach Riverside."

Courtney laughed. "It was just a joke, Cait."

"Oh gawd, I'm too stressed out to find humor in all of this." She collapsed onto my bench like a Hollywood starlet in one of those forties films. You know, Vivien Leigh playing opposite of a young Laurence Olivier, perhaps.

Then Callie floated into the room. "I was just with Mike, and let me just say this: he looks *hot*." She hit the final "t" with emphasis and fell onto my bed. "I'm *so* in love with him."

"Yeah, we know." Caitlyn grumbled from the bench, and

115

Callie glanced over at us with a questioning look. We filled Callie in on the details but had to omit our personal commentary, since Caitlyn was still there, sulking and doing her best to kill our pre-prom euphoria.

Now, if Caitlyn were first in command among our circle of friends, then I would be next in line to take over in her absence, or in this instance, her annoying presence. "Ahem," I cleared my throat in preparation for a speech. "In light of the recent events, I think we should stick to the original game plan and get dressed for prom. We cannot sit around all night and wallow in our misery." My eyes rested on the wallowing one, and then I decided on a big finish. "After all, it's what Brandon would want us to do…so let's do it for Brandon!" I followed it with a rallying coach's clap, and Caitlyn shot up from the bench and marched up to me.

"You have the dumbest sense of humor."

"At least I have one," I fired back.

"Okay, okay, break it up girls," Callie said with a grin, dragging Caitlyn downstairs to my brother's bedroom and leaving us to get dressed in peace. I slid into my ivory gown; Courtney filled out her red satin one; and together, with our tiny purses, painful shoes, and body glitter, we tiptoed into the hallway and peered over the ledge. The landing opened over the family room below, and it was the perfect spot to spy on everyone else in the house. We watched as Caitlyn and Callie joined the moms off to the side while the guys relaxed on the couch, chortling at the flat screen. No one even noticed us, and I turned to Courtney with a grin. "We should throw paper airplanes at our dates."

Her eyes widened. "Yeah, good idea."

We moved stealthily back to my room, pulled some paper from the printer, and made a small fleet of planes. Then we resumed our places at the wall. Narrowing my eyes, I bit down on my lip and fixated on the top of Rob's head.

"*Look out!*" Caitlyn shrieked, foiling our plans.

I faced Courtney. "Seriously, why can't we leave her here?"

She frowned at me. "Just be the bigger person."

"Oh, like that'll be hard."

"You know what I mean, Chlo." Courtney dragged me down the stairs, and we landed in front of our dates.

"Hey," Rob said, gathering me into a hug. He found my ear, and his lips got so close it tickled. "You look really pretty tonight."

"Yeah, you too," I mumbled reflexively.

Then the camera flashed in rapid-fire succession as the four of us crossed into the family room. It all felt surreal. My friends were there, and their parents too, and the room filled with mindless prom prattle. I knew Rob was with me, and I felt his warm hand in mine; but as we plunged deeper into the cacophonous chaos, it all felt differently than I expected, differently than I imagined. And I grew exceedingly nervous.

"Here's your corsage," he said, and I replied with a "Yeah, your thingy is in the fridge." A few moments later, my mother showed up with his boutonnière, and I stared at the two flower-to-go boxes in our hands.

Rob added softly, "I'm supposed to put this on you, Chloe."

"It's okay. I can do it myself," I added quickly, but felt instantaneous regret since women's lib and prom go together like sand and stilettos.

"Sorry," I said and wished my life came with a backspace button. "What I meant to say was, 'Yes, that would be nice.'" Of course, my apology was aimed at his shoes, which were very shiny and black, and I wondered if they were as painful as my golden pair. I had heard about brides having two pairs of shoes for their wedding day, the pair to wear down the aisle and one for the reception, but at prom, most girls end up barefoot—but hopefully not pregnant—by the end of the night.

"Hope you don't mind that I shaved my head."

"*What!*" My eyes darted to his hair, and I was relieved to find his auburn waves gelled back to perfection. Then I narrowed my eyes at his smirking face. "Why would you say a thing like that?"

"To get you to stop staring at my shoes." He smiled some dimples. "And it worked."

"I'm sorry." My shoulders slumped with my admission. "I'm just a little nervous."

"Hey, it's just me."

"I know that." My voice dropped to a stage-whisper. "But I feel like everyone's watching us, and I don't know how we're supposed to act in front of our families now."

"We're not." That statement was both comforting and frightening, and in the crowded family room, he drew me into a hug and kissed my cheek. His kiss calmed me, and I smiled up at him, letting him know I was back to normal again. We stepped out of the hug and exchanged floral boxes. I pinned the boutonnière on his lapel, and he slid the corsage on my wrist. And just like that, my nervousness lifted like the fog with the morning sun.

"Aw, now, that's a Kodak moment!" Aunt Nancy gushed as she dropped by us with her camera. She moved in closer, never quite mastering the art of whispering. "Well, it's too bad your friend's date doesn't have his own tux like Josh. Then he wouldn't be holding up the whole show. Now, would he?"

Caitlyn heard this, and after seeing her pained expression, I felt sorry for her. And I knew she was in no condition to work on scheduling revisions, so I sought the advice of Mrs. Callahan. "I need your help. What should we do if Brandon doesn't get here for a while?"

She smiled at me, and then at an approaching Caitlyn. "Well, you should start taking pictures now. Begin with the four of you, and then with each couple, saving you and Brandon for last. And if you really want to save time, you should plan on eating here." She started walking into the dining room, and the women in the house trailed behind her. "Nance and I could set the table with the…" My mother nodded. "The good china, and we could order take-out from that great Chinese place up the road."

Caitlyn followed Mrs. Callahan as cancellations were made and orders were placed; then everyone migrated to the pool for pictures. My backyard was prom-picture paradise; our pool area

118

had a wooden bridge over a river of rocks, a large gazebo in the back corner, and several garden landscapes.

The four of us girls lined up on the bridge, huddled in the gazebo, and posed one at a time in front of the colorful blooms; and when it was time for the couples to be photographed, Callie and Mike went first, followed by Courtney and Josh, and lastly, it was my turn to be photographed with Rob.

He took my hand and led me to the center of the bridge. I slid my arm around his waist, and he draped an arm around my shoulders. My left arm hung at my side, and then I tried my hand on my hip, but finally decided to rest it on the railing of the bridge. Rob did the same, but my mother, playing the photographer's assistant, crept forward and brought our hands together. "Now, that's much better."

Rob turned toward me. "Your hand's all cold and clammy," he said in a hushed voice, but not without a big grin, since we were being reminded to "Smile!"

I faced him with a plastered grin. "Well, *your* hand is all hot and sweaty."

"What do you expect, Chloe? I'm standing outside in one hundred degree heat and wearing a tux."

"Well, you wouldn't be so hot if you weren't wearing a *black* tux." I smiled broadly, partly out of obedience to the photographers' wishes, but mostly from the sheer pleasure of broaching a debatable topic.

"So, we're back to that again?"

"Listen, I thought we agreed on brown."

"No, *we* did not agree on anything. You and my mother did." He paused, waiting for the comeback that never came and offered me his most adoring smile. "Are we having fun yet?"

"Oh, tons," I said, and then we both turned toward the cameras, which was where we thought we should be looking, but we were wrong.

"Oh, no, no, no…" Aunt Nancy scolded us. "It was much better when you two were looking into each other's eyes."

Rob faced me, arched an eyebrow like a cartoon villain,

119

which only made me laugh uncontrollably, and then as if his look hadn't been amusing enough, he added, "Look, deep into my eyes" in the voice of a creepy hypnotist.

Suddenly, the doorbell interrupted everything, which was fine because we were done with pictures anyway.

"Oh, I hope it's Brandon," Caitlyn exploded and raced into the house. Then Rob turned to me with a half grin. "I hope it's Chinese."

They both got their wish when Brandon walked in the door with several bags of Chinese food and some aptly lengthened tux pants. Apparently, he and the delivery boy met in the driveway. Brandon paid the bill, which was generous of him, but it also placed him back on the "getting some" status for the night. So it was like he paid to have sex, but isn't that how most guys view prom anyway?

After Brandon and Caitlyn had their pictures taken, we sat down in the dining room. Rob and I ate off each other's plates and joked about the Chinese restaurant scene from *The Christmas Story*, and even though we recited the same movie quote every time we had Chinese together, we still found it amusing.

The eight of us wrapped up the meal and reached for our fortune cookies in the center of the table. Rob kept his to himself, but that didn't prevent my curious eyes from drifting in his direction. It said: *Stop searching forever; happiness is right next to you.* His eyes lifted and caught mine briefly; then he shoved his fortune into the pocket of his tux pants—where it would soon be forgotten and returned with the tux the following day.

Later on, as we headed out the front door of my house, Rob asked, "And what did your fortune say?"

I smiled over at him. "Mine said, 'You are in good hands this evening.'"

He offered a broad smile and reached for my hand, filing his fingers through mine. He held my hand down the front steps of my house and during the limo ride, and he was still holding my hand when we arrived at prom.

-19-

Prom Night

The eight of us entered the ballroom, finding a table near the edge of the dance floor, and we reserved our seats with tux coats and wraps before we stepped onto the floor. Rob and I danced together for a few fast songs, smiling back and forth at each other, but not carrying on much of a conversation.

He tilted an imaginary cup toward his mouth, and I nodded. Then we exited the floor with Courtney and Josh in tow, landing at the refreshment table in the back of the ballroom. There were pretzels, mints, bottled water, and bright red punch, and the table was being manned by a couple of teachers. And Mr. Martinez was one of them. Rob paused in front of the physics intern, and they acknowledged each other with a nod. Then my teacher's eyes fell on me. "You look nice," he shouted over the music.

"Thanks," I hollered back and grabbed a bottle of water. I thumbed at Courtney. "She did my makeup."

Mr. Martinez looked at Courtney briefly, but all he said was, "Punch?"

"Uh-huh," she replied and took the outstretched cup from his hand. It was awkward, but somewhat undetectable to the untrained—or should I say unknowing?—eye.

We returned to our table for a few songs, but stepped out onto the floor when the DJ played the first slow song of the night. At that moment, I realized Rob was much better at slow dancing as he twirled me in and out of a few turns with ease. Then he drew

121

me close to him, and I rested my head on his shoulder. We lined up perfectly, and I shut my eyes as we rocked slowly in a circle.

Throughout the night, we took breaks from the dance floor and circulated the ballroom, visiting with different friends from school: our journalism cohorts, his baseball buddies, and toward the end of the night, we crossed paths with our cross country teammates. They were encircling our coach, who actually wore a 5K T-shirt and sweatpants to the dance, and as we came closer, he offered us a toothy grin. "No way! Are you two dating?"

"Yeah, Coach," Rob returned with a smile. "She finally caught me."

The coach chuckled, and then Doug, Riverside's top runner, shot two pointer fingers at my boyfriend. "Yeah, man, couples that run together, stay together." And to this, Lilly, his girlfriend, nodded and took another bite of her organic raw food bar.

"Well," I started plainly. "Rob and I never run together." Lilly dropped her jaw, exposing partially masticated food particles, and I did my best to convey Rob's exact sentiments: "Because if we did, then one of us wouldn't be getting our optimal workout."

I turned toward him and smiled cynically, and he responded with an arm draped around my shoulders. "Yeah, and speaking of running," Rob started. "We should really get back to…"

"Our table," I added.

"Since it's our turn to…"

"Sit there."

Rob and I arrived at our empty table, and he slid his chair close to me, leaning over to talk. "By the way, I made that comment in middle school."

"I know."

"And if it really means that much to you, we could run together."

"Really, Rob?" I returned enthusiastically, thinking how nice it would be to run with him on the beach or along the Riverside Trail. "Maybe we could run down to the pier tomorrow morning."

"Sure," he started with a mischievous grin. "As long as you can slice a minute off your pace."

122

I narrowed my eyes at him, but Rob laughed it off, and a moment later, Brandon plopped down across the table from us. He leaned in toward me and yelled, "Hey, Loser!" Then Caitlyn collapsed on his lap, and their tongues gravitated like magnets. His hand groped at her breast, and she pushed it away, and then he grabbed it again, and she pushed it away again...

Rob shouted near my ear, "I think our turn is officially over."

"You wanna' dance?"

"Sure," he flicked his head at the other side of the ballroom. "But let's talk to Tom and those guys first."

"Grrr."

"Listen, I went to prom with *your* friends. The least you can do is spend some time with mine."

"Yeah, but my friends don't totally suck."

His eyes drifted across our table at the "little" fallacy in my argument.

* * *

I sat down next to Tom Richardson, and Rob pulled up a chair from another table. The table was in the midst of a next-year-at-college conversation, which was completely alienating and allowing me to drift to La La Land, until Kendra put the spotlight on me. "And Chloe, have you thought about where you'll apply next year?"

In an alternate universe where you don't have to be nice to the ex-girlfriend of your current boyfriend, I might have replied, *What are you? My guidance counselor?* But, I just smiled and said, "Well, Courtney and Caitlyn want me to go to University of Central Florida with them."

"Hmm," Kendra deliberated. "You *might* get in there." She was a huge intelligence snob, ranking fifth in the class, but Rob finished second—only because he had fewer AP credits than Tom.

"Are you considering any other schools?" Jessica Jacobs asked, nestled next to her date. "Like anything out-of-state?"

Tom arched an eyebrow. "Georgetown, maybe?"

"Yeah, right. I'm not *that* studious." I thumbed at my boyfriend.

Tom was quick to point out, "But you were the only junior in AP English."

"Well, English is my best subject," I said, and then I thought it would be fun to reveal the truth—just to toy with Kendra a little. "Plus, Rob and I wanted to have another class together, so that's why I took it this year." I draped an arm around *my* boyfriend.

"Yep, and she made all A's." He placed a quick kiss on my cheek, the second one of the night.

Kendra leaned forward, mumbling "Let's see how well she does without her private tutor next year." I smiled back, not because I found her particularly amusing, but because she was at prom without a date and clearly not over mine.

Josh walked across the room, resting a hand on Rob's shoulder. "Hey, you mind if I dance with Chlo?"

"Not at all," I answered quickly.

Josh offered his arm and led me to the dance floor. I rested my wrists on his shoulders, and his hands held my waist; we danced with the agility of two middle schoolers in a dark gym. Josh flicked his head at Courtney while she was being twirled around by Landon Williams. "Did she date him?"

"No, but I did."

"Really?"

"Yup, in the seventh grade. It lasted a whole two weeks."

"But that's long enough to make the no-no list, right?"

"Yup, you know the rules, Josh."

He nodded. "According to page ninety seven of the *Seven C's Handbook*, I can only date Courtney."

I rolled my eyes, since the handbook was only three pages long. "Why? Did you have someone else in mind?" I flicked my head at Caitlyn, who was feeding pretzels to Brandon.

"Way too mothering," he replied. Then my eyes drifted to Callie and her circle of towering teammates, and he answered, "*Way* too tall!"

I was out of friends, and a weird feeling came over me. My face froze, but Josh kept smiling. "No offense, Chlo, but cousins have their own set of rules."

"Then who is it?"

He pushed out a deep breath and leaned in with his answer. "I used to have a thing for Carly Evans."

"Oh, wow, do I have something to show you!" I pulled him through the crowded dance floor toward a dark corner of the ballroom, where combat boots and fish net stockings accentuated vintage formals, and I said, "She's the one with purple hair. It was red a few weeks ago, so maybe she added a little blue."

His eyes remained on Carly for a moment. "What happened to her?"

"She changed."

"I can see that, but why?"

I shrugged and tried not to think about it too much because it only made me sad. I still missed her. We all did, but Caitlyn the most, and having her here was way worse than if she had moved away.

A giggle entered my ear. "Time to switch," Courtney decided. Then Landon spun her toward Josh, and I took Landon's outstretched hand. "Should I get you a step ladder?" he asked with a toothy grin.

"Nah, I'll just stand on my tippy toes."

"Yeah, I guess you'd have to wear *low* heels with your date."

"Hey, he's almost six feet," I tossed back

"That's average."

I stepped back. "Listen, there's nothing average about the size of my boyfriend."

Landon doubled over in hysterics, and I placed my hands on my hips. "Seriously, is *that* all guys think about?"

Two hands found their way through the openings in my arms and encircled my waist. "Want *me* to answer that, baby?"

I stepped out of his arms and whipped around. "No."

Austin stared at me with his dazed expression and slid the tip of his tongue across his lips. "Dance with me."

125

"*No!*"

"Why not?"

"Because I promised Rob the next dance." I thought it was a good reason until I followed Austin's eyes across the dance floor and saw Rob dancing with Kendra. My heart sank into my stomach as Austin patronized, "Aw, I guess he forgot all about you." He stepped in closer and tapped my butt. "But don't you worry, baby. I never will."

Aimee marched over, tossed me a nasty look, and pulled Austin onto the floor for another round of vertical foreplay. I didn't want to watch my ex-boyfriend with his current girlfriend or my current boyfriend with his ex-girlfriend, so I headed for the bathroom while the DJ announced, "And for the last song of the night."

The entire ballroom flooded the floor. I was heading upstream, finally finding refuge at the vacated refreshment table. I grabbed a bottle of water, and Rob sidled up next to me. "What did he say to you?"

I played dumb. "Who?"

He offered his serious stare, which was supposed to intimidate me into submission, but instead, I changed the subject. "Did you have fun dancing with Kendra?"

"She asked me," he replied quickly. "Plus, you were out there with Landon."

"It's not the same."

He looked down. "Yeah, I know."

"Do you?" I paused. "She still likes you, Rob. A lot." His eyes remained on the floor as I continued, "She didn't even come with a date because she's hoping you'll get back together."

He stepped in, his eyes finding mine. "But that's not going to happen because I'm with you now."

"But," I paused, not wanting to relent. "I still have every right to be mad at you."

"Yeah, maybe, but just hear me out, okay? This is the last song of the night, and regardless if I'm right or wrong, you'll probably forget all about why we were fighting in a few days anyway." I rolled my eyes because I had quite the memory for such things. "But I can promise you this: you'll never forget this fight if we spend the last few minutes of our prom arguing about it." He turned up a corner of his mouth and offered an outstretched hand. "Either way, I'm sorry, Chlo," he said earnestly, and then I accepted his hand and his apology.

We found a spot on the edge of the dance floor, and I wrapped my arms around his neck and rested my head on his shoulder. While we danced slowly in a circle, I gazed into the swaying mass. I spotted Mike and Callie. They were linked together in a movie ending kiss, and even Jessica Jacobs was frenching her last-minute date. I wondered if the last song at prom was like "Auld Lang Syne" at a New Year's Eve party, and if so, why was I the only girl not getting kissed?

Wait, I felt something. Rob kissed the top of my head lightly and mumbled, "I had a great time tonight. Thank you for asking me to prom."

I patted his chest. "Yeah, you bet." I refrained from saying "buddy" or "pal" or some other nomenclature that signified we were less than boyfriend and girlfriend. But it was four hours into prom, and the last song was playing its final refrain, and all I had to show for the night were two kisses on the cheek and a slight peck on the top of my head. And as the last song faded into closing announcements, I heaved a heavy sigh.

Prom was officially over.

-20-

After Party

We took the limo back to my house, where everyone changed into shorts and T-shirts, and then headed to the beach. Rob drove his Jeep, and Caitlyn was deemed designated driver for Brandon's Forerunner.

Josh and Courtney rode with us, and it was guys up front and girls in the back. I wasn't very good company for Courtney, since I was still sulking over Rob's inability to get out of the batter's box on prom night. Sure, I had recovered from his dance with Kendra, since it's not his fault that she's not over him. He was just being nice; therefore, I had another reason for fuming in the back seat. I was extremely upset that he never kissed me—I mean, *really* kissed me.

Yes, I was suffering from a bad case of PDA envy, and it didn't help any that I was stuck in a Jeep with Sir Flirtsalot and Lady-is-Willing. The one-hour ride intensified my feelings, since along the highway, Josh kept turning around and smiling at Courtney. My date, however, kept his eyes on the road, and I kept my eyes on the side of the road, reading every billboard like great literature. When we exited the interstate, Rob still kept his eyes on the road, but I ran out of interesting reading material and was forced to watch the amorous interactions of my car mates. At one stop light, Courtney undid her seatbelt and lurched into the front seat and made out with Josh until I offered a helpful comment, "Oh, look, the light turned green."

This, of course, didn't dissuade them from trying similar feats with the many red lights along A1A, which is the main strip along the beach with all those tourist shops and hotels. I looked at Courtney as she buckled her seat belt again. "Should I switch places with Josh?"

"Nah, we're almost there."

Where? I wondered because I was still at 0st base, thinking someone should create an ordinal number for zero, by the way.

A few minutes later, the Jeep pulled into the driveway *after* the Forerunner. It must have been all those red lights, we could say if anyone asked, but nobody did. They had beer and over-night bags in their hands and whooped when Courtney hollered, "And let the party begin!"

I grabbed my bag from the back and headed into the house. Callie and I claimed the back bedroom with the two twin beds. Courtney took the master, and Caitlyn rolled her suitcase into the middle bedroom. Sleeping arrangements were predetermined, and the only boys relegated to the family room were the ones who dated the virgins.

With my overnight bag still slung over my shoulder, I went immediately to the bathroom and started brushing my teeth. Rob showed up in the doorway. "Listen, I know you're mad at me."

With the toothbrush dangling from my mouth, I mumbled, "I'm not mad."

"Then why are you getting ready for bed?"

"I'm tired."

"Then why did we even bother to come?"

"Good question." I closed the door on him, mostly because he was annoying me, but partly because I had a strand of floss caught between my butt cheeks. Luckily, I had packed a spare pair of granny panties in my overnight bag.

He knocked. "Open up, Chloe."

"I can't."

"Why?"

"I'm naked. That's why!"

"I'm sorry. I, uh, didn't realize…"

I finished getting dressed, putting on a Riverside Cross Country T-shirt and a pair of plaid boxers, and flung open the door. "I think we need to talk."

He nodded, and together, we entered the family room. Everyone else was consuming Frito Lay favorites and adult beverages. I wore a look that said, "I'm pissed at my boyfriend," who, by the way, looked completely unfazed as he walked by his cousin's bare feet and shoved them off the arm of the couch. "Get your stinkin' feet off my bed."

Rob's comment started something, and Mike shouted from the kitchen, "Hey Braitlyn! (Yes, my two friends were deserving of a Hollywood compound name.) Stop making out on *my* bed!"

Everyone thought this was hilarious, but I didn't. I officially lost my sense of humor around midnight, and I kept moving toward the sliding glass door. I slid it open, stepped onto the patio, and assumed Rob was trailing behind me like a puppy. He was, and his comment affirmed it. "Sometimes…" He started to growl. "You can be such a—"

"Thanks!" I cut him off and fast-walked down the private boardwalk to the beach. I plodded across the sand and stopped at the water's edge, letting the waves roll over my feet. My arms were folded across my chest, and I stood there, silently brooding.

He spoke first. "You wanted to talk. So talk."

"I'm mad at you, Rob." He said nothing "And do you want to know why?" This was clearly rhetorical; he didn't have to respond. "It's because the whole night, you didn't even…and sometimes I don't think you ever will…and if that's the case, then maybe we should just…" I turned to face him. "You know what I'm saying, right?"

"Nope, not at all." He pushed out an exhale. "Why don't you just come out and say it? Like in five words or less?"

I counted the words on my fingers. "You. Didn't. Kiss. Me."

It was only four, so he added a fifth. "Yet." He stepped in front of me, cupping my shoulders with his warm hands. "Chloe, I haven't kissed you tonight because I was waiting for that per-

130

fect moment. You see, this girl I know made me read all these romance novels, and I actually learned something from them: real kisses don't take place on crowded dance floors or between the front and back seat of your friend's Jeep. They happen at the right place...at the right time..."

"Like on a quiet, moonlit beach?" I looked around us, stars glittering in the clear blackness and waves rolling up on the shore; then I glanced at his face. "But this isn't the right moment, is it?"

He swiped a finger down the length of my nose and rested it on my lips. "I think you already know the answer to that."

-21-

Sweet Dreams

The house was quiet and still as I slipped from the front bedroom and into the family room. I knelt down next to the couch and brushed Rob's cheek with the back of my hand, and as I touched him, his breathing quickened and a slight smile surfaced. I wet my lips with my tongue and pressed my mouth against his cheek. His skin glistened momentarily where my lips had been, and then his eyes opened slowly. "What are you doing, Chlo?"

"Trying to influence your dreams."

He flipped onto his back and rested his hands behind his head, and I sat in the small space on the edge of the couch. He brought his arm around my side to keep me from falling off.

"Guess what? Mike snuck into our room last night," I informed.

Rob glanced at the empty couch and expected the direction of the conversation. "Yeah, but we told our parents we'd sleep in separate rooms."

I eyed the room where I had slept for a few hours and then back at him. "Well, we did that, so we wouldn't be lying if we..." I pulled my lower lip across my top teeth and settled into a convincing look.

"Please don't do that." He spoke in a very serious tone, which only encouraged me more, so I cued the pitiful eyes and pushed out my pouty lips.

"That's probably how Eve looked before Adam took a bite of the apple."

"Well, did it work...this time?"

He shook his head, pulled up the blanket, and closed his eyes.

"Rob, I can't sleep in *there*." I left out the details of what was happening in there, primarily because I didn't have proof, just auditory speculations and an astute understanding of Callie's prom-night mentality.

"Well, you're not sleeping with me." His eyes remained closed as he turned on his side and faced the couch.

"Why not? We did it before, and who knows what would have happened if my dad hadn't called."

At that, he flipped over and opened his eyes, wide. "Do you know how that sounds?"

I mock-glanced around the room. "Oh, no! What will the walls think?"

He mumbled some non-intelligible remark under his breath and sat up on the couch. "What do you want to do, Chloe?"

I shrugged and looked out the sliding glass door at the waves creeping up the shore. "How about a walk on the beach?"

"What time is it?"

"Late or early, depending on how you look at it."

He shook his head and dragged his blanket behind him like Linus from the Peanuts gang, and once outside, he gathered the green blanket into a ball and toted it under his arm as we walked to the beach. We reached the water's edge, letting the cool water crawl across our feet and then slowly retreat back into the ocean again.

"It's a nice night," I said.

"For sleeping," he added with a yawn.

I gave him a little nudge. "Oh, c'mon, Rob."

"Yes, it's a nice night, and you look lovely under the moonlight," he romanced flatly, and then he headed toward the dunes and spread the blanket on the sand. I followed him dejectedly as he continued, "Listen, I'm going back to sleep, and if you're not tired, maybe you should just count the stars." He lowered himself to the blanket. "Goodnight, Chloe. And wake me when you reach infinity."

"Funny," I said and took the spot next to him. I propped up on an elbow and let my fingers glide the length of his arm. "There's something I've been meaning to ask you, Rob." I made a swirl in his arm hair. "It's a real personal question, and there's no easy way to ask it, so I'm just gonna' come out with it. Are you a virgin?"

"Huh?" He turned with a scrunched-up face.

"Listen, you know I am, so I was just wondering if you were. And it only seems fair that we know each other's…"

"Standings," he added. "For a lack of a better word."

I nodded.

"Does it really matter?"

I fell on my back and looked up at the stars, figuring it must have been with Kendra. She was the girl he dated the longest, and I know he really liked her because he avoided answering my annoying "Do you love her?" question whenever I broached it.

"No," I said softly.

"Good," he paused. "Because I am."

I turned my head toward him. "You are?"

He nodded sheepishly.

"Do you believe in waiting until marriage?"

"Yeah." He rolled onto his back and folded his hands behind his head. "I sure as hell don't want to repeat my parents' mistake." He looked away, and I moved in closer to him, resting my head on his shoulder and draping my arm across his chest. Rob's mother was still in college when she got pregnant with him, but I guess his biological father treated the pregnancy as a mistake rather than a miracle. And to this day, his real dad has never acknowledged his existence.

"Rob," I started softly. "You're not a mistake because God doesn't make mistakes."

"Now, you sound like my mother." He pulled me into a hug, drawing me closer to him than I had ever been before, and with my head against his chest, I listened to the rhythmic beats of his heart and breathed in his familiar scent.

"Thanks, because your mom is the best mom I know." It wasn't some secret, but when I was little, I wanted her to be my mom. Their house always smelled like fresh-baked bread, and his mother was like an antidote for boredom, always coming up with fun ways to spend the day. My mother—and this won't come as any surprise—only had one idea in mind: go read a book.

"Yeah, I know," he said, swallowing audibly. "But I hope I was a good enough son. I mean, she gave up everything to have me, and I hope I didn't disappoint her."

"You didn't disappoint her," I said softly and held him close while his heart was open. "Rob, you're probably the best son in the whole world."

"Thanks, Chloe." He kissed the top of my head lightly. "And you're probably the best friend in the whole world." I pulled up from him at the sound of *that* word, but he was way stronger than me. "Hey, listen, friends last a lifetime; but girlfriends come and go. And I *always* want you in my life." He gave me a squeeze. "Because I'll always need you, Chloe." Need is not synonymous with love, but it felt really good to hear him talk in terms of "always."

"You too," I mumbled and placed a kiss on his chest. His hand smoothed back my hair, and he kissed my forehead. "Goodnight, Chloe. And sweet dreams."

His familiar line sent me to a beautiful night of slumber, and when I awoke in his arms hours later, I was still somewhere between a dream and reality, wishing the two were one. I kept my eyes closed, replaying the fragments of a dream in my head.

His lips fell to my ear. "The sun's coming up." He pulled me up with him, and still half asleep, I opened my eyes slowly and watched the cloudless canvas change from a soft grey to a powdery blue as the fiery orb rose from the depths of the ocean. My eyes stayed on the horizon. "It's…it's beautiful."

"I know," he said softly and brought my face toward his. I stared back at him in complete awe. His eyes simmered in

135

the sunlight as the rays turned his eyes into a rich auburn hue, the same color as his gorgeous hair. And without thinking, my fingers filed through the strands of his hair. My heart filled with warmth as we stared into each other's eyes, and very slowly, he leaned forward, pressing his mouth against mine, and very gently, his tongue parted my lips. He drew me closer to him, and we kissed passionately as our bodies fell to the sand.

* * *

"We have to stop," he tried again, but I didn't let go of him, and he didn't keep his mouth or his hands from driving me unbelievably crazy. "Listen, one of us has to exhibit a little self-control here."

I lifted my lips from his and called out, "Not it!"

"Oh, that's real mature."

"Well, you're older, so you be the mature one."

"You're the girl."

"So?"

"Girls like to say no."

"And do you know this from personal experience?"

"Oh, very funny." He flipped onto his back, resting his hands behind his head and smiling over at me. I slid over and nestled against him, whispering in his ear. "You know how you're always telling me to have sweet dreams?"

"Yeah?"

"Well, my subconscious listened to you last night."

"Really?" He flashed a big grin. "What kind of dream did you have?"

I walked my fingers up his chest. "I'm not telling."

"Aw, don't play with me," he said, pulling me in for another kiss, but before his lips found mine, a familiar voice stopped us. "Sheesh, could you two stop for one friggin' minute?" I glanced up to find Courtney hovering over us in all her mood-wrecking glory.

"Hi," I said with a frown.

Her eyes revealed drama. "I need to talk to you. Alone."

Rob pushed up from the blanket and eyed me with a smile. "We'll finish our conversation later."

"Yeah...later."

Rob headed toward the house, and Courtney took his spot on the blanket. "So I did it."

"What?" I asked, since my eyes and thoughts were still on my boyfriend.

"The right thing. So, tell me, Chlo, why do I feel like total crap?" I looked over at her, trying to listen intently. "Last night Josh told me that he loved me. It was so sweet and so sincere, and I don't think any guy has ever said it like that before. But I don't love him that way, and this morning I had to tell him." She brought her legs up to her chest and hugged them. "I really wish I did though."

"But your heart is somewhere else, right?"

"Yeah, where it'll get hurt."

"He won't hurt you, Courtney," I told her like a good friend should.

"Yeah, not intentionally." Her thoughts drifted out into the ocean, and then she turned toward me. "So, what happened out here last night?"

"I shouldn't kiss and tell."

"Yeah, right!"

Softly, I said, "But I think I went to heaven."

She grabbed my shoulders. "Are you in love with him, Chlo?"

I nodded slowly and bit down on my lower lip.

"And he feels the same way about you?"

I shrugged. "I hope so."

She looked out at the ocean again. "Yeah, me too...because if this doesn't end well..."

"Just say it, Courtney."

"I don't want to take sides when it's over. That's all."

"Oh, don't worry. We promised to be friends no matter what."

137

"Yeah." She swatted at the idea. "That *never* works out, and you know it, Chlo." She flicked her head up at the beach house. "Just like Josh and I will never be close again. Sure, we'll pretend to be, but things will be weird for a long time."

*   *   *

Rob and Josh were both packed and ready to go by the time I entered the beach house. I let Josh ride up in the front with the sports radio, and I sat in the back, all alone with my book. I opened up *East of Eden* and wondered if I could finish it by the time we arrived at church.

After a few minutes, Rob turned down the volume on the radio. "Tough break, man."

Josh shrugged it off. "Yeah, well, it was fun while it lasted."

Yep, that was their entire conversation on the subject, very deep and over in a few seconds. Girls, on the other hand, would require an entire car ride and a succession of lengthy phone calls to complete their post break-up debriefing.

In my mind, I reversed their roles, having Josh say the first line and Rob the second. Then my face heated with anger, but I closed my eyes, remembered my dream from the previous night, and cooled off a little.

"I think she's asleep." Josh spoke softly, which obviously I wasn't since I'm retelling this part with great accuracy.

"Then we should talk smack about her," my boyfriend decided, and I knew he said that part just to see if I'd blurt out something. So I concentrated on deep, slow breathing and passed his test.

There was another lull in the conversation before Josh asked, "Where'd you two go this morning?"

"To watch the sunrise."

"Yeah, how was that?"

"Amazing," Rob answered.

Josh heard it in his voice and so did I. I smiled on the inside, and Josh responded, "That's good, man. I'm really happy for both of you." And even though Josh was hurting, I knew he really meant it. Then Rob turned up the volume on the sports radio, and I let my thoughts drift to my dream again…

*   *   *

"It's later," he said as he held my hand through the woods. He and I made it through the church service, but seeing our glazed-over faces, our parents excused us from Sunday school.

"I meant *much* later," I returned.

"How much later?"

"Probably *never*. Why?"

He squeezed my hand. "Well, you talk in your sleep, so I can probably guess what was in your dream anyway"

"What did I say, Rob?"

"Oh, don't worry. I won't tell anyone."

"Tell anyone what?" I asked with widening eyes.

"What you said."

"But I don't know what I said."

"And I won't tell you unless you tell me about your dream."

I looked away from him. "It's rather embarrassing, Rob."

"Well, it's your choice. I can't force you to tell the truth."

"Fine. I dreamt about you and me."

"Yeah, that's what I thought, but don't be embarrassed. I've had that same dream." His smile grew as he continued, "Especially when I'm *not* sleeping."

I gave his shoulder a shove. "Don't be such a horn dog."

"What? You don't want me to think about you that way?"

"Yes!" I considered it for a moment. "I mean no, but regardless, I did *not* have that kind of dream, Rob. It was different… much different." I pulled an oak leaf from a tree and twisted it between my thumb and forefinger. "And it all seemed so real too."

"Tell me about it," he said softly, coaxing the words from me.

139

"Fine." I tossed the leaf to the side. "I dreamt that I was on the beach…getting married."

"To me?"

"Yes," I said with exasperation.

"You know," he stepped closer, putting his hands on my face and touching his forehead to mine. "Some dreams come true."

"In fairy tales," I muttered.

"Well, you do have that damsel in distress act down."

"And I suppose you think you're a regular Prince Charming?"

"Do you have to be that way?"

"What way?"

"So argumentative."

"We like to argue. It's what we do together."

"Yeah, well, I can think of something else we could do now."

"Okay." I was game. "Why don't you tell me?"

"Why don't I *show* you!" He put his hands on my face and pushed me toward the wall of my house, pressing my backside against the rough cedar, and before his lips touched mine, he said, "But first, I want to hear you say it."

"Say what?"

"Say you love me."

I looked into his chocolate eyes and relented quickly, "I love you."

"I love you too."

He kissed me softly, and I spoke against his lips. "Rob?"

"Yeah?"

"Maybe I always have."

He kissed a path toward my ear. "And maybe I always will." He gathered me into a hug, rubbing circles in my back.

I yawned. "I'm *so* tired."

"Yeah, you should get some sleep."

I stepped out of the hug. "And speaking of sleep, tell me what I said in mine last night."

His mouth formed a thin line like he suppressing laughter.

"I think you were conjugating verbs in your sleep. Maybe in Latin, but I can't be completely sure because I took four years of Spanish."

I gave him a little shove. "You tricked me."

"Listen, we can't always climb the tree every time I need to get the truth out of you, so I'll have to get creative."

"Why don't you save your creativity for other things?"

"Like?"

"This." I grabbed a hold of his shoulders and pulled him in for another kiss.

-22-

Sex Talk

When Rob and I weren't in school or studying for finals, we were kissing and kissing some more until we had to pry ourselves from each other; and now, in a remote corner of the public library, Rob and I were working on our technique.

But before the kissing started, I was cramming facts about post-Civil War America into my head—that was until Rob placed a book on top of my history text. "In case you still have any questions," he said and walked away. I glanced at the book, the cover showing a young boy and a girl holding hands in a pastoral setting, and it was entitled *A Child's First Guide to Sex*.

Even after weeks of dating, some things about our relationship hadn't changed; he loved to tease me, and my naivety about the birds and the bees perpetuated many jokes. So I got up, placed the book on the re-shelving cart, and looked for him up and down the aisles like a mother searching for a lost child at the grocery store. I paced down the center aisle, looking all the way to the left, and then all the way to the right, repeating the process until I neared the reference section. There, I spotted him, perusing through a volume of the *Encyclopedia of Science and Technology*.

"Hmm," he said, flipping a page. "You ever notice how some reference books only show one diagram of the male anatomy? It's like teaching the phases of water and leaving out the solid state." He looked at me for a response.

142

I gave him one: my hands went straight to my hips.

"What's wrong, sweetie pie?"

"Listen here, Rob, this is not the right place to talk about—" I was so uncomfortable with discussing it at that library that I couldn't even say the word.

"Why not? They have books on it."

"Yeah, well, in *my* opinion." I pointed to myself. "The library is a lot like church, and there are certain rules: you have to wear shoes, you talk quietly, you refrain from public displays of affection, *and* you don't broach certain topics."

He mock-glanced around the library. "Are these rules posted somewhere?"

"No, it's just common sense."

"Yeah, well, so is turning off the engine before you lock the car door."

I growled at him, but he just stepped closer to me and whispered in my ear, "You see, Chloe, we all have lapses in judgment." He pulled me into a corner and kissed me, soft and gentle at first, but with increasing fervor since I didn't dissuade him to stop.

* * *

Later on, Rob and I returned to our table and abided by most of the aforementioned library rules. Well, except for shoe thing because I had to flick off my wedges to rub his calf with my big toe, but other than that, we were being civil patrons of the public library system.

"Psst." Rob got my attention. "How much longer?"

"I dunno. Why?"

"I don't want to be a bad influence on you, but I don't feel like studying anymore."

I shut my history text. "And what do you feel like doing?"

"I don't know. Maybe we could hang out at my house." I considered it for a moment, weighing the parental rules. His parents didn't have any rule against closing the door like mine did, *but* his bedroom shared a wall with the family room, meaning his parents were often in the next room.

He read my mind. "Just so you know, my dad's spending the night at the hospital, and Mom and Ry went to a play tonight."

"Well, in that case…"

*   *   *

When we got to his house, I made a couple of peanut butter and jelly sandwiches, poured two glasses of milk, and we scarfed down the food at the breakfast bar. He slid his plate toward me and kissed my cheek. "Thanks for dinner."

"Unh-uh." I placed my plate on top of his and slid the stack toward him. "I cooked. You clean."

I found a spot on the family room couch and watched my boyfriend do the dishes, and after a few minutes, he joined me, draping an arm around my shoulders. I fell against him, relaxing in the moment. The whole evening, having the house to ourselves, and now, sitting quietly in each other's arms was like pressing the fast-forward button on life. I could imagine a future with him: he would come home from work, and I would have dinner ready for him. By then I would have expanded my culinary expertise, and after a meal, we would cuddle on the couch and discuss the day. But my musings were interrupted by his less-than-subtle reach for the remote control. "I just need to check a couple of scores."

"And then we can turn it off?"

"Why? What did you have in mind?"

"How about a game of Scattegories?" I suggested that particular game since it was on the top shelf of his bedroom closet.

*   *   *

We sat down in the middle of his bed, and I distributed the game pieces. "Why don't we just play our favorite category?"

"Terms of Endearment," he said with a smile.

"Uh-huh, you flip the timer, and I'll roll the alphabet dice," I decided. "Ooh, it's an L." We scribbled a list of terms that *someone* may find endearing while sixty seconds slipped through the timer.

"Time," he yelled, and our pens hit the bed. We leaned forward, ready to fire our answers back and forth.

Rob started, "Lipstick Lesbian."

"Ooh, just rumors, Limp Libido."

"Sure, they are Little Lush."

"And a string of doubles from the Long-winded Lexiconophiliac."

"Whatever, Liar." He smiled.

"Well, isn't that the truth, you Listless Lover?"

"Ow, Latin Loser."

"But at least I'm not a big Loner." I peered across at his empty list. "*And* I still have Lamo and Landshark, so who's the Loser now?"

"Austin," he said with a wink.

"Oh, very funny, my little Love Muffin. Now, come here and get your sympathy kisses." He crept forward, sweeping the game pieces onto the floor, and tackled me. *I love game night!* I decided as I ran my nimble fingers through his auburn hair, against his warm neck, across his shoulders, and down the length of his back. And while I pressed my lips against his mouth, I tugged up on his shirt. He pulled it off the rest of the way and tossed it onto the floor.

He rolled over onto his back, and I nestled against him, tracing his happy trail with my fingers and sticking my pinky in his belly button. Then I ran my fingers along the waistline of his shorts and tried to slide my hand under his boxers, but he grabbed my hand before my fingers crossed the equator.

"Sorry," I muttered as he rolled off the bed and walked toward the window. He stood there with his hands on his hips, and I joined him, threading my arms through his. "What's wrong?" I asked softly.

"Nothing."

"Just tell me."

"I'm, uh, frustrated. That's all."

"Oh?"

"Because you can't do that."

"Why?"

"Because I won't want you to stop." He stepped out of my arms and turned around. "You drive me crazy, Chloe, and I've never wanted anyone as much as I want you. But at the same time, it's you, and I know you want to wait until marriage."

"Maybe I've changed my mind." I looked up at him. "And maybe I want you to have it."

"It?" he teased.

"Yeah," I returned. "But I don't mean right now…just sometime before you leave for school. I don't want to regret my first time, and that's why I wanted to wait until I got married. But if it were with you, then I would never regret it. I love you, and you love me. So shouldn't our first time be with each other?"

He nodded slowly.

"And waiting until marriage seems so easy until you actually fall in love with someone. And I love you so much, Rob, and I will never feel this way with anyone else." I stepped closer to him. "No one could ever replace you in my life. You were my first friend, my first boyfriend, and…" I swallowed down the knot. "I want you to be my first lover."

"But waiting until marriage also means you intend to make love to only one person."

"I know, and I want you to be that person."

He rested his hands on my shoulders and studied me. "And you're absolutely sure about this?"

"Definitely," I said, since he was standing there without a shirt on, and if *People* magazine spotted him, they'd put him on the front cover of their "Sexiest People" issue. My fingers went into his chest hair, soft and wiry, and I remembered the summer I first noticed the hair on his chest. That's when I started calling him a Gorilla, and he, in return, nicknamed me Bird Legs.

"But we're still so young, Chloe."

"I've known you most of my life, so as far as relationships go, ours is very old."

"But—" I placed a finger on his lips.

"Rob, we both know all the reasons why we should wait. Religious, emotional, developmental, whatever, but maybe we should focus on the other reasons too. The ones that make it okay for us."

He pulled me into chest, and I breathed in his intoxicating scent. He rubbed his chin against the top of my head. Then he pushed out an exhale. "I've made up my mind."

"And?"

"I'll let you know on your birthday."

-23-

His Answer

Several weeks had passed, and with finals behind us, we were now enjoying the carefree days of summer. It was the end of June, and Rob and I had just returned home from church. I sat on the edge of his bed and watched as he hung his tie back in the closet. Then he faced me as he unfastened the top buttons of his dress shirt, and I wished his parents weren't home. Seeing him undress down to his boxers would have been a very nice present, especially if he were wearing those stretchy, grey ones that I spotted in the top drawer of his dresser. But the fact was he never took off his jeans or shorts when we were alone, and my imagination only took me so far.

As he unbuttoned his shirt, I asked, "You want some music?"

He responded by biting down on his lower lip and rolling his shoulders slowly one at a time as he finished with the last few buttons. Then he lifted his hands over his head and rolled his hips a little. He smiled and slid off his shirt, twirling it above his head a few times before he released it in my direction. I picked it up and took a whiff like a groupie at a rock concert, and then he stepped forward and kissed the top of my head. "Okay, show's over."

"Seriously?"

He nodded.

"But it's my birthday," I whined.

He frowned at me, crossed the room, and opened the door. I left his bedroom, feeling needlessly dejected, and entered the kitchen. His parents were still dressed in their Sunday best and pulling trays of food from the fridge.

"Want some help?"

"Nonsense, it's your big day. You shouldn't lift a finger."

"Mind sharing that philosophy with my mother?"

Rob's mother leaned on the counter. "Why? What did she make you do today?"

"You know, the usual long list of chores in case the camera crew from *Better Homes and Gardens* shows up unannounced."

"You have it rough, kiddo."

"So I won't be getting any sympathy from you, will I?"

She shook her head and pulled out a bottle of cleaner. Apparently, *BH&G* had scheduled the Callahans instead.

Then Rob rested a hand on my shoulder. "Chloe and I will be back soon."

"What? Where are we going?" Surely, I looked dumbfounded. "Shouldn't I be here for the party?" After all, it was my seventeenth birthday, and silly me, I thought I was the guest of honor.

He smiled down at me and then over at his parents, and I realized I was the only person not in on the secret. Then he offered his hand and led me out of the sliding glass door.

"I'm not a fan of surprises, Rob."

"I know, but I am."

"That's just like you." I smirked over at him. "You're always thinking of yourself." He squeezed my hand a few times, and we walked through the woods that separated the houses in our neighborhood. Our feet crunched on sticks and leaves as we headed toward the river. Once there, he took a seat on the end of a fallen log and patted the other side. I sat down, remembering the first time we found the log. It appeared years ago after a big lightning storm, and whenever we journeyed down there as little kids, mainly to fish or toss rocks into the water, it had been our place to sit.

"That night before finals when we were, uh…talking in my

149

room," he started slowly, his hands wringing nervously like before a game. "I decided to give you something today. It's my answer, Chloe, and I hope you like it."

Then he reached into the pocket of his shorts and pulled out a black velvet box, and like any girl about to receive jewelry, I extended an eager palm. But as soon as he dropped the box in my hand, all the parts of the equation added together, and I realized what the box contained. The box, still unopened, grew heavier and heavier in my hand. Of course, I wanted to marry him, spend my entire life with him, but those were someday dreams. I was just seventeen, a whole year from high school graduation, and I still didn't know where I was going to college.

I took a deep breath as I opened the box, finding an intricately designed golden ring. Two tiny hands held a heart, and on top of the heart was a crown. I couldn't remember the name of the ring, but I had seen it before in family photos and on the hands of his relatives.

"I like it," I said.

"Do you know what it is?"

"A ring?" I asked, not intending to play the sarcastic card.

"Yeah, but it's called a Claddagh ring." He slid it onto my right ring finger, facing the crown outward. "And when it's worn like this, it means a girl is available."

"Should I wear it this way?"

"No," he chided playfully and turned the ring so that the crown faced inward. "Now, it means," he started slowly, finding my eyes, "that you have given your heart to me."

"Oh," I breathed out, and he continued on, holding my hand lightly in his. "And not only that, each picture is a symbol. The hands represent friendship whereas the heart stands for love, and Chloe, we have been blessed to have known both in our lives." He looked directly into my eyes as he continued, "You were my first friend as well as the first girl I ever loved."

He leaned in, his nose brushing mine a few times, and then he settled in for a soft kiss, warm and buttery. He pulled back slowly and smiled.

150

"And what about the crown?" I wondered.

"It stands for loyalty."

"Like a promise for next year?"

He nodded. "Or longer."

I took a deep breath, since our impending separation caused sadness to spread in my heart. I didn't want to think about it and changed the subject. "What does it mean if I wear the ring on my left hand?"

"Uh, we're not ready for that."

I didn't heed his warning and slid it onto my left hand anyway. I looked at him, awaiting his response. "Now, we're engaged." I thought about my earlier musings, and then turned it around so that the crown faced inward, thinking I knew the significance of the ring's last position. "And now?" I bit down on my lip.

"And now," he repeated, shaking his head. "We're married."

"Well, if we're married, then it's okay to—"

"Chloe," he started, laying a gentle finger on my lips. "I love you." It was one of those really sweet ones that comes out all breathy and shaky, and I felt the words enter my heart and knew they would remain with me forever. "And because I love you so much, I want us to wait. It won't be easy, but it's the right thing to do."

"I know," I conceded softly, falling into his open arms. He wrapped me up tightly, and I spoke into the crook of his neck, "I love you too."

He kissed the top of my head. "I wish we could stay out here longer, but we have to get back to your party."

* * *

Back inside the house, Rob leaned on the arm of the couch, and I plopped down next to Grandpa. He examined the ring on my hand. "It looks nice on you, Chloe."

"Thanks, Grandpa."

Josh sat on the other side of his grandfather and glanced over at me. "Yep, that's the ring that means so many things."

My father scooted to the edge of the other couch and gave Rob an eye-narrowing look. "And just so we're clear on this, I don't want to see it on her other hand any time soon."

"I guess a summer wedding is out of the question then?"

I frowned at my boyfriend, but my father decided to play along. "Well, do we have to invite the entire Callahan clan?"

"Yeah, think of the bar tab alone," Brad said, gesturing toward the collection of Guinness bottles on the coffee table. "Maybe you should write another book, Dad."

"Yeah, how about *Preston's Principles for the Father of the Bride*?" Grandpa added, eliciting hearty laughter from the room.

I slumped back against the couch and folded my arms, wishing we were showing off my ring to the women in the house. I glanced up at the moms; they were getting lunch ready in the kitchen. "I think they need my help in there," I said.

Jake gave Rob a slap on the back. "Now, that's a good woman, Cous. She already knows her place in the house."

I got off the couch and turned my head slightly. "And do you really wonder why you don't have a girlfriend, Jake." My comment elicited a couple of low ooh's from the room as I traipsed into the kitchen.

* * *

After lunch, we had cake, and I started opening the rest of my birthday presents: a laptop from my parents, a magnetic hide-a-key from my brother, and some gift cards from Rob's family. Then I spied the center of the table, figuring the last two presents were both books. Grandpa picked up the one wrapped in the Sunday comics and handed it to me. "This will remind you of what brought you and Robert together."

Slowly, I slid my fingers under the tape and opened the package, pulling out a leather edition of *Much Ado about Nothing*. I smiled, knowing that was one theory. My brother had the other.

"Now, *my* gift reminds them of the real reason why they got together. Chloe broke up with Austin the same day she locked her keys in the car. Coincidence? I think not."

Rob faced my brother. "Well, if that's the real reason, then it's a good thing you didn't give it to her sooner." Rob picked up the hide-a-key thing and slid it across the table to my brother.

"Oh, you men have it all wrong!" Mrs. Callahan decided, and then she muttered an aside toward my mother, "Which is usually the case when it comes to love, isn't it?" She raised her voice again, "Chloe and Rob are dating because we—" She gestured between my mother and herself, causing her emerald-cut diamond to glisten under the bright kitchen lights. "—have spent the last fifteen years praying it would happen."

I turned toward Rob. "So, do you have a theory?"

He leaned back in his chair and rested his hands behind his head. "Sure, the reason why Chloe and I started dating is because it was the only way to settle a bet." He glanced at me and winked. "And *I* won."

"Only because I let you win."

"You did not."

"Did too."

Aunt Nancy piped up. "Listen, if you two keep at it, then there'll be no question about why you stopped dating."

"Oh, no," Riley squashed that silly notion. "Their fights are pure foreplay."

My father coughed. "And this one is from your grandmother." He pushed her gift toward me, and I opened it hastily, glad for the diversion. Every year Grandma Preston sent me a book. I received *Rebecca* by Daphne du Maurier for my twelfth birthday, and in the years that followed, she gave me novels by Bronte, Austen, and Hardy. When I was a young girl, she read me sonnets by Shakespeare and Rossetti while other grandmothers recited fairy tales, and as I unwrapped her gift, I wondered which classic it would be. I slid out the book; it had a blue suede cover with my initials embossed in silver lettering. I opened the front cover and read a message from her:

A place for your own story.
-Grandma

Later on, when Rob and I sat alone at the table, I stared at the words on the inside cover of the journal. "So Rob, if I wrote our story, where would I begin? With the night of the bet?"

He shook his head. "Nah, you'd start with the whole key incident."

"Why? Then that proves my brother is right."

"Nope, it just proves that I'm a great guy, and Austin's a colossal jerk." He draped his arm around my shoulder and whispered in my ear, "But if you're really going to write about us, then you should omit the parts where our clothes come off."

"Why? That's the best part."

"Yes, it is, but I don't want your dad to find your journal and have a reason to kill me."

"Aw, Rob, my dad loves you. Remember?"

"I feel like we've had this conversation before."

I folded my arms and leaned back. "I guess we've just run out of things to say to each other."

"Maybe, but we still haven't run out of things to *do* with each other." He rose from the chair. "You ready to go out?" He smiled. "By ourselves."

"Yeah, but I need to check something first." I left the kitchen and headed toward the stairway. There was something I had to see, something that had been in the back of my mind ever since he had given me the ring. I examined the wedding photo of his parents and saw a Claddagh ring on his mother's hand, and as I took each step up the stairs, I could trace the lineage back to his great grandparents, each one wearing the same style of ring.

"There you are," he said.

I joined him at the bottom of the stairs. "Hey, can I ask you something?"

"Sure." His hands encircled my waist.

"Why doesn't your mom wear that ring anymore?" I pointed at her wedding photo on the wall. "Like on her other hand or something?"

"She can't."

"Why? Did she lose it?"

He shook his head. "No."

"It doesn't fit her anymore?"

"Nope, that's not the reason either."

"Then why, Rob?"

He smiled. "Are you out of guesses?"

"I think so."

He held my hand lightly and turned my ring with his thumb. "I'll give you a hint." His eyes dropped to my ring, and then climbed the wall of photos, and returned to my hand again.

I gasped, loudly, but he smiled as he brought me in for a hug.

-24-

Last Kiss

Later that night, Rob and I walked along the river eating ice cream under a darkening summer sky, and he told me the story of the Claddagh ring. Many years ago, his great grandfather, who resided in Northern Ireland, bought the ring for his bride-to-be on her sixteenth birthday. She wore the ring for eleven years before dying in childbirth with their sixth son. When her eldest son came to the States for school, he met his wife in Boston, fell in love with her and the city, and on her twentieth birthday, he proposed with his mother's ring.

As the story goes, Grandma Callahan wore the ring for over thirty years, but one Christmas Eve, she slipped it off and handed it to her oldest son, and on the next morning, and in the presence of his family, David Callahan proposed to Tracy Wesley. It was her twenty-first birthday, and a few months prior, she had given birth to a child out of wedlock.

David was a young doctor, fresh out of medical school, and with only a few deliveries behind him, he felt an unusual surge of emotion during her son's delivery. At first, he chalked it up to the novelty of his profession, but in the weeks that followed, he grew more and more eager for Tracy's follow-up appointment. He knew she was his patient, and he understood that certain lines shouldn't be crossed; but still, he kept her needlessly long with questions. At the end of her check-up, he asked, "Do you have any questions for me?"

"Yes, just one." She looked up at him with a smile. "Do doctors still make house calls?" He nodded and had dinner at her house the same night, and even though they only dated for a few weeks before he proposed, he suspected that he had fallen in love with her well before then.

She wore the Claddagh ring until her tenth anniversary when she received an impressive emerald-cut diamond to mark the milestone event, and following tradition, she gave the ring to the eldest male of the next generation, which was her son, my boyfriend.

One night, as she tucked her son into his bed, nestled in a room full of baseball paraphernalia, he begged for the story of the ring again. After she explained how the ring moved from one generation to the next, she asked, "So, who will get the ring now, Robbie?"

"Probably Chloe because she doesn't throw like a girl," he said, rolling over.

His mother laughed and brought the covers up to his chin. "Is that the only reason?"

"Yeah, what else is there?"

That, of course, was the part his mother had told me, the part he had forgotten, and now, several weeks after my birthday, as we walked through the woods that connected our houses, he reassured me that there was something else. And like any curious girlfriend, I asked him to tell me what was on his list.

It was our conversation on the night before he left for the annual bike trip. All the guys, along with my mom, who drove the support vehicle, were headed to North Florida in the morning; whereas, Mrs. Callahan and Riley had already left for NYC. They invited me, of course, but I was saving my money for other flights—like ones headed to Washington-Reagan in the fall.

At present, Rob was opening the gate to my backyard and leading me onto the back porch, and once there, we nestled next to each other on the wicker bench. "You want to know what else, huh?" he asked nonchalantly. I bit down on my lip and nodded eagerly. "Well, you're very smart, and extremely well read—

157

not many kids read the classics just for fun." I smiled, knowing intelligence ranked high on his list of dating prerequisites. "And you're naturally beautiful, which is why you look so pretty first thing in the morning. You know, when your hair is all over the place?"

In an effort to recreate my morning allure, I did a quick hair flip, but when I leaned over, I forgot to take into account the wicker table in front of me. "Ow," I said, rubbing my forehead. I got up slowly, heard him laughing, and added quickly, "But don't worry, Rob. I'll be okay."

He chuckled a little more and continued on with his list, "Of course, you make me laugh—and not always on purpose." He leaned over and kissed my forehead. "But most importantly, you're not afraid to feel. Your heart is so tender, and by knowing you all these years, I have experienced life differently than I would have without you. You have opened me up and filled me with love, and for that, I am most grateful."

I stared back at him. "You should write that down, Rob."

He shook his head gently and brought my hand to his heart. "It's all right here." But to me, his lines belonged in romance novels, and sometimes after a night with him, I wrote his words down in the journal that my grandmother had given me for my birthday.

I rested my head on his shoulder and sighed. "This'll be our last kiss then."

"Forever?" he teased

"*No,*" I chided back and pressed my lips against his neck. My mouth traveled up to his jaw line, and I started kissing the corner of his mouth. Rob had a serious five o'clock shadow by nightfall, so my lips burned a little as I kissed his sandpapery face. I left his mouth and came at him from another direction, a little more vigorously this time, and he emitted a low groan. I answered him with a softer, longer one, and we settled into a rhythmic kiss.

"Hey, guess what?" He pulled back suddenly. "We don't have to do this."

"But I *want* to do this."

"No, I'm talking about this weekend. Since you're not going to your grandmother's house, you should come with us." I nixed my annual trip to Kentucky because Rob and I only had two months left of summer, and I couldn't bear to spend a whole week away from him.

I grimaced. "And do what?"

"Be with me."

"But you're going to be on a bike all weekend, and when you're not riding, you'll either be sweaty or sleepy."

He turned up a corner of his mouth. "You want to stay home, don't you?"

"Yeah, maybe." It was the first time my parents had ever let me stay home by myself, and naturally, a little freedom intrigued me. "Plus, I should really hang out with my friends every once in a while."

He folded his arms across his chest and leaned back. "Yeah, what are you guys going to do while I'm gone?"

"Just hang out at Courtney's."

"I'm sorry I'll miss it."

"Yeah, I'm sure you are." We used to sneak out of Courtney's house in the middle of the night and play "knock-and-run" on his bedroom window. But several years ago, when Josh was spending the night at Rob's house, they were waiting for us up in the old tree house. And when we tiptoed to his bedroom window, they were moving stealthily behind us. When they tapped our shoulders, we squealed like thirteen-year-old girls are prone to do. Then the two of them doubled over in hysterics as we marched back to Courtney's house, defeated.

He glanced at his watch. "Listen, I should probably get going."

"How about one last kiss?"

"Tomorrow." He slid a finger down the length of my nose and rested it on my lips. "Good things come to those who wait."

* * *

The next morning, I rose with the sun and shuffled into the kitchen. My dad was pouring ice into a cooler, and my mom was making sandwiches in assembly-line fashion. Brad, however, looked like a statue as he cradled his head in his hands at the kitchen table.

I plopped down across the table from him and poured some wheat crunchies into a bowl. My eyes remained on our backyard, watching the sun glisten like a diamond through the trees as Rob and his father emerged from the woods and into our kitchen.

Mr. Callahan helped my parents pack the car, and Rob joined me at the kitchen table. He wore his Red Sox cap backwards, and his auburn hair curled up at the ends. He hung an arm around my shoulder and whispered, "Good morning, Beautiful." His lips stayed close to me, softly sucking on my ear lobe, since he discovered it had an exceedingly titillating effect on me.

Meanwhile, Brad remained at the table, his head in his hands as he ate his cereal. I slid my hand up Rob's thigh, finding the soft place where his hair thinned out and his skin felt the smoothest. I wriggled my fingers there until he emitted a low chuckle. It was his coveted ticklish spot. In return, Rob slid his hand down my back, his fingers inching toward my butt. He gave it a playful squeeze, and I giggled back.

"I'm glad we don't have a glass table," Brad announced without moving an inch.

"I know," my mother said as she reentered the kitchen. Rob and I put a little distance between us, and my mom sat down at the head of the table with her cup of coffee. "Your father and I had a glass tabletop when we first got married, but we had to get rid of it because you—" She singled me out with her icy blue eyes. "Kept running into it."

"That explains a lot," Brad said, bringing his bowl to his lips and slurping up the milk.

"Bradley," my mother scolded. He just shrugged and walked over to the sink, and my mother took another sip of coffee. "Maybe we should see if they need our help out there."

They left us alone at the table, and Rob rested his hand on top of mine. "I'll give you a call before I go to bed tonight."

160

"Okay," I said.

He leaned in and kissed me tenderly on the mouth.

I pushed out my lower lip. "Will I see you tomorrow?"

He shook his head. "It'll be too late."

"Not 'til Monday then?"

He nodded. "Remember, good things come to those who wait." He lifted me off the seat and pulled me into a corner of the kitchen. He put his hands on my face and placed his warm lips on mine. Then he kissed me, *really* kissed me, and I felt a sudden surge of pleasure in my secret place. And even though our kiss only lasted a few minutes, it was long enough to take me someplace else, a place where only he mattered, and I could stay in his arms forever. In other words, heaven on earth.

"It's time to go," he said sadly and led me out of the house. He leaned against the side of my dad's SUV, which was all packed with gear and had four bikes hanging off the back. I gave him a tight squeeze, and into the crook of his neck, I muttered, "I'm going to miss you so much."

"I'll miss you too."

My lips fell against his neck, feeling the warmth of his skin. "I love you."

"Love you too."

Brad popped open a back window and stuck out his head. "Hey, he's not leaving for college for another two months." At the thought, I whimpered and held him tighter, but Rob reminded me softly, "I'll only be gone for two days."

"Which is only forty-eight hours."

"Or 2,880 minutes," he calculated.

I stepped out of the hug and spread my hands to the side, and he smiled. "Or 172,800 seconds." He smacked one last kiss before he got in, and I stood in the driveway for a few more minutes, watching as they rolled slowly down the driveway— and completely out of sight.

161

-25-

Trouble

I walked back inside and rubbed my hands together. The house was all mine. I blasted the music from the surround sound speakers and headed into the kitchen. Once there, I opened both doors of the fridge, peering inside for a *really* long time before deciding on some chocolate chip cookies out of the cookie jar. I washed them down with some milk. No cup though. I drank right out of the jug, swiping the milk moustache off with the back of my hand—something I had seen my brother do, but had never actually tried myself.

Back in the family room, I plopped down on the couch and rested my feet on the table. I clicked on the television and noticed the time. It was only nine thirty. I wondered what Rob was doing and if he was thinking about me. I thought about him, slowly undressing him down to those stretchy, grey boxers and wasting a good hour with some varying scenarios on how to get there and what to do when we arrived.

But thinking about him made me ache inside. I heaved out a heavy sigh and rose from the couch. "Next year's gonna' suck," I grumbled and headed upstairs. Once there, I took a quick shower and packed my overnight bag, arriving at Courtney's door an hour later. She and I headed out to the pool, and soon, Callie and Caitlyn joined us. The four of us lay on chaise lounges under a hot summer sun.

Callie turned to Courtney, "When are you heading back to the beach?"

"Sometime tomorrow, because I've made some new friends this summer." She winked. We knew Courtney was fond of summer flings because they always ended before the monotony set in, and she had given up on Mr. Martinez after he accepted a permanent teaching position at Riverside. She took a sip of water and continued on, "But there's always an open invitation for all of you. Come whenever you want." She looked over at Callie. "How long are you going to be at basketball camp?"

"Four weeks."

"That's a long time to go without Mike," Caitlyn chimed in.

"I'll be home every weekend," Callie returned.

I looked over at Caitlyn. "Are you still going to Hilton Head with Brandon's family?"

"Yeah." Caitlyn looked over at me, and her eyes fell briefly to the ring on my hand. "What about you? Any big plans that we should know about?"

"No," I returned sharply.

Later when the sun started to fall behind the trees, we moved inside to shower, eat pizza, and put on a movie. Courtney made some strong frozen concoction. I had one, knowing I shouldn't have, and after I finished my drink, I felt the alcohol working its way into my system.

My cell chirped next to me, and I answered, "Hiya' sexy."

"Have you been drinking?" Rob accused quickly.

"Just one."

"Yeah, well, that's all it takes."

"Hey now."

The girls made kissy sounds in the background, and I covered the phone, rushing into the bedroom at the back of the house. Since I arrived first, I got the best room, the guest bedroom with the adjoining pool bath.

"I'm alone now," I informed him.

"Good." He paused. "Listen, I wasn't trying to lecture you—"

"Then don't." I was well aware of his stance on drinking. He came from a household that had wine with dinner and beer at family events, but he never drank when he was out with friends. "And you're not my father, by the way."

"Speaking of fathers, do you want to talk to yours?"

"*No.*"

I heard him take a deep breath. "I miss you."

"I miss you too," I returned.

"And I can't wait to see you."

"Monday's too long, Rob."

"What do you suggest?"

"We should meet up at the tree house when you get back."

"And do what?"

"You know what."

"Okay." He cackled in an adorably sinister fashion. "Twist my arm."

"Call me when you get home."

A fist pounded on the door and was followed by Courtney's voice. "Are you two having phone sex?"

"What did she just say?" he asked.

I was surprised at the auditory capabilities of my cell phone. "She said 'Are you two done yet?'"

"Done?" he parroted. "I haven't even started."

"Now, stop it."

"Stop what?"

"Argh."

He chirped me a kiss. "I love you."

"Love you too."

"Goodnight, Chloe."

"'Night, Rob."

"And?"

"Yeah."

"Sweet dreams."

* * *

After I hung up with Rob, I returned to the family room, plopping down next to Courtney on the couch. "And to answer your question: No!"

She leaned in and whispered, "You should really try it. It's completely safe, and it will get you through those lonely months while he's away at school."

My face burned with embarrassment. "I am *not* having this conversation with you."

"Fine," she relented with a smile. "I'll have it with Rob then."

"Oh, no!" I grabbed her arm and felt a familiar feeling like when she used to run off and talk to my crushes.

"Listen, I worry about you two," she said with a little pout. "Chloe, do you know why most long-distance relationships fail?"

I shrugged. "Because people stop loving each other?"

"Wrong."

"Okay, enlighten me then."

"It's not because people stop loving each other; it's just so easy to fill that void with someone else."

"Listen! Rob is the only guy who could ever fill my void!"

Courtney's eyes popped open. "Your void, huh? I thought you were a virgin."

I picked up a throw pillow from the couch and hit her upside the head. "Shut up, slut."

She picked up a pillow and yelled, "Prude!"

"Stop it!" Caitlyn shouted. "I'm trying to watch a movie here."

Courtney and I had no intention of stopping until one of us got hurt or something got broken. She pushed off the couch and ran into the middle of the family room, armed with a golden throw pillow, and I chased her with a brown one. We made a circuitous route around her house, running at top speed, giggling and swatting each other. We ran through the kitchen, into the dining room, through the living room and back into the family room, and by the second lap around the house, she detoured toward the couch. I caught her. Her head was facedown, and I sat on her legs, pounding her mercilessly with the pillow.

"No freaking way," Callie said as she pointed to the sliding glass door. Brandon, Austin, Ricky, and a few other guys from the team peered into the family room like little kids at a candy store window.

Caitlyn crossed the room, slid open the sliding glass door, and bid them entrance with a graceful wave of her hand. Then she walked her fingers up Brandon's chest. "Aw, you couldn't stay away, could you?" He replied with a long kiss as the guys got comfortable on the couches.

"You guys out there long?" I asked.

"Long enough to see you and Courtney make nice." Austin held up his phone in my face. "And I got it all right here."

"Yeah, so?"

"So—" He licked his lips and smiled. "A little girl-on-girl action always gets plenty of views on the 'Net."

"Pervert," I said as I reached out for his phone.

He bolted into the kitchen and lounged against the counter with a grin on his face. "Ah, come and get it, baby?" He slipped the phone down the front of his pants, and his nimble fingers unfastened the top button of his jeans. "Go ahead. Grrrrab it."

"You...*you*...I don't know what you are!"

"But I know what you are." He glared at me as he fished the phone out of his pants. "You're a little tease."

I narrowed my eyes at him. "I don't know why I ever dated you."

"Puh-lease, you've had a thing for me since the day we met. You couldn't hide it then, and you *still* can't hide it now." He wheeled around and pulled a couple of beers from the fridge. "Here, catch." He chucked one in my direction. "You're more fun after you've had a few."

I put the unopened beer on the counter and entered the family room. Courtney was on the couch between Ricky Sampson and Morgan Harris. Morgan was the place kicker on our team and the go-to guy for party favors (if you know what I mean). The two of them were playing tug-o-war for her affections, and

I fell into the easy chair next to them and decided to watch the match. I was betting on Ricky. Morgan was a little wild—even for Courtney's tastes.

The sliding glass doors opened again. More familiar faces entered, and I realized our girls' night-in was turning into quite the party. "Hey!" I got Courtney's attention. "I think I'll head home."

"Why?" she pouted.

Austin hung an arm around my shoulders. "Because Chloe still wants me and can't handle being around me."

"You wish," I pelted at him.

And then I decided to stay, just to prove him wrong.

*　　*　　*

Later on, Courtney and Caitlyn slipped back into their swimsuits, enticing the guys to the pool like the mythical Sirens luring the sailors.

But Callie and I remained at the kitchen table, chatting about next year. "Are you and Mike worried about the whole long-distance thing?" Mike was going to Florida State, like his brothers, and even though it was a four-hour drive, it still meant seeing each other on holidays and the occasional weekend.

She shrugged. "Nah." I expressed my shock, and she patted my hand right hand. "We're not like you and Rob."

"What's that suppose to mean?"

"Mike and I live in the now, and we don't talk about the future."

"I thought you loved him. I mean, he was your first."

"And I don't regret it." She gave me a slight smile. "Losing your virginity is not that big of a deal. Someday you'll understand." I felt like a child when she said that, knowing it would be a long time before I fully understood what it meant to be with a guy. Rob and I talked openly about our sexual urges, but he remained adamant about leaving some things until marriage and continued to restrict our explorations to the northern hemisphere.

167

"What are you girls drinking?" Austin entered the room and started rifling through the liquor cabinet.

"What are you making?" Callie quipped back.

"For you…" He turned and gave Callie a wink. "Anything."

"Rum and Coke," my friend decided.

He looked at me. "The same?"

"Nah, how about a Coke? Hold the rum."

A few minutes later, he handed us our drinks and took a seat at the table. And it was pretty sad but after years of being friends and months of dating, I had no idea what to say to him. I sipped the soda slowly, and he didn't bother to start up a conversation as he stared off into the family room.

Mike arrived, pausing for a minute to chat with Austin before he pulled Callie off the chair, and with a smile, he led her to one of the bedrooms at the back of the house.

I went to get up, but Austin placed a hand on mine. "Hey, can we talk?"

"Uh, I guess so," I said quietly and sat back down.

"I don't want things to be weird between us."

My eyes fell downward. "They're not."

"Really? When's the last time we talked, Chlo?" I shrugged, and he continued, "We used to be real close, you know."

"I know," I admitted, and maybe it would be better if I didn't hate him. Next year, we could eat lunch at the same table, and life could go back to normal. After all, we had both moved on. Or in Austin's case, on and on and on, since he and Aimee only lasted a few weeks.

He leaned forward. "How's your family?"

"Good. Your dad?"

"He's the same. He's still dating Whitney, which means he's never home. But I don't mind. I get the whole place to myself."

"You ever see your mom?" I wondered as I cradled my chin in my palms. I felt a wave of fatigue wash over me, thinking I should call it a night soon.

He shook his head. "No, but I'm thinking 'bout going to Texas this summer. It's a really long drive, but it's not like Mom'll come here. She still hates my dad's guts."

I nodded slowly and yawned. He was trying so hard to talk to me, and it reminded me of our *second* first date, where he showed up at the door with a pale blue polo and a red rose in his hand. He took me to a little Italian place downtown, and he tried so hard to be someone he wasn't. And I wondered why he was making that same effort now, but it didn't really matter. I was too tired to analyze Austin Walker's twisted mind. I glanced up at the clock. The numbers blurred, and I blinked to make things clearer. I pushed out an exhale and mumbled, "I'm going to bed now." The words sounded funny like when I played back one of my voice mails intended for someone else. Sure, it was me, but I didn't like the way I sounded.

Austin's fingers travelled up my arm. "Are you drunk?"

"Unh-uh… juss had one." I held up a finger and stared at it for a moment.

"Then you're a cheap date."

"Shu…up," I managed inside a yawn.

"Aw, baby, you look so sleepy," Austin said, but I was more than sleepy. I felt like I had the flu, and the symptoms presented themselves with an uncanny speed. Austin leaned in closer to me; his lips fell to my ear. "But don't you worry. I'll take you to bed tonight."

"No," I murmured, maybe. I wasn't even sure if the words left my lips.

Then Austin was at my side, lifting me off the chair and helping me like an injured player off the field, and together, we weaved through the crowded family room and down the hall of closed bedroom doors.

He opened the door to my bedroom and lowered me to the bed, swiftly climbing on top of me, and then I couldn't escape the scent of his cologne or the taste of alcohol as his tongue slid into my mouth. I started sobbing, and eventually screamed for help, but my sounds never made it beyond the bedroom door. The entire house was loud, pulsating with techno, and I knew no one could possibly hear me back here, especially not now as I grew even more tired. I started slipping in and out of conscious-

169

ness like a patient with anesthesia coursing through her veins. And the whole time Austin kept his mouth on mine, kissing me in a way no one—including him—had ever kissed me before. I could feel his tongue, his lips, and even his teeth as his hands slid down my body, deftly untying and unbuttoning any obstacle in his way, and as my nearly naked body lay under his pressing weight, his hot breath entered my ear:

Hush-a-bye, don't you cry
Go to sleepy, little baby

And like an infant succumbing to sleep in her mother's arms, I drifted into the darkness, sleeping for hours like a baby.

-26-

The Light

The sun slipped through the bedroom sheers, and I awoke to the horrible realization of what happened the night before. I don't know why, but I didn't cry or run to tell any of the girls; I simply got dressed and stripped the sheets off the bed, wadding them into a ball for the Valentine's maid to discover on Monday morning.

I picked up my overnight bag off the floor, rushed through the pool bath, and raced across the patio. Without glimpsing at Rob's house, I ran through the woods frantically like a fawn in the height of hunting season, and once inside my home, I checked all of the locks on the doors before I turned on the alarm system and headed up the stairs.

I entered my bathroom, stripped off my clothes, scented from the night before, and tossed them onto the cold floor. As I stepped into the shower, the water hit my body, dissolving the caked-on blood into a rusty stream. And searching for its redemptive powers, I remained under the warm water until the river turned to crimson and then pink; and finally, it ran clear, washing the evidence down the drain.

Inside the white tiled cell, I released unheard screams and fisted uncaring walls, waging a fight of futility hours too late. The crime had passed quietly in the night, taking my most guarded possession; and no matter how hard I cried or searched, and no matter who listened or helped, my innocence would never come

171

back to me. My virginity had been pilfered like love or dignity in a crime of abstraction where objects are easily taken yet impossible to return.

Slowly, I stepped out of the shower and wrapped myself in my pink robe and fell to the floor. The tiles felt cool against my skin, and I curled into the fetal position. I cried like a newborn afraid to face her harsh new world outside her mother's womb, and alternating between screams and cries, time traipsed by slowly. Eventually, I pushed myself off the floor and walked into my bedroom. I fell onto my bed, staring at the whirling blades of the fan. "No one has to know," I whispered.

The phone rang again and again, and finally, I turned off the ringer, drowning out all sounds with some music, playing it real loud, loud enough to muffle the thoughts in my own head. Then I got up and started pacing in circles, and I even wondered if it really happened. I soothed myself with that possibility until I touched the tenderness between my legs and fell victim to the hot tears again.

"Just accept it," I said out loud. It wasn't really rape; he was my boyfriend once. He had seen me in just my unmentionables before and ran his fingers across my skin. He had whispered affections in my ear and told me his secrets while in my arms. I had done more with him than I had with anyone else. And I had even thought about him *that* way countless times.

"But why now?" I shouted at the ceiling, at the whole world. My heart belonged completely to Rob. My eyes fell to my right hand, and I twisted the ring again and again, watching the heart disappear and reappear, thinking how quickly things could change.

I descended the stairs and trudged across the front hallway, ending up in my parents' room. I walked across the thick California loop, feeling the softness of the plush carpet against my bare soles, and entered my parents' spacious bathroom with the high clerestory windows. The rays of light splashed onto the marbled countertops, making the fancy bottles of perfume glisten in the sunlight. I picked up my mother's signature scent

172

and sprayed the spicy floral into the air. It drew me close to her, and I imagined my mother hugging away my sadness like when I was little girl.

I spied the medicine cabinet on the wall, remembering the reason I had crossed the house in the first place. I reached for my mother's sleeping pills, hoping they would erase the remaining hours of the day, and after dropping a few tablets in my hand, I headed back to my room. I took an Ambien and turned on my cell. Since my mother was driving the support vehicle for the bike trip, I knew I could reach her, and her alone.

"Hello, Chloe," she chirped cheerfully. I imagined her driving along the curvy country roads, sipping slowly from her cup of coffee and completely immersed in a book on tape. A long Michener, perhaps.

"Mom," I spoke softly. "I'm going back to bed, and I turned off the ringer."

"What if I need to reach you?"

"You won't. I'm fine." I dismissed her maternal paranoia quickly.

"You girls stay up late last night?"

"Yeah."

"Nothing ever changes, huh? You girls will never grow up." She laughed momentarily. "I'll never forget the time when I picked you up from Caitlyn's slumber party and drove you to the mall afterward. Remember that? We had to buy you a pair of shoes for Uncle Doug's wedding, and you actually fell asleep in the middle of the Macy's shoe department."

"I remember," I said softly.

"Well, go get some sleep then." She stopped and remembered, "Oh, and would you like me to give Rob a message?" The mention of his name gripped at my heart, and I swallowed down a knot before I answered, "Um, no."

"No?" she teased.

"Mother, please. I'm really tired, and he knows how I feel about him."

But as I hung up the phone, I started to wonder how Rob

173

would feel about me. Me: defiled. Him: perfect. And I hated to think where that would leave the two of us.

-27-

The Truth

"Good morning, sleepyhead." Rob's voice entered my room on Monday morning. My family was gone for the day: Dad caught a 9:40 to Chicago-O'Hare; Brad headed to the beach with some guys from the tennis team; and Mom had already left for work.

"Are you awake?"

"Yeah," I answered groggily like I was thick with sleep. I remained under the covers, facing the window as he lowered himself to the other side of the bed.

"You know," he said, his voice moving closer. "I should be mad at you for standing me up last night. I kept calling you, but you never answered your cell. And I even went to the tree house just in case you were already there."

"Sorry," I mumbled.

"Well, I need more than an apology." He inched closer to me, the antique bed registering every movement with low-pitched creaks. "What I really need is some—" His voice cut into a low chuckle. "No, seriously, Chlo. I started thinking about next year, and if I miss you this much after two days, just imagine what I'll be like after a month or two."

His hand rested on my arm, but with a deft reflex, I brushed it away.

"Hey, what was that for?"

I said nothing, and Rob tried to touch me again. He stroked

175

my hair. He caressed my back, but I swatted at his every advancement like pesky flies on a hot summer day.

Without a word, he rose from my bed and started pacing around my room. I listened to his footsteps, and my heart raced faster and faster until the beats crept into my head, and I felt so scared, not knowing what was going to happen next. He lowered himself to my side of the bed, but as I tried to turn from him, he grasped my shoulders and held me in place, his face inches from mine. "What is wrong with you?"

I turned my head and squeezed my eyes shut; hot tears burned a path down my cheeks.

"Did something happen on Saturday night?" he deduced correctly. "I talked to Courtney on her way to the beach, and she said you left her house without saying goodbye. Why? What happened, Chlo?"

I wriggled free from his grasp and faced the other wall, knowing that the truth was creeping to the surface like drops of oil in a pan of water, and I had to tell him what happened. Sure, I had tossed the conversation around in my head countless times in the last twenty-four hours, but no matter how I phrased it, I knew that the next few minutes would be exceedingly painful. And by revealing the truth, I would hurt him, and he was the last person I ever wanted to hurt.

"Talk to me...*please*."

"Rob," I started, but instead of more words, I heaved out heavy sobs.

"Chloe," he paused. "Just tell me what happened." He leaned in closer, careful not to touch me again. "Listen, I hate to ask this, but did you..." His voice trailed off, and I listened to each breath he took, one and then another. "Did you cheat on me or something?"

I flipped over and faced him, anger raging inside me. "How could you think that!"

"What else am I supposed to think?"

"I don't know," my voice weakened. "But not that."

He got up and paced, and as he moved back and forth across my room, he spoke, "Fine, then just tell me why I can't touch

176

you. And why you won't stop crying." His voice faltered, "Just tell me the truth, because nothing in the world could be worse than thinking you were with someone else."

"I know," I muttered weakly. I sat up in my bed, pulling my knees into my chest. "On Saturday night...Austin...uh..."

"What?" he asked harshly.

The tears rolled freely down my cheeks, and my stomach twisted into a row of knots.

"He...uh..."

"What?" he repeated, his tone revealing his rising anger.

I pulled my legs tighter into my chest and sniffed back the tears. "I can't say it," I protested with more tears, shaking my head. "I just can't."

"Chloe," he spoke uneasily. "Just tell me the truth. I can handle it."

I tried several times to swallow the impossible knot growing in my throat. "He...uh..." My mouth went completely dry, yet the tears flowed freely down my cheeks. "He r-r-raped me."

"How could you let this happen!" he roared. "How could you!"

I said nothing, not knowing what to say.

He walked across my room and seethed, "I swear I'm gonna' kill him." And then I heard a loud thump, figuring he had punched my wall. I glanced up at him, watching as he fisted the wall relentlessly until he just fell against it, motionless. Eventually, he pushed himself off the wall and crossed my room. He sat down on the bench, dropping his face into his hands, mumbling.

As his anger receded, sadness took over him, and for the very first time since his grandmother's funeral, he didn't hold back the tears. The sound of his sobs wrenched at my heart, and all I could do was watch my boyfriend, my very best friend, cry. Occasionally, he would lift up his brown eyes and look at me, and then he would return his face to his hands again. The sight of me was more than he could bear, and I remained in bed, alone.

I stared at the space between us on my bedroom floor and thought about the Berlin wall, which divided Germany for over twenty-five years. There, two parts of a whole were separated by an impervious force, and as the minutes slipped from the day and the distance grew between us, I wondered how long it would take us to tear down the wall and be reunited again.

*　　*　　*

After a while, his hands hit the top of his thighs. "I should read you a book or something." He stood up, examining my shelves for a few minutes, and then returned to the bench, opening the book to the first page. He read out loud to me:

> *You don't know about me without you have read a book by the name of THE ADVENTURES OF TOM SAWYER; but that ain't no matter. That book was made by Mr. Mark Twain, and he told the truth, mainly. There was things which he stretched, but mainly he told the truth...*

Rob read *The Adventures of Huckleberry Finn* all morning and well into the afternoon, only pausing to prepare me a plate of food, which I did not feel like eating, or to go to the bathroom, which he did with more frequency than me. And by the time his mother phoned him, soliciting his help with moving some furniture around the living room, he had finished the entire book.

"That's still one of my favorites," he said, sliding it back on the shelf, where it had remained since he gave it to me for my sixteenth birthday. "So, did you like it?"

"Yeah, it was okay."

"Of course, you should have read it in English this year. Do you feel like you missed out by taking AP this year rather than next year?"

"No."

He slipped into his brown Crocs and paused by the side of my bed. "Which English class are you going to take next year?" Really, it was a simple question, but I was tired of answering them. He kept asking them all day long—Are you hungry? Do you need to go to the bathroom? Are you cold? Are you hot?

I looked up at him. "Stop asking me a million questions!"

"Sorry." His voice was strained, and his swallows were audible.

"It's okay."

He stood by me, and we both didn't know what to say to each other. "So, I'll see you later," he said finally.

"Yeah…later," I mumbled. Then the words just came out of nowhere. I had no intention of using them, and when I said them, they felt foreign on my lips. "I love you."

He waited a moment. "I love you too." But it was the worst "I love you" in the whole world because it was completely conditional. It was what he had to say, and as I climbed under the covers again, burying my face into my pillow, I wondered if he would ever truly love me again.

-28-

The Aftermath

The following morning, Rob appeared in my doorway. I was at my desk, trying to get lost on the Internet, but no matter where I went, my mind remained on Saturday night.

"Hey," he said like he had been waiting for me to speak first.

I lifted my eyes from the screen and acknowledged him.

"Listen," he said, entering my room slowly. "You need to tell someone about what happened to you ."

"I did."

"Besides me." He rested a hand on the edge of my desk. "Because I'm not really sure what to say to you, and I don't know how to help you get through this." He handed me a folded piece of paper. "This is the number for a support group, which meets at the hospital. I've heard my dad talk about it." I took the slip of paper and tucked it under my laptop. "But first, you'll have to tell your parents, and then you should report it to the police…" He went on, rambling off a post-rape to-do list while I stared blankly at my computer screen. I wanted him to stop talking about it. I wanted things to be normal again, but he just continued with more questions. "When does your mom get home?" I shrugged even though we both knew she would arrive home shortly after five o' clock, the same time as always. "And what about your dad? When does he get back?"

"I don't know." I paused. "Can we talk about something else?"

"Like what?"

"Anything."

"You can't pretend this didn't happen. You have to—"

I lifted my eyes from the screen and stared at him, fighting the temptation to yell. "Listen, I don't *have* to do anything."

"You're right. It's probably too late anyway. You should have gone to the police right away."

"Is that all you care about? Getting revenge?"

"No! I care about you!" he contradicted quickly. He walked around my room and mumbled, "But revenge would have been nice."

"You're not helping, Rob."

"What? Am I not allowed to have feelings?"

"No, you're allowed to have them, just not entitled to express them." I soon repented my words, but rather than retract them, I just stared at the screen.

He said nothing at first and then decided, "Maybe I should go get some coffee." He started toward the door. "You want anything?"

I shook my head and tapped on my keyboard, continuing with my ruse of busyness.

* * *

Rob returned with some fresh croissants from the bakery up the road, and the following mornings, he continued with his daily visits, and each day, I felt more and more like a sick patient at the hospital. He came armed with breakfast food and the morning paper; the food was for me, and the paper for him.

On Wednesday, he brought me a blueberry bagel, but on Thursday, he opened the paper bag from the previous day, shaking his head at the bagel still inside. He ate it himself and commented, "I guess I'll eat this muffin too." He sat down on the bench and opened the paper. "What do you want to do today?" he asked from behind the front page.

181

"Same thing as yesterday...same thing as Tuesday...same thing as Monday," I returned, sitting up in bed and completely absorbed with the lint between my toes. I extracted a fuzzy pink remnant from my five-day-old socks and dropped it to the floor.

Noisily, Rob folded the paper and placed it next to him. "How long are you going to stay holed up in your room?"

I turned toward him with a pronounced pout. "I'm too sick to go anywhere, Rob." I offered a fake cough.

"I can't believe your mom buys that crap."

"Why? I'm a very good liar," I returned boastfully.

He lifted up the paper again, hiding his expression. "Yeah, it's such an admirable quality of yours." At that, I stuck out my tongue at him, yet it went unnoticed. He was too preoccupied with the world news.

*　　*　　*

For the rest of the day, we barely spoke to each other, and if we did, the conversation seemed to find its way back to Saturday night. And no matter how hard he tried, I never revealed any more details to him. I decided it was one story better left untold, since it was an awful tale with a beginning and an end, and that part in the middle, of which I did not know.

Yet it was the unknown that caused those wretched nightmares, and every night I awoke with visions so terrible that I often wondered if my subconscious had conjured up the truth in my slumber. So, in the blackest hours of the night, during those unbearably long moments before dawn, I lay awake, restless and frightened, while the possibilities played in my head.

I produced a series of loud yawns, and he asked, "You tired?"

"No," I lied. "Just bored."

"We could go somewhere," he suggested, lowering his paper.

"I don't feel like it." I offered another pathetic cough. "I'm too sick, remember?"

The conversation, with its uncomfortable lapses, had gone full circle again.

"But you'll be there tomorrow night, right?" he asked.

"Yeah, I said I would."

He offered a half smile and picked up the paper again. I extracted another ball of pink fluff, released it over the floor, and watched it float to the ground.

*   *   *

On Friday afternoon, I stood in my steamy-hot bathroom, fully wrapped in my pink robe. I combed the tangles out of my long hair, lathered body milk on my smooth legs, and dabbed perfume on my pulse points. Slowly, I opened the door and found Rob waiting in the hallway. His arms were folded across his chest, and he wore his best dimpled grin. "Hmm, what's that smell?"

"Clean," I returned quickly and with a slight smile. "It's something new I'm trying. You like it?"

He stepped forward and lifted an eyebrow. "Yeah, I *love* it." But it was the way his voice dropped when he said "love" and the expression that made me feel uncomfortable.

"Um, I should get dressed," I said, closing the bedroom door behind me. I entered my closet and ran my fingers along the row of dresses, examining the colors, patterns, and fabrics of every occasion. I didn't know what to wear to Grandpa Callahan's seventieth birthday party. Desperately, I wanted to slip back into a pair of boxers and an oversized running T-shirt, but I promised him I would attend. I selected an Easter dress from a few years ago. It was a blue floral, ankle length, and tied in the back. I grabbed a hair clip from the bottom drawer of my jewelry box and drew my hair off my face. I examined myself in the mirror, noticing my eyes, which were sunken and swollen and embellished with purplish grey circles under them. I heaved out a heavy sigh, crossed the room, and opened the door. Rob was waiting, still smiling. "Wow," he paused. "You look beautiful."

I stared back at him. "Wow," I paused. "You're a terrible liar."

Quickly, I brushed past him and bolted down the stairs, heading out the garage and stepping into fresh air and sunlight for the first time in almost a week. I felt like a prisoner being let out of solitary confinement, and still squinting, I walked over to his bright yellow Jeep. I leaned against it, feeling the hot metal through my thin cotton dress, and with folded arms, I waited for him.

Rob approached me. "You're right, Chloe. I am a terrible liar, and that is why I have always told you the truth." He opened the door for me, and I climbed inside. "And the truth is: you will always be beautiful to me." He closed the door, and while he walked around the front of the Jeep, I mumbled, "Yeah, right."

He got in, started the engine, and backed down the driveway. "We need to run a few errands for the party tonight." He reached over, switching the radio station to one with music. "But it shouldn't take too long."

My eyes remained on my hands, which were clasped tightly in my lap. I felt uncomfortable outside the house; the natural light seemed too bright, and the streets seemed too busy. I wanted to be in my own room, where I controlled the light and could crawl safely under the covers.

"Perfect day, isn't it?" He drove past the gatehouse and waved at Clyde. "My mom's planning to set up some tables on the patio. She figured we'd want to go swimming."

"I don't want to go swimming."

"That's okay. We don't have to."

"But *you* still can."

"I know."

"Do you?" I countered.

"Listen." His voice was gentle, and he placed a hand lightly on mine. I stared at his hand as it invaded my personal space. "All I care about is being with you tonight."

"Why? Because I'm so much fun to be around?"

The light turned red, and he turned toward me. "You're

hurting, and you need time to heal. I'm not expecting you to be yourself yet."

"So you expect less from me? Like a teacher does with her special-needs kids? What am I? Relationship-challenged?"

The light turned green, and he proceeded through the intersection. "Why don't we talk about something else then?"

"Like what, Rob?" I asked sardonically, since he had spent the last five days focused on that one particular topic.

"I don't really know anymore." His voice was strained as he veered into the right lane and pulled into a bank parking lot. He cut the engine and faced me. He took a deep breath and spoke, "Maybe we can't talk about anything else because we're both thinking about the same thing, and until you deal with what happened to you, then things will be like this between us."

"Like what, Rob?" I repeated angrily. The whole time my gaze was out the passenger-side window, watching as a mother unloaded her children from a minivan.

"Are you even listening to me?"

"Yeah," I retorted. "You said blah, blah, blah, blah..."

He started the engine, looped around the building, and began backtracking down Riverside Drive.

I glanced at him. "Where are we going now?"

"We," he emphasized, "are going nowhere." And with that said, he sped back to my house and zipped up my driveway. He was simmering mad as I reached for the door handle.

"Listen, I didn't feel like going to the party anyway," I admitted.

"That's nice, Chlo, but what am I supposed to tell my family?"

"Tell them I'm still sick."

"I'm tired of covering for you...tired of all your lies."

"Why? Everybody lies." He said nothing, and I took it as my cue to continue. "Think about your life, Rob. You have a biological father, but you don't even know who he is." I looked over at him; his eyes narrowed into slits, daring me to continue. "And years ago, when you found out that Dr. Dave adopted you, you had lots of questions for your mom. You wanted to know

185

what your real dad looked like, and if he loved baseball too. You wanted to know if you had any half-brothers or sisters, and if you would ever meet any of them. And I still remember what your mom told you. I remember because I was sitting there at the kitchen table, wondering the same things as you. And she said you would be better off if you didn't know. I believed her then, but I don't anymore. It was all a lie." He remained in silence as I pressed on, "And the whole thing still bothers you. That's why you never talk about it. Even with me."

"Actually, I don't care who he is."

"Really?" Our eyes met, and I tossed back, "Now, who's the one lying?"

He held up a hand. "Please don't say anything else."

"Why not?"

"Because I don't feel like talking about it."

I pulled on the door handle. "Now, you know how *I* feel."

"Wait a second." I froze, but didn't turn around. "You brought that up just to prove a point, didn't you?"

I opened the door, letting the humidity creep inside the air-conditioned Jeep.

"Answer me, Chloe," he demanded in a voice that I hadn't heard in fifteen years of knowing him.

"Yes," I whispered back and slipped off the seat, but before I closed the door behind me, I heard him utter a nasty name under his breath. It was more than just the harsh tone and the word he chose. It was everything; but most of all, it was the realization that a part of him hated me. And that hatred was like an incurable cancer, and with each passing day, it would spread, eating the love between us, and very slowly, and very painfully, our entire relationship, a friendship of many years and weeks of something more, would eventually die.

*   *   *

That night, my mom had her book club and wouldn't be back home until after nine o'clock, and if I timed it correctly, I could enter her room as if I had just gotten home from the Callahan's house. I listened intently as her car pulled into the garage, and then I waited a few minutes before I walked into her bedroom. For a moment, I stood in her doorway, watching her take off her jewelry. She unclasped her charm bracelet and removed her cross necklace, gently laying them in the crystal dish on top of her dresser. She turned and noticed me. "Oh, are you just getting home?"

I nodded.

"That dress looks nice on you."

"Uh, thanks." I paused. "So, how was book club?"

"Oh, fine." She walked into her closet, and I sat on the edge of the bed. "How was the party?" she asked, putting her shoes back on the shelf and sliding into her slippers.

"It was nice." I improvised some generic details. "Mrs. Callahan had enough food to feed an army, and Grandpa really appreciated the scrapbook."

"Well, I hope so. Tracy has been working on it for over a year." She paused in the doorway of her closet. "Did he get pretty emotional?"

"Yeah, as emotional as old guys get."

She shook her head and grabbed a book off the nightstand. "I'm going to relax in the tub, so I'll say goodnight to you now." She walked over and kissed the top of my head.

"Mom?"

"Yes?"

I took a deep breath. "I was thinking of going to Grandma's tomorrow."

"Tomorrow?"

"Yeah, I feel bad that I didn't go last weekend, and I already checked the flights."

She sat next to me on the bed. "And?"

"I booked a 10:20 into Lexington."

"What if I had said no, Chloe?"

I shrugged. "Dad said it was okay."

"Of course, he did."

187

"So, could you drop me off at the airport in the morning?"

"Me?" She gestured to herself. "Why isn't Rob taking you?"

"It's Saturday, and he'll be out riding."

She looked at me for a minute, examining me with her narrowing eyes because she wasn't sure if I was telling her the whole truth. "I thought you and Rob couldn't bear to be apart this summer."

"Well, Mom." I gave her a half smile. "I thought 'absence makes the heart grow fonder.'" I borrowed my father's favorite parting words even though I didn't believe the old adage any more than she did.

In actuality, I was hoping absence would make the heart forget, or at least forget the bad stuff, and in the end, maybe our hearts would only remember the good.

-29-

Grandma's House

Ilanded at the Lexington airport before noon, and my grandmother arrived with a huge smile on her face. As we drove
along the highway, I stared at the endless white fences
sprawling in every direction, and Grandma chattered on about
our plans for the week. She talked up the summer carnival, the
fresh vegetables from her garden, and how much the cat was
looking forward to seeing me, which was my Grandma's idea
of a joke since Spike was a feline octogenarian and also quite
blind.

Nevertheless, the cat was good company, and when I entered
my room at the top of the stairs, he was already there, curled up
in a ball at the end of the bed. I started unpacking, transferring
my clothes from my suitcase to the old oak chest and topping the
bathroom counter with my essentials. When I finished unpacking,
I removed my journal from my personal carry-on and lowered
myself to the bed. Lying on my stomach, I rested my bare feet on
the pillow, and faced Spike. I scratched him under the chin and
got his motor running, and then I opened my journal, finding the
next blank page. I decided to write a letter to Rob, remembering
Mrs. Rivers's advice after Carly left our circle of friends. She
told us to write a letter, one we would never send, and in the
waning hours of a very long week, I wrote this:

189

Dear Rob,

You taught me the meaning of love, and for years, you spoke it to my heart, not with words, but with every action as my friend. And I cannot recall a time in my life when I didn't love you, since I cannot remember my life before you, nor can I remember when I didn't feel an affectionate warmth in your presence. I loved you like a brother, yet secretly desired you in ways that I never allowed myself to feel. For so long, I denied my feelings for you, since I could not understand them; but I know now that I always had a love for you, and no matter what, I always will.

Yet I wonder if we will ever find our way back to those hopeful days, and perhaps, that is why I had to leave. I wanted to give us a chance.

I know you, your heart, and your immense goodness. You would have done the right thing and stayed by my side regardless, patiently waiting for the healing process and waiting for the time when you could love me with the unyielding passion of a lover and not distantly like a defiled friend. You would wait, and I love you for your patience, but I also love you too much to watch you go through the days with me. I don't know how long this will take, since I do not know the future—just the past.

So please forgive me, for all I have said, and for all I have done, and though it may not seem like it right now, I did this because I love you.

Always,
Chloe

I closed my journal and cried, wasting the final hours of the afternoon with more tears, and after dinner with Grandma, I retreated back to my room. I turned on my cell phone for the first time since the flight attendant instructed, "Turn off all cellular phones and electronic devices." I scanned the call log. It showed five missed calls, but before I reached the end of the list, my phone rang.

"Hello," I answered.

"Hey, I've been trying to reach you all afternoon."

"Sorry," I mumbled.

"Uh, listen, when we got back from the ride this morning, Mom was just pulling up the driveway. Rob asked her where she had been, and well, you can imagine the rest of the conversation…"

"What did she say?"

"I don't think she knew what to say, Chloe." Brad got quiet for a moment before he asked, "So, what happened with you and Rob?"

"I don't want to talk about it." Or think about it. I had envisioned the moment when Rob found out about my trip, and as much as I didn't want to hurt him, I had to leave without telling him. It was the only way.

"Yeah, well, I think I can put two and two together."

I changed the subject. "Is Mom mad at me?"

"For what? Lying to her?" He paused. "I don't know, but she should be used to it by now."

"Thanks a lot, Brad."

"Anyway, Mom wants to know when you're coming home."

"Uh, next Saturday," I answered, but I never made my return flight. I never went to the airport. I never packed my suitcase. I just decided to stay with my grandmother for a while longer.

In the days that followed, Rob never wrote me—or even called. And I knew he had every right to be upset with me, and I had every intention of picking up a pen or a phone, but unfortunately, it just seemed easier to avoid him, to avoid everything.

I barely spoke to anyone, and Brad acted like a liaison for my mother, who acted passive aggressively and barely spoke to me. My father, on the other hand, called me every Wednesday night, since "Call Chloe" remained a repeat event on his phone's calendar.

191

As for my friends, Caitlyn called me once from Hilton Head, and Callie phoned a few times from basketball camp, but they both jabbered on about their lives, interjecting only an occasional inquiry into mine. I revealed nothing to either of them, and eventually, Courtney sent me a text—*btw i took his side.*

At first, I felt lonely, but that feeling only forced me to create a new life for myself. In a place where I had spent one week every summer, I reinvented myself like the new student at school, and since no one knew my past, I could pretend it never happened. I spent the days going on long runs through the hilly countryside, chatting with my grandmother on the front porch, or visiting with summer acquaintances. But at night, I often retreated to my room, finding solace in my reading and writing.

I was healing, slowly, and I started to feel something strange inside me: a slight twinge of happiness. I was in no rush to return home, and I talked to neighboring kids about their high school, wondering if my parents would let me complete my senior year under the tutelage of my grandmother.

Some days, I would drive my grandmother's silver Cadillac into town by myself, and one morning, I entered the corner drugstore and switched the Claddagh ring to my left hand, just in case the cashier cared about my marital status. I purchased a two-pack of pregnancy tests, since I had missed my last period, which for most girls would be a tell-tale sign. But I ran on a runner's cycle, and when I trained heavily, logging an excess of thirty miles a week, I didn't have a period at all.

I slipped the box into my purse and crossed the parking lot to the McDonalds. It was a quiet Thursday morning crowd. A few moms ate with their children in the play place, and a group of elderly men sat in the back corner by the bathrooms. They dressed in similar fashion with overalls and dungarees, and while they chatted, they sipped on their coffees slowly. Most wore ball caps, pledging allegiance to a Kentucky team or their favorite farm equipment, and they filled the back corner like a group of regulars.

"Morning, Miss," a few said as I passed by them.

"Good morning," I returned with a slight smile.

"Wait, aren't you Mark Preston's daughter?" It was still a pretty small town.

"Why, it sure is! She looks just like a young Emmy Sue." That was my grandmother. She was quite pretty in her younger years and had been crowned the queen of one of those fruit or vegetable festivals in town.

"You got a boyfriend back home?" asked another.

"Oh, she's a bit young for you, Homer."

"Shoot, George. I got me so many grandsons. She could have her pick of the litter."

I smiled, finding the whole group pretty amusing. I liked the way they talked. Like Grandpa Preston did. And had I not been in a rush to get to the bathroom, I might have pulled up a chair, so to speak. But that would have been a Herculean feat since the McDonalds organization believes in bolted-down furnishings, which I assumed was a preventative measure against theft or a more heinous crime—reconfiguring the dining area.

"Take a look at her hand, boys." The lone supporter of the Louisville team stood up. "You see, I still remember to look at a young lady's hand before I ask that question." He glanced down at my left hand. "Engaged or married?"

I blushed and moved the ring back to its rightful place. "Neither, but it's from my boyfriend. His name's Rob, and he's going to Georgetown next year."

"Well, that's a fine school." His accolades were meant for Georgetown College in Kentucky.

"The one in Washington D.C.," I said apologetically.

"Well, I'm sure he's nice boy anyway." He shrugged. "Listen, Miss Preston, you say hello to your grandma for me." He gave me a little wink. "My name's Willis. First name, Douglas." He lifted his hat off his head, revealing a surprisingly full head of silvery hair.

"Nice to meet you, Mr. Willis." I shook his hand.

"Likewise." He pumped my hand and examined me for a moment. "You sure do look a lot like your grandma, and it seems to me you have her same sweet disposition too." My grandma

193

was a real fine Southern lady, but I never imagined anyone comparing me to her. I always thought I took after the Preston men: bull-headed and outspoken.

"Thanks," I said quietly and headed into the bathroom. I sat down on the toilet seat and opened the box of tests. I pulled out the directions. There were several diagrams on the front and a lengthy Q & A section on the back. But really, how many different ways could the pamphlet authors say, "Pee on the end of a stick"?

Still, I read each word carefully, and with trembling fingers and a swirling sickness in my stomach, I unwrapped the testing stick. I followed the steps verbatim, recapped the test, and set it on the silver box next to the toilet. I glanced at my watch and rested my forehead on folded hands.

Dear God, I started with tears. *I don't pray enough, and I ask for too much when I do, but I don't want this.*

I wiped the tears with the back of my hand, and then I looked at the ring. I thought back to what Rob said about having children—even though it was a taboo subject at sixteen—and he said seven. He created names similar to the seven dwarfs, and according to him, I was going to be the mother of Whiney, Weepy, Stinky, Fluffy, Snotty, Scruffy, and Wesley.

"Wesley," I repeated with a knowing smile.

He nodded. "Yeah, and we could call him Wes for short."

Meanwhile, I kept turning the ring with my thumb, and periodically, I glimpsed at my watch. I still had another minute left, and it took willpower I didn't have to keep from looking at the test. So I watched the lethargic second hand sweep around in a circle. It was like waiting for the minutes to elapse from pre-calc class.

Finally, time was up.

I picked up the test. Luckily, I bought one with words rather than with lines or colors, not thinking an unwanted pregnancy was the best time to be deciphering a code that would change my life. The test read: *Not Pregnant.* I wrapped it in toilet paper and tossed it in the trash.

I repeated the test. The second one revealed the same result. Satisfied, I left the stall of the bathroom, slipped through an empty back corner of the restaurant, and drove across town to my grandmother's house. She lived in a white two-story house with a wrap-around porch, and in the front yard, there was a small pond, which my grandpa stocked for recreational fishing. As I came up the drive, I spied her on the front porch, watering her hanging plants, and as I walked up the steps, I heard her humming a familiar tune.

"What is that song, Grandma?" I asked as I neared her side.

"Oh, your grandpa wrote it for me a long, long time ago. He could be a real Romeo, you know?"

"Yeah, I know." I smiled at the memory of my grandparents holding hands into their seventies. In the evenings, they would take walks along the side of the road or swing on the porch swing, and their hands would be fused together in a bond as strong as their love.

"So," I started. "I ran into Mr. Willis at *the* McDonalds." It was a small town, and unlike Riverside where every chain had to be identified by a cross section, there was only one of everything here.

"Yeah," she said, getting a little schoolgirl grin on her face. "He comes by here every now and then. He likes to check in on me."

"He seems real nice," I said, noticing I used "real" a lot more often when I visited her. "And I think he really likes you, Grandma."

She waved her hand dismissingly. "Oh, he's just a big, old flirt."

"Well, at least he's a big, old flirt with hair and teeth," I clarified as I sat down on the swing.

She took the seat next to me. "I tell you what, young lady!"

"C'mon, Grandma." I gave her a gentle nudge. "Do you *like* him?"

"Oh, heaven's no, Chloe!" Her gaze drifted off into the distance, and then she answered quietly. "After all, I still have your grandfather."

195

"But he's gone, Grandma. And it's been almost four years."

"Yes, dear, but his memory still keeps me good company." I thought about Rob and how I took him to bed with me at night, holding onto his memory like nothing had ever changed. I looked at my ring and sighed.

My grandmother's eyes followed mine. "Why don't you tell me about him?"

"You've met him many times."

"Yes, when he was your friend, but tell me about him as your boyfriend."

"It's not much different. We just make out, that's all."

She cracked a smile. "Does he write you poetry? Sing you songs? Does he make you laugh?"

I answered her quickly, "No. No. And only sometimes."

She rested a hand on my knee. "Listen, dear, I can't help but notice that he hasn't bothered to call or write. Do you want to talk about what happened?"

"No, Grandma." My voice cracked. "I really don't."

"Fine, fine. We have lots of corn that needs shucking, and we'll get it done faster if you're not jabbering on about your love life anyway."

Then we moved to the front steps, peeling off the fresh corn husks and dropping the remnants into a paper bag. Grandma believed in cooking in bulk, freezing or canning summer's bountiful harvest in preparation for the winter, I suppose.

Occasionally, we'd glance up at the kids passing on bikes and wave. A few neighbors would stop on the porch and ask how my family was doing, since my father was the local celebrity and the townsfolk were proud of him. Whether or not they ever read his books never seemed to matter; they just liked having their own success story in town.

"Well, I'm heading into the kitchen," Grandma announced with a smile and a stock pot full of fresh corn.

"Need any help?"

She shook her head. "Did you pack that journal I sent you?"

I nodded.

"Well, I was thinking," she said, resting the pot on her hip. "If you can't talk about what's going on inside that head of yours, then maybe you can write about it." It sounded like one of the phrases she used on her own children, seeing how my dad makes a good living from expressing his thoughts on a page. And like a good little girl, I headed up the stairs to the bedroom and grabbed my journal.

I returned to the front porch and found a spot on the swing. I watched the sun dip behind the rolling hills and noticed how the soft illuminations turned the small pond into a sheet of glass. Light could change the way things appeared, and with a sigh, I remembered the morning on the beach when the sun transformed Rob's eyes into a warm auburn hue. I turned to a blank page and jotted down these words:

AUBURN EYES

A rush of words poured out of my heart and filled my head, and I knew I might never feel the same inspiration again in my entire life, but as a writer, I would always remember my first time, the first time the words flowed effortlessly onto a page, and how those words consumed me and time held no importance. I was in a world without minutes, and when the porch light went on, I brought my legs up to my chest and rested my journal on a knee. I couldn't keep up with the words in my head, and the feeling inside my heart was invigorating. It was like a runner's high, and I had reached the covetous plateau where my pen scrawled effortlessly across the blank lines of the page. And when I emptied the last words from my head, I heaved a sigh of satisfaction and closed the journal.

Then I got up, opened the screen door of the house, and walked into the kitchen.

"Grandma?"

"Yes, dear?" she asked as she sliced cooked corn off the cob.

"I'm ready to go home now."

197

-30-

Homecoming

My mother pulled into the arrival side of the Orlando International Airport. My flight arrived shortly after seven o'clock on Friday evening, making it almost three weeks since I had left home, and as I neared the Civic, she popped the trunk. I lowered my suitcase full of clean clothes into it. Grandma had spent the morning doing my wash, saying she didn't want to send me home with a bunch of dirty clothes.

"Hi, Mom," I said quietly as I opened the passenger door.

She offered me a slight smile. "Did you have a nice visit with your grandmother?"

"Yes, it was nice." I glanced in the back seat. "Where's Brad?"

"He went to the movies with Lisa."

"Who's Lisa?"

"I think she's his girlfriend."

"Oh," I paused. "Anyone I know?"

She shook her head. "Probably not."

"When's Dad coming home?"

"Wednesday, I think."

"Anything new with you?"

"Nope."

We had reached the end of our conversation; my mother leaned over and clicked on the radio, and I pulled a book out of my bag. But as I stared at Steinbeck's *Cannery Row,* I only saw Rob.

*   *   *

Once home, I hauled my suitcase up the stairs and unpacked my makeup bag. Quickly, I freshened up in the bathroom and bolted down the stairs, finding my mom in the family room. She had her feet up on the coffee table and was flipping through a magazine.

"I'm going out for a walk," I informed.

"It's a little late, don't you think?"

"I don't know, Mom." I took a deep breath and headed toward the French door.

With my hand on the brass handle, she uttered, "Why don't you wait until the morning?"

"Because it's been three weeks."

"I don't expect you to start talking to me now, Chloe, but what you did to him was inexcusable and don't think for a moment that I have enjoyed the imposition that you have placed on our entire family."

"You're right, Mom. I'm not going to talk to you." I shut the door behind me and ran into the woods. The light from the Callahan's back porch lit the path, and I started to feel giddy, imagining our reunion. It was going to be like at the end of a movie or a book. He'd see me and start running in my direction, and all would be forgiven. He wouldn't ask any questions; he would just hold me tightly.

As I walked along the path, I spied the tree house in the boughs of the old oak, but as I neared his house, I heard voices. I stopped at the edge of the woods and peered around the tree, recognizing the faces of each person sitting on the patio. Tom was next to Rob at the table. Jessica was standing next to her prom date. And then I saw Kendra. I heard her distinctive laugh, and I felt like she was laughing at me. *Stupid Chloe,* I could almost hear her say, but I turned away before I saw or heard anything else. I felt sick all over, and I bolted through the woods and down to the river, finding a seat on the fallen log. It was where he had given me the ring, and now I twisted the ring with my thumb as the chills ran down my arms and legs. My face dropped into the palms of my hands, and I cried.

After a few minutes, I cut back through the woods and edged up to my house. Looking in the window, I found my mother in her room. She was leaning against a pile of pillows and reading. Then I crossed my backyard and entered the family room as quietly as possible. I didn't want to talk to her, to anyone, since I completely regretted my decision to come home.

I headed up the stairs, never turning on the lights and collapsed onto my bed. "I hate my life," I murmured into my pillow, and for the first time ever, I contemplated ending it, mostly because I had the words to a letter floating in my head.

-31-

Routines

The morning sun shone brightly through the blinds in my bedroom. I rolled out of bed, gathered my hair into a pony tail, and grabbed a running outfit from my suitcase. I put on a sky blue pair of shorts and white tank, which I had worn countless times while in Kentucky.

I stepped into the garage, noticed my brother's missing bike, and grabbed a bottle of water from the fridge. Then I bolted down the driveway without saying a word to my mother. She was gardening, which was her typical Saturday morning routine, and I was about to do mine.

I jogged to the front of the neighborhood, and Clyde leaned out of the gatehouse. "Welcome home, Miss Preston. We sure missed you." I wanted to say, *Yeah, you're the only one*, but instead I issued a standard thanks and crossed the street. I entered the trail, which was less popular in the scorching hot summer months, and joined the other die-hards who were maintaining their strict training regimens.

I had decided to train for a marathon, and after running every day for the last few weeks, I was running a 10K at a sub-seven mile pace. As I ran the familiar course, I kept peering at my GPS watch, noting my time with a certain satisfaction. I concentrated on my breathing, and as I reached the best part of the course, the canopied trees, I pushed myself, dropping into the mid-sixes. I could feel the burn on the top of my thighs as I neared the loop, the coveted halfway mark. I glanced at my watch again and calculated my finish time, hoping I could maintain the pace on the second half of the course.

But when I glanced up at the course in front of me, I saw someone sitting alone on the park bench. My heart lurched as he stood up and grinned. It was him. He had on a sleeveless Riverside Football T-shirt and a pair of bright orange running shoes.

I froze for a moment, and then pivoted around, bolting at top speed down the course. I didn't look back. I knew the course would come out of the woods again and run alongside the road. My heart pounded in my chest, and my throat tightened. With the adrenaline rushing through me, I sprinted along the trail, pumping my arms and keeping my eyes on the road ahead of me. I heard the words of my coach: "Keep your eyes on the finish line, and never *ever* look back!"

But just like in a race, where I could always feel a runner gaining on me, I could sense him getting closer and closer. I could hear the distinctive rhythm of his run—his slapping footsteps and his short pants—growing louder and louder as he sidled up next to me.

"I caught you," he teased.

But I can outrun you! I answered in my head and pumped my arms. And together, we whipped around corners, keeping pace like old running chums. But I knew the road ahead; I knew the constant curves would come to an end as the path emerged from the woods and ran parallel to the main road again. I concentrated on the trail ahead of me, and as we veered around the last turn, the road straightened into an open stretch, a beautiful sight at the end of any race, yet disheartening now since the course was completely open, completely empty, and not another person shared the trail with us.

Then he grabbed my upper arm and flung me toward the side of the trail, where the grassy easement rolled toward the trees. I scampered forward on all fours, but he tackled me from behind, his arms around my waist. I kicked my legs frantically, but he pressed down on top of me, flattening me to the ground. He crooned in my ear, "Yeah, you like it rough. Don't you, baby?"

I screamed, but he covered my mouth quickly with his sweaty palm.

"Shush," he hissed in my ear. It was hard to breathe. Tears spilled from my eyes as that night flashed in my head. Even though I didn't have concrete memories from the whole night, I had those vivid speculations that had manifested into a painful reality.

He kept his hand on my mouth, and I squeezed my eyes shut, pushing out more tears.

"Ooh," he moaned. "You want it bad." His tongue encircled my ear, and all I did was cry. I didn't fight back even though I could this time; instead, I lay there like I was dead because so much of me was already gone.

His hand left my mouth, and I gasped for air. He lifted me off the ground, cradling me in his arms. He started walking, and I watched the woods advance toward me. A feeling crept up in me, a will to fight, and I screamed—this time much louder than the first.

He admonished me in a low, gravelly voice, "You shouldn't have done that!" He pressed me tightly against his chest and proceeded quickly down the grassy easement and toward the trees. I kept screaming and started wriggling my way out of his arms.

"Wait!" my brother yelled. "Stop! Wait! Chloe, is that you?"

Austin turned slowly but was quick with an explanation. "Hey man. Your sister fell, and I was just helping her up." He kept me in his arms while my brother and Mr. Dixon advanced toward us, leaving the rest of the riders on the side of the road.

Being a detective, Mr. Dixon took the inquisitive role. "Chloe, is that what really happened?"

I said nothing, keeping my eyes on the ground, since I knew very well who else was there. I didn't have to look up to see him; I could just feel his eyes on me.

Mr. Dixon continued his investigation. "Why were you screaming?"

Austin spoke on my behalf. "Aw, she was just screaming for help. She twisted her ankle real bad, and I was gonna' carry her all the way home."

My brother tossed a skeptical glance. "Through the woods?"

"Yeah, I guess I forgot where you lived."

My brother rested his bike in the grass. "Just put her down."

Austin lowered me to the ground, and I walked over to my brother's side. "Aw, look, you're all better now. It must have been all those kisses I gave you."

"Hey! Don't go near my sister again!"

Austin stepped toward my brother. "Don't talk to me that way, Preston, or I'll make practices a living hell for you."

Mr. Dixon intervened, "I need to speak with you. Alone."

"About?"

"About what just happened?"

"I already told you what happened," Austin returned nonchalantly.

"But I don't believe you."

"Well, that's too bad." Austin started walking away. I lifted my eyes slightly, watching the bright orange shoes head up to the trail, and then they paused in front of a yellow bike. "What? After all these years, you don't have anything to say to me, Callahan? Well, maybe you shouldn't have let her out of your sight." Austin's voice paused, and then with a low snicker, he added, "Again."

A yellow bike fell to the road, but before anything else happened, I just turned and sprinted toward my house. I don't remember much about the run home, but when I reached my bedroom, I kicked off my shoes and climbed into bed fully dressed. I cried continuously. The tears soaked my pillow, and my sweaty body stuck to the sheets, but I didn't really care. My brother had been there, and soon my father and mother would find out too.

*   *   *

204

Later that night, my father entered my room and sat on the edge of my bed. I was cocooned under my covers, and my face remained in my pillow. My father's hand rested gently on my back. "I just got home, Chloe."

I said nothing, swallowing back the impulse to cry.

"I'm so sorry," he offered.

"S' okay," I managed.

"Maybe this wouldn't have happened if I had been around more. Your mother doesn't always—" His voice broke off before the full accusation left his lips. He exhaled loudly, his hand circling my back. "Anyway, Mr. Dixon will be over tomorrow to ask you some questions."

"Great," I muttered.

My father's voice was softer now. "It'll be okay, Chloe. Just try to get some rest." He rose from my bed. "I love you, Sweetheart. You know that, right?"

"Yeah, I know," I said, wondering if he would still love me if he knew the whole story.

-32-

The Ending

The following afternoon Mr. Dixon showed up at my house. The four of us congregated in the living room: my parents sat on either side of me on the couch, and Mr. Dixon took a wing chair across from us. He leaned forward, resuming the detective role. "I already took a statement from Austin, and now, I need one from you."

I shrugged. "I'm sure he told you everything."

"Not really." He paused. "Why was he taking you *into* the woods?"

"I don't know."

He fired another question at me. "Why were you screaming?"

"I was hurt."

"And then the pain miraculously went away?"

"Yeah, I guess so."

"Why are you covering for him?"

"I'm not."

"What are you afraid of, Chloe?"

"Nothing," I returned emphatically.

"Then why won't you tell me what happened?"

"I did." I looked up at my father. "Can I go now...*please*?"

"No, sweetheart," my father returned with a few successive pats on my thigh, but I wanted to push off the seat and escape from the room. I wanted to run out the front door and never look back.

"Listen, Chloe." Mr. Dixon rested on his elbows. "I spoke with Rob yesterday because I know you two were…" I hated hearing about us in the past tense, and my eyes welled quickly with tears. I brushed them with the back of my hand as Mr. Dixon continued, "And he would be willing to make a statement on your behalf, but he wanted me to talk to you first…to give you a chance to tell your side of the story."

I sniffed audibly, wishing I had never told Rob anything. How hard would it have been to pretend it didn't happen? Now, I had lost everything, since I had told the truth. Rob never cared about how the truth would affect me; he just cared about upholding his principles. And at that moment, I felt a sharp pang, just thinking how he loved integrity more than he loved me, and how he would still be revered in my parents' eyes. Anger rose up in me, and I felt such a strong hatred for him. And I wondered how it all turned out this way.

"Okay, fine," I started, the anger coaxing me to continue. "It all started on that Saturday when everyone went on the bike trip, and I went over to Courtney's house—"

"Wow, you mean you were actually where you said you were," my mother interjected, but my father snapped back, "Oh, just let her talk, Liz."

"So anyway, I was over at Courtney's when Austin showed up." The night played in my head as I spoke, "At first, we were all just hanging out, talking and stuff, but then I started to feel really tired and…" I looked down, losing momentum.

Mr. Dixon spoke next. "Were you drinking?"

"No, I just had one," I defended. "That's all."

My mother heaved a sigh of disappointment.

"What happened next?" Mr. Dixon prompted.

I copped out. "I don't remember."

"And why not?"

I couldn't come up with a good lie. "Because I just don't." I dropped my face into my hands, frustrated.

"But Rob knows, right?"

"No," I said angrily, wishing he didn't keep playing the

"Rob" card. "He doesn't know everything." The only person who knew everything was Austin, but he was the last person who would ever tell it.

"Okay," my mother wondered. "What *exactly* happened that night? And what does this have to do with yesterday…on the trail?"

No one answered her, exactly. I offered more tears, and Mr. Dixon sat back in his chair like he already knew the rest of the story. It was on his face, and he wore a look of compassion as his eyes traveled from my mother and then back to me. Maybe it was his detective nature that enabled him to complete a puzzle with so many missing pieces. Or maybe my story wasn't any different from other victims, since rape was something so horrible, so humiliating, that a girl would hide it from everyone. The only person she would tell was her boyfriend, since his touch, no matter how gentle and loving, would catapult her back to that exact moment. Yet, when she told him, it would probably rip them apart, and no matter how hard they tried, they might never get past it.

"Chloe," Mr. Dixon addressed with a gentle voice. "I think I know what happened that night, and I also know what would have happened on the trail had we not shown up. But do you think you can tell your parents now?"

"No," I said softly, staring at my folded hands.

My father hung an arm around my shoulders, and my mother uttered two of the greatest clichés in parental history. "You know you can tell us anything, and we'll still love you no matter what."

But I knew my parents would look at me differently, treat me differently, as soon as I told them the truth. I was holding on to their untarnished view of me for as long as possible since I didn't want to disappoint them.

Then my father drew me into his chest. I could smell his cologne and feel the softness of his T-shirt against my face. At first, he said nothing. He just took a few deep breaths, each inhale and exhale so deep and rhythmic it rocked me back and forth, and then he squeezed me tightly. "This whole time I kept hoping—no, praying—for another answer, but I know what he did to you." My father sniffed back the tears. "He had his way with you, didn't he?" I nodded meekly. It was easier to tell the truth from inside my father's arms.

I heard my mother's gasp, and it was all out in the open. As the truth filled the room, I did not feel relieved; instead, I felt cold, frightfully cold, like a person experiencing the chills of death. It was suffocating, actually, and then I closed my eyes, picturing myself running through the woods behind my house and leaping across the river. I kept going, running faster and faster, creating a path to a safe unknown.

*   *   *

Eventually, I escaped, only making it as far as my bedroom. I walked over to my bookshelf and glanced at my team photos and my red varsity letter adorned with golden pins. I felt like Ebenezer Scrooge from *The Christmas Carol*, glimpsing at life's artifacts from inside a foggy dream. I picked up a picture from prom night, the one where the girls and I lined up on the bridge in my backyard, and I realized that I was never going back to Riverside. It didn't matter if Austin went to another school because I didn't want to be known as *that* girl. I thought back to the morning when I locked my keys in the car or the day when Austin spread those lies about me, and at the time, I thought nothing could be worse. But this was much worse, because everyone would find out what happened, and it would be a long time before anyone would forget.

Shortly, a knock came at the door. "I brought you something to eat," my mother said as she entered with a plate of pasta salad and tall glass of ice water. She placed the food on my desk, and I offered a listless thanks.

She took a seat on my bed, patting the spot next to her. "I was hoping we could talk."

"I'm fine, Mom," I said, still standing.

She continued, "I know we're not that close anymore, and you tend to confide in your father more than you do in me. But I wanted you to know that—as a woman—I understand how you feel."

"How could you possibly know how I feel!" I contradicted, and then I let out the words that I had kept inside for weeks. "I feel dirty. And ruined. Because I was saving myself for marriage, and he took that away from me. You could *never* understand what I'm going through, Mom, so don't come in here and think you can talk to me and make it all better."

I expected her to leave; but instead, she remained. "Then I won't talk. I'll just listen."

"You really want to hear this, Mom?" I questioned as I sat next to her. "Most of the time, I feel angry because I lost everything, and I can never ever have it back. I made a choice—one that few girls make, but in the end, it really doesn't matter."

"Yes, it does," my mother said genuinely, "because you're still pure in God's eyes." She reached over and held my hand. "And it matters to Him."

Her words lifted some of "the yuck" from inside me, and she gathered me into a hug. I remained in my mother's arm for longer than I could remember. Neither one of us pulled back as the tears slipped from my eyes.

"Oh, hi," my mother said abruptly. I expected to hear the voice of my father next.

"Uh, hello, Mrs. Preston," he returned, and I held on tighter. I wasn't prepared to face him. I was riding an emotional rollercoaster, climbing with anger and falling with tears. "May I talk with Chloe?" he asked tenaciously.

"Sure," my mother said, rising slowly. I reached for a pillow, hugging it for comfort. "Can I get you something to eat or drink?"

"No, thanks. I just had dinner."

"Well, I should get going," my mother returned, her voice travelling across the room "I have a sink full of dishes waiting for me."

"Okay, see you later," he said to my mother, and then he took her spot on the bed. "You should try to eat something."

I obliged quickly, getting up and chucking my pillow across the room. I sat down at my desk and pushed pasta around the plate like a defiant two-year-old. "What do you want, Rob?" I asked coldly.

"I just wanted to see how things went earlier."

"It went great. It was the highlight of my life."

"Don't act this way."

"What way?"

"Like a—" He censored himself.

I turned toward him, looking at him for the first time in weeks, and I wish it didn't hurt so much to see his face. "Like a what, Rob?"

"Listen, I didn't come here to fight with you."

"Then maybe you should just leave," I suggested.

He sounded hurt. "I thought we promised to be friends."

I held up my hand, the one with the ring on it. "Yeah, well, we made lots of promises that we'll never keep." I pulled at the ring, but I couldn't get it past my knuckle. The damn Florida humidity made my fingers swell to epic proportions, so I eyed the ice water and dunked my fingers into the glass. Quickly, he was at my side; his hand grabbed my wrist, and he yanked my fingers out of the icy water.

"You left me!" he pelted.

"You made it worse!"

He found a spot against the wall by my desk and folded his arms across his chest. "I wanted to help you. I just didn't know what to do."

I pushed out a deep breath, trying to avoid an all-out emotional explosion. I wanted to scream at the top of my lungs, yell so loud that my throat would burn afterward; but instead, I spoke calmly. "Just forget about it...forget about everything."

"Everything, huh?" His voice faltered, and I watched him swipe a tear with the back of his hand. "So we're just nothing now?"

"Yeah, I guess so." I said, without crying. I left all my tears for him down at the river.

211

"This is *your* decision, Chloe."

I was flabbergasted; the thought of him with Kendra fueled my next response. "Me? You made *that* decision."

"What's that suppose to mean?"

"Don't play games with me, Rob?"

"Games?" he repeated. "You went to Kentucky without even telling me."

"I had my reasons," I said plainly.

"Yeah, and hurting me must have been one of them!" He left his post at the wall and started pacing around my room.

My eyes followed him, back and forth. "Well, you didn't look like you were hurting last night...at your little pool party."

"Last night? Why? What was I doing? Trying to act normal?" He paused. "When you left, I was stuck here. And I got questions from everyone. My mom would sit on the edge of my bed and ask me what happened, and even Riley looked at me like maybe *I* had done something wrong. Everyone thought you left because of *me*. Did you ever think about that? And I tried to be there for you, but I didn't know what to say, and I still wonder if I'll ever say the right thing to you again."

"Listen, I saw her," I blurted out.

"Who?"

"Kendra."

"Yeah, so?"

"You went back to her, didn't you?"

"No, of course not!" he exclaimed ardently. "Tom and Katie broke up a week ago, and Kendra and Tom are both going to school in Boston. *He* brought her."

"Oh," I murmured, and the world spun around so I could view it from a different perspective.

After a moment, he asked, "Why? Were you coming to see me last night?"

"Yeah." I bit down on my lip. "I just wanted to say hi."

"Hi," he said softly. "So, did you run up at your grandmother's house?"

"Yeah, it's what I do when I'm upset."

212

"I know," he said gently and crossed my room. He tilted my blinds and looked into my backyard. "It turned out to be a nice day. Your dad's outside skimming the leaves off the top of the pool, and you can tell Brad is giving him a hard time about something."

I answered his musings. "Yeah, probably about the fact that we don't have a screened-in pool, because if we did, then no one would have to skim off the ever-present layer of leaves."

"That's because you know the two of them so well." He sat down on the window seat. "But do you ever watch two strangers and try to guess what they're saying?"

"You mean, read their body language and facial expressions?"

He nodded, and as we talked, it started to feel easier, less strained. I wanted him to stay, so I got up and crossed the room slowly. I sat down across from him on the bench, but when our eyes met, they soon traveled elsewhere in the room.

"What would people say about us...if they saw us right now?" he asked.

"That we're friends...probably."

"And what would we be discussing?"

"Books," I paused, lifting my eyes up to his chest, reading Georgetown on his light grey T-shirt, and then I stared at my hands. "By the way, I'll probably finish Steinbeck's literary career by the end of the summer."

"Really?" he returned.

I nodded.

"Any recommendations?"

I got up, removing two books from the shelf, and handed them to him. We chatted about books for a while, and then the conversation turned toward running and biking. We discussed our separate training regimens: he wanted to complete a half-Ironman in the fall, and I told him I was training for a marathon. We discussed music and movies, but when we reached a lull in the conversation, he glanced at the clock. "It's getting late. I should probably get going."

I nodded, and he stood up, placing a tentative kiss on my forehead. It was soft and warm, and somewhat familiar. It brought me back to a night in late April. It was the night I asked him to prom and the night I told him why we had never kissed. It was a lifetime ago when I was a different girl, and I knew then that the kiss belonged in my past, and those feelings were gone, completely lost with my innocence.

"Rob?"

He stood in my doorway. "Yeah?"

"I'm sorry about everything."

"Yeah, me too, Chlo. Me too."

After he left, I crossed the room and turned off the lights, returning to the window seat where we had talked for hours. The back porch light cast a dim glow around the pool area, and I watched him walk into view. He did not glance up at my window. He did not offer a wave or a smile. But still, my finger travelled across the warm glass, following him into the encroaching darkness.

-33-

A New Beginning

The case against Austin Walker consumed most of my summer, but by the end of it, he was charged with physical assault with the intent to do harm for what happened on the trail. The rape, however, was just his word against mine, and since there was no evidence to link him to the crime, he got away with it. Well, sort of. He ended up going back to Texas, taking Riverside's chance of a repeat state championship with him.

As for me, I decided against returning to Riverside. I needed a fresh start—a genuine tabula rasa, and I transferred to Central High where Cynthia Westwood's father was the principal. At least, there I'd have one friend, and one "C" was better than none.

With days separating summer from the start of another school year, I spent my evenings on the back porch with a book and a journal on my lap. My father usually slipped out with me, milling around the backyard. He had cancelled his speaking engagements and was using his time off to complete my mother's honey-do list. My mother cut back on her hours at the library, and Brad hung around the house most evenings—and even his girlfriend Lisa joined us for family fun nights.

A puzzle had taken up permanent residence on the dining room table, since we were still sorting the infinite shades of blue that made up the sky. Some nights we opted for Monopoly; other times it was Scrabble. For years, the puzzles and games had been neatly stacked in the closet, collecting dust, but now, our family was on constant game-night mode.

My friends came back into my life slowly. Callie was first, since of the three of them, she was the most removed from the situation. Caitlyn felt exceedingly guilty, since if it weren't for her, then Austin wouldn't have been there in the first place. Then there was Courtney, whose house would always remind me of that night.

But in the end, Courtney was the most dedicated to me, visiting me every day, and as I started reading Steinbeck's *The Winter of Our Discontent*, I heard the familiar squeak of the gate's hinges. I lifted my head and smiled as Courtney took the seat next to me on the wicker bench. "I head back to the beach in the morning."

I nodded and forced up a corner of my mouth.

Her voice grew softer, like when we were telling secrets in the back of the classroom. "Are you going to be okay without me?"

"Yeah," I said quietly, knowing Courtney had helped me through some rough moments. I thought back to a few weeks ago when she removed a duct-taped shoebox from my closet and toted it through the woods. She lit a fervent blaze in her fireplace. And on a hot July night, we offered my painful past to the zealous fire. Then she sat beside me on the couch, and together, we watched the cackling blaze lick at the shoebox, eating away at the vile memories, until all that remained of my past were a pile of feathery ashes.

She put her hand on top of mine. "I'll call you every day."

"I know." I lifted my eyes and found hers. "You've been a great friend."

"You would have done the same for me." I nodded, and she continued, "And I think you should come to the beach this week. It would be really good for you."

"I'll think about it," I returned as my father sat down in a chair on my left. "Phew, I'm beat," he said, wiping his brow.

216

"Why don't you hire a pool guy, Mr. Preston?"

My father gave his standard response: "Because it costs money."

I rolled my eyes and noticed a broad oak leaf floating toward the pool, then another, and another. There was a warm breeze, and my eyes watched the dance of more falling leaves like they were the fireworks on the Fourth of July. I did not ooh. I did not ah. Instead, I smiled inwardly at the senselessness of my father's nightly chore. It was like making a bed that would be unmade later that night or polishing silver that would only tarnish over time.

Now, my life was like a list of chores, and each day was essentially the same; consequently, my parents knew my exact whereabouts at all times. Every morning, I went for a run, but never alone and never along the trail; instead, I took a left, weaving safely through my neighborhood, and sometimes, if I had the energy, into the next. In the afternoon, someone would lure me from the house with a movie, or a trip to the mall, or a stroll through a museum. The goal was always the same: to keep me busy. And each night, I returned home to the same end; following dinner and family time, I retreated to the porch, trying to waste the last few hours before bedtime.

As I sat on the porch, I sighed at the approaching night, knowing that my unpleasant past would seek me in my sleep, and in the background, beyond my thoughts, I heard my father's low chuckle and Courtney's soft giggle. Soon, my friend would leave for an evening of frivolous possibilities, and my father would retreat to his office to work on his latest manuscript. And I would remain, all alone, with only the written word to keep me company.

Then out of the corner of my eye, I noticed him coming through the woods. I had seen him less than a dozen times in the last month: every Sunday at church, a neighborhood barbecue, two trips to the movies with Courtney, a chance meeting at the mall, and a few visits on the back porch.

He opened the gate, and my eyes remained on him. His tight-fitting T-shirt evidenced a summer of fervent exercise. His

217

shoulders seemed broader, and his arms seemed stronger; his body was much different from when it last held me. I thought back to our final goodbye, that last hug before the bike trip, but sadly, I couldn't recall how it felt to be in his arms anymore; I could only remember how awful it was to be with Austin.

Slowly, he entered my backyard, and I noticed his walk, confident and fluid, completely unchanged. He received an immediate hello from my father, and Courtney rose to her feet and hugged him like he had been off at college for months. I lifted my eyes slowly and tried to smile. Yet my greeting went unnoticed, and I dropped my eyes to my lap, where my book and journal waited patiently for me.

He took the vacant chair on Courtney's right and then leaned forward, placing *Cannery Row* on the table. My eyes remained on the book. Maybe I should have asked him if he liked the novel or if he needed another one from my collection; but instead, I said nothing.

"Rob, you should come to the beach this week," Courtney decided. "And I asked Chloe to come too."

"Yeah, what did she say?" he asked.

"She said, 'I'll think about it'"

"Then I wouldn't hold my breath."

I looked up at him, annoyed. "What's that supposed to mean?"

"What do you think it means?"

"I don't know. That's why I asked you."

"Asked me what?"

I let out an exasperated huff. "Are you trying to irritate me?"

"Maybe?" He smiled.

"Some friend you are!" It was just a simple reply, but for some reason, it resonated in my head. The last few weeks had been enough to mend our broken friendship, yet nothing more.

He ran his fingers through his hair. "Sorry, Chlo."

"Well, listen, I should get back inside," my father said, his hand tapping my forearm lightly. "I have to work on my book."

"What's the title?" Rob asked.

"Preston's Principles for the—" He paused to create a moment of suspense, and I filled in the blank. "College Student."

My father offered a synopsis, "Yep, it's a guide to making sound economic decisions during those first four years away from home."

"I'm thinking it'll take five," Courtney added.

"Yeah, if you're lucky," Rob retorted.

My father departed as the banter ensued, and Courtney decided, "Well, I better get home and start packing." She turned and held me tightly before she slipped into the woods; then Rob and I were completely alone.

"By the way," he said, gesturing at the table. "Thanks for lending me the book."

"Oh, you're welcome," I said plainly, searching for more words, but the moment passed, and we entered into a period of uncomfortable silence.

Rob ended it. "Do you have any plans for tonight?"

I shrugged a shoulder. "I was just going to read…maybe write."

"Yeah, I get it. You just want to be alone?"

I pressed my lips together and shook my head.

He tilted his head toward the woods. "Do you want to hang out at my house?"

I shook my head again.

"You want to stay here then?"

Again I shook my head.

"You want to give me a hint?"

I let out a happy breath, almost a laugh, and nodded

"You know I'm terrible at Charades, so can you use some words, Chlo?"

I shook my head one last time, stood up, and took my journal with me—not wanting my emotions to fall into the wrong hands. Then I curled my finger at him; and he rose from the chair and followed me into the woods.

"I feel like Lewis and Clark following Sacajawea into the unknown," Rob declared.

I turned and offered a scrunched-up face.

"I'm surprised Disney hasn't done a movie on her yet. I mean, they did Pocahontas and stretched that into a love story, but we all know it wasn't. They couldn't even speak the same language. And I think talking is important, don't you?" He waited. "Obviously not, because you're still ignoring me."

I suppressed a laugh, and soon, he sidled up next to me. "So, if it's not my house or your house, then where are we going?" I said nothing, figuring he probably knew the answer as we walked along the familiar path. When we reached our destination, I placed a palm on the base of the old oak tree.

"Our house," he said with a smile. "It's been a while, huh?"

"Four months," I said, and then added, "to the day."

He looked down at the ground. "Yeah, I should've known that."

"It's okay," I returned as I started climbing up the tree. He followed me, and together, we settled into the quiet corner of the tree house. True, it had been four months since we ventured into our childhood home, the last time being the night of our first kiss, and like so many memories of our relationship, the months felt more like years.

He started the conversation, "It sure is hot up here."

"Yeah, but it didn't seem to bother us when we were kids."

"That's because kids don't mind a little sweat."

"Or dirt," I shot back.

He tousled my curls. "Or knots in their hair."

We both laughed, which felt nice, but the brief laughter was replaced by silence again.

"So," I began, "you want to go somewhere else?"

"Nah, I like it up here."

I drew my knees into my chest. "Yeah, me too."

"Everything's better up here."

"Yeah," I agreed. "It's just us..."

"And our past," he finished. "Some of the best moments of my life happened here." He offered a half smile, and I reached out a hand, slowly, and placed it on his cheek. His skin felt like warm sandpaper, and I stared at him, witnessing a smile that I had missed greatly, the kind of smile that started in his mouth and spilled into his beautiful eyes. I kept my eyes fixed on him as his childlike dimples sunk deep into the stubbles of his handsome face, and it was like glimpsing at the boy inside the man.

I smiled back at him, knowing this was a small step in the right direction. Yet he started toward me, and reading desire in his eyes, the panic stirred inside me. I was not ready for intimacy, since I knew we could never start over again with simple kisses. So, before his lips met mine, I turned my head swiftly to the side.

"Great," he muttered and fell back against the wall. "I feel like I'm six all over again."

"I'm sorry, Rob."

"Yeah, I know." He gazed out the window.

"I'm just not ready yet," I defended.

"Maybe you never will be." He kept staring out the window. "You know I leave for school in a few weeks."

"I know," I returned softly as a tear crept down my cheek, falling into the crevice by my nose and remaining there until it dropped into my lap. A few more followed the same path.

"And if I leave while we're just friends, then that's probably all we'll ever be. We won't be able to rebuild our relationship, and when you're ready to be with someone, I'll be some 846 miles away from you. So, you'll find someone here, and then I'll find someone there. At holiday breaks, we'll see each other, and it'll hurt. A lot. But as time passes, we'll forget about each other. And eventually, a whole day will pass, and you won't think about me. Soon a week will pass. But then you'll see something—a tree house, perhaps—and you'll remember me."

I faced the opposite wall and brushed more tears from my face. Then I returned my hands to my lap as he spoke again. "You'll always be my first love, Chloe." His hand rested on top of mine, briefly. "I hope you know how much I care about you and that I'm sorry I wasn't a better boyfriend for you. Maybe if we had been older or together longer. Maybe a thousand other things that keep me up at night, but the truth is—"

"Are you trying to break up with me?"

"Actually," he paused. "We can't break up because we're not even together anymore."

"Oh." I bit down on my lip. This was the exact moment where I had to speak, where our entire relationship depended on my response, but all I said was, "I don't know what to say."

He exhaled loudly. "That's okay. You don't have to say anything at all." He leaned over and kissed my temple, speaking softly against my skin. "Goodnight, Chloe." He left my side and crawled across the planked floors.

"Wait," I shouted at his backside. "That's it?"

He turned around and faced me, finding a seat against the opposite wall.

I spoke again. "I thought you loved me?"

"I do," he said softly.

"Then why are you leaving me?"

"Because it hurts to stay."

"That's *not* a good enough reason."

He spread out his hands, repeating my earlier line, "I don't know what to say."

I stared back at him, fuming. "You frustrate me! You know that! I came up here, hoping we could talk. Hoping this place would be like crawling into a time capsule, and we could go back to the way it used to be. But you know what? I can't find my way back there anymore, and when I read my journal..." I reached over and picked it up. "It's like reading a work of fiction because I don't think it really happened to me." I swiped more tears from my eyes. Then I opened my journal, flipping past my first few entries, and Rob returned to his normal spot next to me. "See, right here," I said, placing my finger on the exact paragraph. "I wrote about our first kiss." I turned the pages, naming off the events as I went. "And here's prom...and the night on the beach...and my birthday..."

Then I stopped.

"Did you stop writing after that?" he asked.

"No," I said sadly.

He reached over and turned the pages for me as I looked away. "And you wrote while you were in Kentucky?"

"Yeah." I faced him again. "And when I got to my grandmother's house, I wrote you a letter." His eyes were on me, not the page. "Like an apology...for hurting you so much."

"Hmm," he said like he was censoring himself. Then his eyes returned to my journal, and he turned the pages slowly. "And what about this?"

I glanced down, and then grabbed the journal. "Oh, that... that's nothing."

"Wait!" He yanked it back. "Is it a song?"

I tugged harder, revealing nothing.

"Let me read it," he replied, his voice deep and demanding.

"No way," I shot back, pulling back with all my might that even my arms started quivering.

"Okay. You win," he said abruptly and let go of my journal. I, of course, demonstrated Newton's Third Law of Motion and fell over.

This amused him, and inside his laughter, he decided, "Well, I didn't want to read it anyway."

"Gee, thanks."

"Aw, it's not like that. It's just that if it's a song, then you should sing it to me."

"Yeah, right."

"Why not, Chlo?"

"Because I'm scared. That's why."

"Of what?"

"A million things, actually."

He paused. "Do you know what scares me more than anything?"

"What?"

"Living the rest of my life without you in it."

"Then why were you going to leave me?"

"Because I knew you would stop me." He continued, "I knew you would never let me walk away without a good fight."

I looked down, suppressing a smile. "So who won?"

223

"Well, you won because you got me to stay, *and* you also won our little game of tug of war." He laughed, and I offered a playful "grrr" before he continued, "But I intend to win the next round."

"What next round?"

He smiled and scooted into the corner, resting his hands behind his head. "Because I am *not* leaving this tree house," he said, jabbing a finger into the planked floor, "until you sing that song to me."

"What if you need to go to the bathroom?"

"Well." He spread his hands to the sides and did a quick glance-around. "*I* can always go in the woods."

"Yeah, great." I rolled my eyes and tried again. "What if you get hungry?"

He pulled a protein bar from his pocket. "Then I'll eat this."

I stared back at him, wondering if he had a response to everything, and then his eyes narrowed into slits. "And you won't win a staring contest either."

"Is that so?"

"Yeah, it is." He put on his accomplished mean face, and I felt a tickle inside my belly. Eventually, I caved in, laughing.

He smiled. "Just sing your song to me."

"No!"

"Aw, c'mon. You said you wanted to go back in time, so just pretend you're playing that little guitar of yours, and you won't be afraid anymore." He leaned over, nudging me with his shoulder. "Plus, I've always been your biggest fan."

"Yeah, my only fan," I retorted.

"Well, if I'm your only fan, then I guess you wrote the song *for* me."

He was right, actually. I wrote it for him and about him, and the song was what brought me home to him. Still, I felt terribly afraid, since it would be easier, and much safer, to keep my love for him hidden inside my journal than to express it with my song. And as I grappled with my reservations, I realized fear was definitely love's greatest enemy, and at that moment, I had to determine if "fear" or "love" had a greater hold of my heart.

Nothing but Trouble after Midnight

"So?" he asked, and I relented quickly with a smile. "Okay, you won, Rob." Or should I say "love" did? Then taking one last breath, I sang my song for him:

-AUBURN EYES-

I see the past in your eyes
Tender touches with long goodbyes
Friends without secrets or lies
Hid their love in dim disguise

Splash in the waters of our youth
Climb that tree to tell the truth
Cross the woods in the dark
Open the gate into my heart

With you I know, with you I see
A life without uncertainty
For my past, my present, my future lies
Hidden inside those auburn eyes

I saw heaven in your eyes
Caught a glimpse of paradise
More than ever I realize
A love like ours never dies

Open your eyes
(And see me)
Open your mind
(And know me)
Open your arms
(And hold me)
Open your heart
(And love me)

Open your eyes [spoken]

Chloe Preston has the perfect teenage life: great friends, a full social calendar, and the ideal boyfriend.

But *perfect* never stays that way.

One night, Chloe's life is shattered, and all she can hope for is that the memory will fade like a bad dream. But secret truths are dangerous, and Chloe discovers that keeping things hi[...]m than good—especially when t[...]d comes back for more.

Will Chloe find the strength to face the truth, or will she remain a victim of her own fears?

Insightful and compelling, author Kimberly Blackadar's *Nothing but Trouble after Midnight* is an unprecedented battle between true love and ill-fated circumstance.

Cover art by Jonathon Engelien

WWW.TWOHARBORSPRESS.COM

ISBN 978-1935097976
51595
US $15.95
9 781935 097976